{A NOVEL}

BRAD WHITTINGTON

BROADMAN
&HOLMAN
PUBLISHERS

NASHVILLE, TENNESSEE

0-8054-3158-6

Published by Broadman & Holman Publishers,
Nashville, Tennessee

Dewey Decimal Classification: F
Subject Heading: CHRISTIAN LIFE–FICTION
                  DISCIPLESHIP–FICTION

Scripture citation is from the King James Version of the Bible and the
Holy Bible, New International Version, © 1973, 1978, 1984 by
International Bible Society.

1 2 3 4 5 6 7 8 9 10 09 08 07 06 05

For Mom and Dad:

Mastery of words fails me.

Thanks.

ONE DAY in the fall of 2000 the phone rang. It was Gary, an editor who had read my manuscript and was interested in publishing it. This came as a shock to me because it had been ten years since I had touched it or sent it to anyone. Even greater was the shock that he thought it should be expanded from a novel to a trilogy.

His first suggestion was, "Tell us more about the father." So I did. His presence pervades all three books to varying degrees, growing more profound as the series progresses.

Of course the family in the trilogy draws from my own family. My father was a preacher; I have two sisters. Regardless, it is still a work of fiction. I built the characters to suit myself, not to document my family life. They sometimes have characteristics in common with my family and sometimes not.

For example, consider this paragraph from book 1: "That was part of the mystery of Dad: the gritty underside of life didn't seem to bother him. Not that he didn't realize it was there. Whatever he was, he wasn't naive. It just seemed to have no effect on him. The gum on the shoe, the pencil lead that breaks in the middle of a difficult problem, the elevator that stops at every floor when you're late for an appointment on the 37th—all the things that I was doomed to notice and chafe against, Dad seemed to take as part of the equation."

This was not true of my own father. Little things bugged him even more than they bug me. He was very particular about things being done properly. There are other characteristics of Matthew Cloud as described in the book that are not in alignment with my father. As I said, I built the character to suit my purposes in the story.

However, I can't deny that, despite the alterations, the spirit of Matthew Cloud that rises from the page and has moved so many readers is the spirit of Richard Whittington. I think Gary caught a whiff of it in the original manuscript and, like many who have met my father, he wanted more.

In the early nineties when I first wrote what later became *Welcome to Fred,* I viewed it as the story of a kid finding his way through a sticky patch of adolescence rendered more difficult by the multiple complications of culture shock and PKness. Then last night I realized I was wrong.

It was 3:00 a.m. The first draft of book 3 lay beside me on the floor of the hospital room, the pen resting on top after completion of the first edit. By the light coming through the bathroom door, I watched the ragged breathing of my father as he slept, every breath taking unconscionable effort. I was concerned about how long the pain medication would last. I was wondering if he was getting any rest. He was working so hard to breathe, although he appeared to be asleep, that I feared he would be even more fatigued when he awoke.

And I was thinking about what people had said to me over the past few hours about my dad and my book. I was thinking about the last thirty pages I had edited. I was learning something.

It wasn't a story about a kid. It never was. It was a story about a father. Whatever else it might be, it was a tribute to the man who lay dying in the bed in front of me.

Gary knew this from the start. He didn't say, "Tell us more about the kid." He said, "Tell us more about the father."

So I did.

Brad Whittington
Fort Worth, Texas
August 23, 2004

I want to look more like you
But my flesh just keeps on showing through
I try so, so very hard
But I just keep getting caught off guard

Circumcise my heart
Make my life be set apart

I want to act more like you
And not the things that I always do
It seems like each time I try
I find a 2x4 in my eye

Circumcise my heart
Make my life be set apart

I want to be more like you
I want to live what is pure and true
I want to, sometimes I don't
I say I will, but sometimes I won't

Circumcise my heart
Make my life be set apart

—Brad Whittington, *Circumcise My Heart* © 1999

CHAPTER ONE There are times in life when you wonder if you have screwed everything up—when you think that if some bored biographer decided to chronicle your existence, it would turn out to be a dismal account of one mistake after another.

I was in the midst of such speculations. It was after midnight, the perfect time. I was in Dad's study, the perfect place. I was organizing Dad's stuff in preparation for the estate sale, the perfect occasion.

Heidi and Hannah, one at a time, had peeked in to check on me and had gone away. I knew this even though I had not looked up. Each time the door had a distinctive creak that told me who was peeking. Heidi's squeak was fast and high, like someone annoyed. Hannah's squeak was slow and creepy, like someone opening the door with something else on her mind. Both times the door had closed slowly without a sound.

I had been there for some time, a little black notebook in my hand, thinking back on 1972 in Barstow, California, when I had made a choice. It had seemed the right choice at the time. I was still pretty sure it had been.

I had been a scrawny sixteen-year-old preacher's kid in search of Nirvana in the form of the California girls the Beach Boys had sung about. The perfect embodiment had appeared in my mind in hip-hugger, bell-bottomed, patch-covered jeans, wearing a headband to hold back straight hair that hung long enough to sit on. And that was where she stayed. In my mind.

I did not find Nirvana. Instead I found two roads branching out before me. At the head of each road was a man.

One road began with logic and science. I had a fondness for this road. It was clean and unambiguous, free from the messy chaos of emotion. But the Mysterious Stranger inviting me down this road had caused me to suspect that the randomness and chance lurking beneath the surface led to cosmic indifference, thence to nihilism and despair, and ended with death.

The other road began with death. A great cross cast a shadow across the fork. On it hung a bleeding, dying God, a human parchment upon whom was written an unbelievable message of love and forgiveness. This road was messy and laden with emotion. But beyond the death was the promise of redemption and meaning. Life with a purpose.

I chose the second road.

Then I returned to Fred, the microscopic East Texas town where I thought I knew everybody and everybody thought they knew me. I told no one of my choice. Not Dad or Mom, not my sisters Heidi and Hannah.

I hadn't thought out the next steps. The thought of blurting out that I got religion seemed awkward. I was a PK, a preacher's kid. I was already supposed to have religion. Besides, I didn't know how my friends would react.

Ralph was my oldest friend in Fred, the first to befriend me when I was dropped into this hick town four years earlier. We had shared many experiences but didn't discuss religion much. C. J., also a transplant from a big city, was my closest friend. We discussed religion not at all. Jolene, the beautiful but incurable practical joker, and Bubba, her hapless brother, were sporadic at our church. Darnell, the Terror of the Back Roads, had one religion—driving fast.

I might have considered telling my Sunday school teacher, Mac, but he wasn't my Sunday school teacher anymore. A truck driven by his best friend, Parker, had hit his car while he was changing a tire. Mac's wife and daughter were killed instantly, and he was in a wheelchair for life. Scooter and Brenda had taken over the class. I didn't even consider telling them.

2

I suspect Dad knew something in me had changed. But I always suspected Dad knew a lot of things. That was one reason I was now
indulging in a fit of sentimental reflection. Here I was, about the age Dad
had been on that vacation, and I still felt like a sixteen-year-old kid.
Where was the wisdom, that prescient certitude that he wore like an
undershirt? That was one thing he hadn't passed down. Or if he had, I
hadn't discovered it. Perhaps it was in a drawer I hadn't cleaned out.

I began that summer long ago with a life-changing decision. I didn't
realize at the time just how life changing. But in the next few years I was
going to find out.

CHAPTER TWO Returning to a routine after a three-week vacation is at once alien and familiar, but the first Sunday back in Fred was more alien than I expected. There was no hint of strangeness when we arrived. The building looked the same, the people looked the same, the routine was the same. But when I got to the Sunday school class, I entered alien territory.

The first clue was that it was crowded. Heidi, Hannah, and I arrived together. Heidi would only be around for a few more weeks before she went off to college. Hannah was preparing to enter high school. I split the difference between them. When we walked into the room and had trouble finding an empty seat, we looked at each other in wonder.

Bubba and Jolene were there. That was all wrong. The class hadn't even started. They usually arrived late or missed Sunday school completely. Even worse, there were new faces. Squeaky was there, Ralph's alleged girlfriend. I was miffed. After all, I was the PK. This was my turf. I had been there every Sunday for four years with little to relieve the tedium. I missed two Sundays for a long-deserved vacation, and suddenly there were strangers in the camp, very chummy with the regulars. Talk about nerve!

Scooter opened with a prayer. Scooter and Brenda Brown had replaced Mac and Peggy after the wreck. Scooter was a deacon with a blond flattop, seemingly precision cut with the aid of a framing square. He wore boots and a bolo tie. I had pegged him as "Most Likely to Go to Bible College." His kids already had vestiges of the begrudged celebrity and instinctive wariness that marks a preacher's kids. It was only a matter of time.

I looked down at the scuffed, salmon-colored tile and positioned the front legs of the metal folding chair precisely two inches in front of the third tile, a spot determined by years of experience. It allowed me to lean back against the institutional green wall at the proper angle. From this position of repose I pondered in my heart the meaning of this great host before me.

Something had happened while we were gone. During the first half of the class I searched for an explanation. I was mystified until I traced the timeline back to the events just before our departure. Reverend Bates. Six nights of hellfire and damnation. Forty verses of "Just As I Am." People streaming down the aisle with tears streaming down their cheeks. Revival.

I was attending a postrevival class with an infusion of new blood into the congregation. My moment of enlightenment was interrupted by Scooter asking me if I knew the story of the rich young ruler.

"Uh, yeah. He was very sorrowful because he was very rich."

"Come again there doll." Ralph was leaning against the wall on the opposite side of the room. "If yer daddy was rich, he wouldn't be sorrowful." By which he meant he would not find an abundance of material goods to be an undue burden. (If you spend much time in Fred, you learn quickly that when people say "yer daddy" they're not talking about somebody in your family, they're talking about themselves. And when they say "doll," they're talking about you.)

Several others voiced their agreement with Ralph's position. Then Bubba spoke. "For what shall it profit a man, if he shall gain the whole world, and lose his own soul?"

My head jerked around so quickly that it upset the balance of nature and my chair collapsed with me in it. As I painstakingly extracted myself from the wreck, Jolene whispered to me, "Don't pay him no mind. He's been talkin' like that fer three weeks."

I looked at her closely for signs of jest but only detected exasperation verging on resignation. I scanned the room. Heidi's lips were pressed together. She shook her head. Hannah looked at me and raised one eyebrow.

I looked at Bubba. He looked like the same old Bubba, laughing along with everyone else as I set the chair back up and reduced my formula by one inch for insurance.

Scooter took the reins. "Bubba, yer on the right track. But I expect we might should begin back at the beginnin'. Let's look at the verses in Mark 10." He scanned the room over his drugstore reading glasses. "Ya do have yer Bibles, don't ya?" A few kids nodded their heads and flipped around looking for Matthew. Most avoided eye contact and flipped to the lesson in the Sunday school quarterly.

Bubba had a Bible that must have served most of its life holding down a very sturdy coffee table. The kind that has pages in front to record the family tree and significant life events. I looked at Jolene.

"I think he done read that thang through three times in the last three weeks," she muttered in my direction.

"Bubba, read verses 17 through 20."

Bubba cleared his throat.

"And when he was gone forth into the way, there came one running, and kneeled to him, and asked him, Good Master, what shall I do that I may inherit eternal life? And Jesus said unto him, Why callest thou me good? there is none good but one, that is, God. Thou knowest the commandments, Do not commit adultery, Do not kill, Do not steal, Do not bear false witness, Defraud not, Honour thy father and mother. And he answered and said unto him, Master, all these have I observed from my youth."

"Good," Scooter said. "So, what do y'all think? Did he really keep all the commandments since he was a boy?" Several heads nodded automatically, no sign of thought on their faces. These were the folks who automatically answered "Jesus" to every question in Sunday school, figuring the odds were better than even.

"There is none righteous, no, not one." This time I was ready for it. I just eyed Bubba carefully and kept my balance.

"Good point, Bubba. What do y'all say? Have y'all kept all the commandments?"

Some kept on nodding, like those little bobbleheaded dogs in the back car window. Others avoided eye contact.

This question had never crossed my mind. I had certainly never killed anyone or committed adultery or stolen. Did false testimony include the time I broke a lamp and blamed it on Hannah? Maybe. Defraud? I think not. Honor my father and mother. Well . . . who's asking?

Jolene spoke up. "I ain't never killed no one."

Ralph snorted. "Not yet, anyway. Give her time; she'll get around to it."

"So, y'all agree? Think yer doin' OK?" Some shrugs around the room. "As good as the next guy?" A few nods. "OK then, sounds like yer in the same boat as this guy. Let's see what Jesus says. Squeaky, read verses 21 and 22."

"Then Jesus beholding him loved him, and said unto him, One thing thou lackest: go thy way, sell whatsoever thou hast, and give to the poor, and thou shalt have treasure in heaven: and come, take up the cross, and follow me. And he was sad at that saying, and went away grieved: for he had great possessions."

"OK, so what does that tell us?"

"You mean now I gotta give away all my stuff?" Ralph demanded. "Can I at least keep the dirt bike?"

"No," Jolene said. "You can give it ta me. That way you can go ta heaven. I'll just take my chances."

"That except your righteousness shall exceed the righteousness of the scribes and Pharisees, ye shall in no case enter into the kingdom of heaven." Three guesses where that came from. I didn't bother to look.

Squeaky looked confused. "Wait a minute. Brother Bates said the directions to heaven are to 'turn right and go straight.' This guy did ever'thin' right, but he's not goin' ta heaven? That doesn't sound fair."

"Who said life is fair?" I asked.

She glared at me, her little mouse-ears poking through her thin red hair. "Well, at least God ought to be fair!"

"Touché." I should have kept my mouth shut.

"Squeaky, you should be careful about accusing God." Scooter looked reprovingly at her. "Like Jesus said, 'there is none good but God.' He knew this guy thought he was good. Why else would He say that?"

"All have sinned, and come short of the glory of God."

"Yes, Bubba, we know that. The point is that ya can't work yer way to heaven. This guy came in all cocky, thought he had it sewed up, and Jesus took him down a few pegs."

I wasn't sure about this interpretation. It said, "Jesus beholding him loved him." That seemed a little strange to me.

"For by grace are ye saved through faith; and that not of yourselves: it is the gift of God: Not of works, lest any man should boast." Scooter looked on the verge of throwing a quarterly at Bubba.

I leaned over to Jolene. "How does he know all this stuff? I know the Bible pretty good, but I can't pull them out like that, word for word like a tape recorder."

"Bubba was always good at memorizin' stuff. He knows all the players on all the World Series teams since the beginnin' of time. And their battin' average and all that stuff. He's got a photogenic memory."

My correction was interrupted by Ralph trying to work out his salvation.

"You ain't answered my question yet. Do I have to give all my stuff away to get to heaven?"

Scooter turned on Ralph. "Do ya love yer stuff more than ya love God?" he asked in a snarl.

Ralph blinked rapidly four times and said, "No."

"Then ya don't have ta give it all away."

Brenda broke the tension by announcing it was time to split into groups.

In the church service I took my usual seat, far enough back for comfort but close enough to maintain appearances. I noticed Parker right off. He was on the front row, hair slicked down, wearing a new leisure suit, dark brown with light stitching. Sonia was next to him. The strap from his eye patch cut across his hair in the back.

Thankfully, the service was a lot tamer than Brother Bates's revival. As usual, Dad called on somebody to lead the benediction and sneaked to the back to greet folks as they came out. Dad collared me as I squeezed through the crowd.

"Mark, it seems Deacon Fry has a proposition for you." He nodded at the large bald man standing next to him.

Deacon Fry blinked at me benignly and flashed an odious, ingratiating smile. I had an instinctive dislike for this man. His prayers reeked of the ponderous piety of King James rendered with an East Texas accent. He was a tall man, well over six feet, with a bulk to more than match, making for an intimidating physical presence. He was as hairless as an egg. You couldn't even see eyebrows unless you looked closely for the vestigial line of fuzz brushed above his steel gray eyes.

He frequently snoozed through the second half of the sermon, propped against the end of the pew, his index finger running alongside his eye, the rest of his fingers fanned out across his face. I didn't know whether his failure to conceal his sermonic slumbers was incompetence or insult. Consequently, I didn't know whether to hold him in contempt or resent him. But I was sure one of those attitudes was the proper one.

He sang a sonorous, booming bass on all hymns, which might have redeemed him in my eyes had he not scooped the notes like a geriatric Elvis.

"Yes," he droned in his growling drawl. "We find that the feller who has been doin' the janitor work for us is goin' ta be out fer a spell. We have a mess of folks that could do the job, but we thought we might could give you a chance ta earn yerself some pocket money."

For once I had an interest in something Deacon Fry had to say.

"OK."

"That's mighty fine. It's five dollars a week, cash money. Pastor Matt, I mean, yer pa can show you the ropes."

He nodded at us, detached his wife from her conversation, and led her to a black LTD.

Parker and Sonia were next. Since I was standing next to Dad, Parker grabbed my hand and shook it. "Welcome back."

"Thanks." The patch was there over his left eye. The white scar was visible from hairline to jawbone. I tried not to think of the sunken eyelid that lay beneath the patch.

Sonia nodded at me. She seemed calm and content under a generous apportionment of makeup. Some things remained reassuringly constant.

Parker moved on, grabbing Dad's hand with both of his. "Welcome back, pastor. We're glad ta see ya."

"Parker, I am very glad to see you here." He grabbed Parker's shoulder. "It's been a long three weeks since we last talked. How are you doing?"

Parker's smile eclipsed the scar on his face. It almost disappeared. "Never been better. You were right with that new creature thang. I don't even recognize myself anymore. I'm not always sure how to act."

Dad looked to Sonia for confirmation. She pushed Parker out of the way and hugged Dad, to everyone's surprise, including hers.

"I been waitin' for three weeks to say thanks. He ain't took a drink the whole time y'all been gone."

"That's great news, but don't thank me. I didn't have anything to do with it. I just showed up; God did the rest."

Parker shook his head. "You can act all modest if ya want ta, Pastor Matt. But we're mighty proud ya showed up, if that's what ya want ta call it."

"He's quit workin' on that truck and started buildin' a gazebo. It'll be a lot nicer when it's finished out and painted, but it's a nice place to sit in the mornin' with a cup of coffee. Parker comes out before he goes to work and reads the Psalms and all."

"Well, I am impressed! We'll have to get together next week sometime."

Everybody nodded their heads, and we all stood around for a few seconds, awkwardly. Then Parker said a few more welcome backs and Dad said a few more thanks, nice to see yous and they walked off together much like the Frys, only to an old F-150 pickup.

It seemed the Fred we had returned to was somewhat different from the Fred we had left. Which was only fair. The Mark Cloud who returned was somewhat different from the one who had left. Although nobody knew that but me.

CHAPTER THREE My newfound janitorial profit center was not of sufficient magnitude to allow me to retire from my former career as purveyor of the news. I resumed my *Grit* route on the Spyder bike, new driver's license notwithstanding. Adding gasoline expenses to the overhead would have obliterated my profit margin.

Three weeks of back issues in the pouch threatened to topple me every time I took a corner. To my surprise, most of the usual customers opted for all three, and some even gave me a dollar and told me to keep the change. I hit a windfall at the Walker estate. Parker was in the half-finished gazebo drinking iced tea, a Bible next to him on the bench seat. I scored an extra dollar tip. In the euphoria of a capitalistic ecstasy, I pointed my chopper handlebars toward the river bottom, expanding my territory.

Predictably, my success rate fell. The river bottom is its own country. Despite the fact that I was a four-year resident of Fred, I had never seen the people who answered the door. Or who were sitting on the porch when I wheezed up the driveway. Greeting a stranger with something besides a shotgun was unusual for this demographic. Fortunately, a skinny kid on a bike posed little danger, but buying something from a stranger went against the grain. Particularly reading material.

I started to turn back several times, but I was seduced by what might be around the next corner. I might stumble upon a backwoods reading club searching for fresh material and move the entire stock!

But as each succeeding corner failed to reveal such a cultural anomaly, I was forced to consider a retreat. The light was failing, and I would have to turn back to get home before the prolonged East Texas twilight bled into night.

What lay around the last corner was a rarity in Fred—a hill denuded of pine trees, affording a panoramic view of the sunset. On the left side of the road, a rough plank house held the sun on its chimney. I viewed it with a critical eye, appraising it for telltale signs of the literati. It wasn't a promising prospect. On the right side of the road, a green Pontiac Bonneville faced the house and sunset. A hand hung limply from the driver's window. A thin tendril of smoke rose from a cigarette, like incense to the dying sun god.

Here at least was a sign of life. I leaned to the right and rolled to the open window of the Pontiac. With a practiced motion I pulled a paper from the pouch while extending a leg for support. "Would you like to buy a *Grit?* It's a newspaper."

The flaccid hand backed with coarse black hair rose slowly. My eyes were riveted to the cigarette resting in the center of the hand, between the middle and ring fingers. Or half fingers, I should say. The hand covered the bottom of the face as if to prevent a secret from escaping.

He took a drag from the cigarette and blew the smoke out his nose. I held up a *Grit* with my right hand, steadying the handlebars with my left. In the silence of the gloaming, we evaluated each other.

There wasn't much for him to process—a skinny blond kid with hair in his eyes, shoving a paper in his face. The view from my side wouldn't stop the presses either. Jet-black hair with a trace of gray at the temples, wide face with plenty of room for the wrinkles, bushy eyebrows, flat nose. He raised a Coke can to me with his right hand as if proposing a toast.

"Good evenin'." He nodded and took a sip of Coke. I nodded back. "How much is yer paper?"

"A quarter."

"What's in it?"

"Human-interest stuff, puzzles, recipes, jokes. That kind of stuff."

"No news of the war?"

"No, it's not that kind of paper."

He contemplated the purchase with another pull at the cigarette, fished a wad of bills from his shirt pocket, and peeled off a Washington. "Where you from?"

I dug in my pocket for some change.

He frowned and shook his head. "Keep it." He tossed the paper into the passenger's seat.

"Thanks!" That kind of tip didn't come often in Fred. When it did, it was always from guys who were a little rough around the edges. Women were either exact in their purchase or gave me an extra quarter. "I live over near the school."

"No, I asked where you from, not where you live. Yer not from around here, that's fer certain."

"I was born in Fort Worth." I didn't see the need to mention the four years in Ohio.

He regarded me with a penetrating stare that told me he suspected the four years but was too polite or lethargic to challenge my confession.

"OK." A long silence hung between us, and I turned my bike. He flicked an ash toward me. "I ain't seen ya out here before."

"Nosir. I haven't come down this road before."

He nodded, admitting the factual nature of the statement. "How often does this paper come out?"

"Weekly."

"Come a little earlier next time."

"Yessir."

He dismissed me with a nod and turned his attention back to the sunset. I turned my bike toward home and pedaled like mad.

―――

The next week I directed my bike to the knobby knoll on my river bottom route. The Pontiac was absent. A girl in her early twenties was sitting on a glider swing on the porch at the house across the road. I stopped in the weeds that carpeted the yard and flashed a paper in her direction. "Would you like to buy a *Grit?*"

She sized me up without breaking her rhythm on the swing. "Nope." She wore short cutoffs and a work shirt with the tail tied in a knot over her stomach. She might have been a prom queen at one time. Now she was just a girl on a porch on a Saturday afternoon, bored.

"Where's the guy in the car?" I jerked my head toward the field.

The swing slowed to a stop. "What?"

"The guy in the Pontiac. He was parked over there last week."

Her eyes narrowed. "He usually shows up a hour before sunset."

"Oh." I shoved the paper back in the pouch. "Thanks."

She gave me a last look and kicked the swing back into action. I returned late in the afternoon. The Pontiac was there, the left hand hanging out the window, smoke rising from the cigarette. The girl was lengthwise on the swing leaning against an armrest, facing the old man in the car. She didn't acknowledge my arrival. I returned the favor by veering to the car.

The man pulled his attention away from the sunset and raised the cigarette in my direction. I pulled out a paper in anticipation of another lucrative sale. He responded by pulling a Coke from a cooler in the backseat. It was glistening with moisture, unopened.

"I brought an extry in case ya showed up." We exchanged the Coke and the paper. He tossed the paper in the back and a dollar on the passenger's seat. "Hop in and take a load off. Enjoy the view." He waved vaguely with the cigarette. I couldn't tell if he was gesturing at the sunset or the girl.

I collapsed into the Pontiac. It smelled of stale smoke, dust, and a faint sweet, pungent whiff of whiskey. I looked around but didn't see any cans or bottles. Just a pack of Lucky Strikes and a gold lighter on the dash, and a square medal with blue and white diagonal stripes hanging from the rearview mirror. I peeled the ring-tab off the Coke. It wasn't Dr Pepper, but in the wilderness one cannot be choosy. I slid the ring-tab up my index finger. Heidi collected them, making chains she hung in her room.

"Thanks."

He nodded in my direction, dismissing my appreciation without breaking the silence or his gaze toward the sunset and the swing. I followed his lead, staring at the clapboard house silhouetted against the yellow-orange sky and sipping the Coke, feeling the carbonation burn down my throat. We admired the view in silence for several minutes.

"Long way from"—he glanced sideways in my direction—"Fort Worth to Fred, ain't it?"

"Pretty much." I took another sip.

"Especially when it ain't in a straight line, I figure." He took a drag on the cigarette in the same fashion I had seen the week before, clapping his hand over his mouth. I noticed that most of the fingers on his left hand were lacking a joint or two.

"Yep." I didn't see any point in volunteering information. Besides, it wasn't the fashion in Fred to grow garrulous on any given point.

He nodded as if satisfied with the answer, set his Coke on the dash, and shot his right hand toward me. "Vernon Crowley."

I wiped my hand on my pants. "Mark Cloud."

It was a firm grip on both sides; mine slightly calloused from bike handlebars, push brooms, rake handles, lawn mowers, and other random evidences of my serfdom as a teenager. His was smooth.

A few minutes later he broke the silence again. "Not a bad rag. What's new this week?"

"Not much. A guy in Oregon grew a giant turnip. Won a prize or something."

Vernon nodded. After awhile, he nodded toward the house. "Now there's a fine specimen, all things considered. I believe she even won a prize in her time." I followed his gaze. The girl reclined on the swing, studiously ignoring us. I grunted a response, relying on ambiguity to be interpreted as his leanings dictated.

"She does that ever' time. Like a cat paradin' in front of a dog on a leash, just out a reach." He lit another cigarette, releasing the aroma of fresh tobacco. "Funny how they learn that without nobody teachin' 'em. It's the same the world over."

I tried the idea out in my head. My experience of the gentler sex was limited. I had never considered the possibility that they might be disingenuous. A surprising ignorance, considering my knowledge of Jolene's escapades.

He blew a twin stream of smoke through his nostrils. "I know; I seen it in enough countries."

Most Fredonians could count the number of *counties* they had visited on one hand and still have fingers left over to pick their nose. This guy was talking about *countries*. And he had fewer fingers available for nose excavation than the average citizen. "Yeah?"

"Oh, yeah. England, Africa, Italy, France, Germany, Austria, Mexico . . . Texas. They don't change, no matter where you grow 'em." I studied him a little closer. He noticed. "The war. WWII."

"Ah."

"You can't swing a dead cat in any city, no matter where nor how big nor small, without hittin' two or three just like 'er. Full a themselves, like a ripe peach that'll split open as soon as it hits the ground. But it's all downhill fer her.

"High school is a playground fer the likes a her, but now she's stuck out here, no stage ta strut around on. Soon enough her pa will get his fill a her sass and marry her off ta someone."

He took a long contemplative draw from the cigarette. "Or she'll get bored and run off with one a the punks down the river."

I grunted to acknowledge his peroration. My contemplations of the opposite sex tended to focus on their physical attributes. And, from the look I had earlier in the day, I wouldn't have objected if she had come throwing rocks at my bedroom window, proposing we run off together.

We sat in the gloom for awhile. Then he suddenly reached up and cranked the Pontiac to life. "I guess I better be gettin' on home." He shoved the car into gear and lurched forward.

"Hey!" I hollered, spilling Coke on my jeans. "Let me out first."

"Oh." He slammed on the brakes and jerked the car into park. I shot a hand against the dash to avoid a flat nose and jumped out. I held up the Coke. "Thanks."

"Sure." He slapped the car back into gear and rolled forward briefly before stopping with a thunk. He gunned the engine. The back wheels kicked up a cloud of dirt. I looked around the front of the car. He had run up against a stump about two feet high. He shoved the gearshift around, hit park, gunned it, and went nowhere. He slapped it again, hit neutral, and gunned it with the same results. He squinted at the gears and tried drive again, creating another cloud of dust.

"Hey," I hollered through the passenger's window. "You're up against a stump." He looked at me with a confused expression. I realized he was drunk. I took a chance. "Hey, how about if I throw my bike in the trunk and drive you home?"

He glared at me for a few seconds and nodded, the fierce expression still on his face. "Yep, I reckon that's a doofer."

"Huh?"

"It'll doofer now."

He got out of the car and walked with deliberate concentration around the front of the car to the passenger's side, stumbling over the stump on the way. I pulled the keys from the ignition and opened the trunk. It was full of glass gallon jars, the kind with a small neck with a handle on it. I slammed the trunk and maneuvered the bike into the backseat.

"Which way?" I asked as I rolled past the stump.

He nodded to the right toward the river bottom. I followed the road until I came to a trailer up on blocks in front of a decaying frame house. I extracted my bike. He met me behind the car. I handed him the keys.

"This'll just be our little secret." He winked at me.

"Sure."

I watched him climb the cinder-block steps to the door of the trailer. It was locked. He called through the open window. A dark-looking woman, black hair jerked back in a severe bun, threw the door open, began cussing, and backhanded him. He tumbled from the cinder blocks into the dirt. Before he hit the ground she had already turned away. I ran over. His lip was bleeding, but he waved me away and got up, brushing the dust from his clothes.

"Don't pay Gina no mind," he said softly. "I'm terrible hard ta live with. She does the best she can, but sometimes it gets too much fer her."

"Are you OK?"

"Yep, yep, right as rain." He shook my hand slowly. "Now you best git on out a here."

He didn't have to tell me twice.

CHAPTER FOUR School years are marathon runners; summers are sprinters. It seemed I had just returned from California when I realized a single week remained until my junior year.

On Friday I worked through my janitorial chores at the church in the zombie trance that I retreated into while doing menial work. I lurched into my Sunday school room with a mop and bucket and almost fell into Mac's lap.

"Whoa." I was transfigured from my undead state into an unnatural animation, dancing with the mop to avoid a collision with the wheelchair. "I didn't know you were here."

Mac didn't acknowledge my presence. I waited, unsure of the protocol for addressing unresponsive former Sunday school teachers.

I began stacking chairs against the wall. "I was just mopping the floors."

Mac looked up. "Oh, it's you. Hey."

Hardly a greeting designed to make one feel welcome. I fielded it as best I could. "Yep, it's me in the flesh. As usual."

"Sorry, I didn't realize anyone was here. I'll get out of your way." He fingered the tread on his wheelchair but didn't move.

"No problem. You're not in the way."

"What? Oh." He suddenly seemed self-conscious. "I was just checking out the old room. We had a lot of good times in here."

"Yeah." The good times I remembered were the cookouts at his farm. By my recollections the Sunday mornings were akin to extended sessions in the Lubyanka. I kept stacking chairs, watching him surreptitiously.

"Yeah. Good times." He gazed into the middle distance, beyond the puke-green walls cluttered with maps of the ancient Middle East and missions posters. It was like I wasn't there. "I was alive back then."

I began mopping. Mac continued without regard to my movements.

"Funny how a guy will go through life, never noticing he's alive. It's only after, when he has no life, that he sees what life was really like."

I dragged the mop across the floor as quietly as I could, having no desire to turn this monologue into a conversation. I figured I was as close to having no life as anyone in Fred, but I was pretty sure I realized I was alive. If I quit being alive, that I would notice.

Mac stared into the afternoon gloom, talking quietly, as if to himself.

"Even after the wreck I felt alive. I walked through the valley of the shadow of death and climbed out the other side." He closed his eyes. "I was under that car fer a few hours that felt like years, but I felt alive. I was in the hospital fer months, half dead, but I felt alive." His voice grew louder. He gripped the armrests, reliving the moment. "I had ta feel alive. I had ta stay alive, ta deal with the monster that put me in the valley in the first place. It was the only thing that kept me alive."

He released his hold on the armrests and stared out the door down the empty hall. "But then I found out I was the monster. That I wanted ta kill; that I could kill if I had the chance." He sounded surprised at the thought.

His gaze had turned inward. It didn't look like he was seeing anything at all. His voice sank to a whisper. "And the monster I had ta kill became the hero. And I wasn't the hero anymore. And I wasn't even a monster anymore. I was just a . . . a nothing," he said in a voice scarcely louder than a breath.

I realized I was holding a dripping mop and my breath. I slapped the mop on the floor. It roused Mac.

"Hey." He looked around as if I had just come in the room. "Hey, Mark. Old Deacon Fry got you ta moppin', I see. How is the class comin' along?"

"It's OK. Nothing like before, you know." Sufficiently ambiguous to protect me from breaking any commandments. "And you?"

Mac dismissed the question with a wave of his hand. "The same stuff, runnin' the farm, all that."

"Right." I found sanctuary from the awkward silence that followed in the routine of mopping the floor.

"Well, I better get back ta the house," Mac said, spinning around toward the door.

"OK. See ya." After he left, I watched from the window as the hydraulic lift put him behind the wheel of his converted van. I returned to my chores. The afternoon dragged on in a credible impersonation of eternity. I chafed at the thought that my last few days of freedom were so woefully empty.

I wandered through the vacant building like a family ghost in a British manor—comfortable, benign, and bored. I was out of reading material, a situation that, unlike my friends, I viewed as a minor crisis. I was in a macabre period. During the spring I had discovered Poe and had read everything I could find in the high school library. After returning from the California vacation, I had haunted used bookstores, picking up the odd volume of H. P. Lovecraft, material that lent a chill that cut through the sultry summer nights in Fred. I had finished the last book in my possession the night before. The prospect of a weekend without reading material loomed before me with all the allure of a mandatory visit to a mildew-ridden nursing home to sing Stamps-Baxter hymns with a group of chunky, tone-deaf pep squad members snapping Dubble Bubble.

I absently noted that fate or habit had drawn me to the church library, which was little more than an elongated closet. It was scarcely wide enough to allow the despairing visitor to pace in front of the unfinished pine shelves searching for something capable of dispelling the ennui of a weekend in Fred.

I scanned the options. Most I had read during previous bouts with boredom: *Ben Hur, The Robe, Quo Vadis, The Gospel Blimp, Run Baby Run, The Cross and the Switchblade, God's Smuggler, God Is for Real Man,* and the oddly present *Return of Sherlock Holmes.* I had successfully avoided *The Greatest Salesman in the World* for at least five visits. Couldn't bring myself to check out a book by someone named Og.

I opted for light reading and pulled out the illustrated Bible encyclopedia. A very worn brown book thumped across the gap. The spine was so worn the title was illegible. I picked it up and looked on the front. *In His Steps.* Not a promising title. I opened it up and looked at the copyright. It was very old, older than my parents. Older than my grandparents! That could swing either way, to Charles Dodgson or Charles Lamb. No telling from the date or the cover.

I didn't ponder long. I had picked over these meager shelves many times and knew they held little promise. If nothing else, the book would provide an hour of diversion in the Fortress of Solitude while I discovered if it was worth reading. I signed the checkout sheet and locked up.

I took a Dr Pepper and a jar of pickled okra out to the Fortress, the isolated tree house I inherited from the previous PKs. It had two walls facing the house and was open toward the woods. A half roof protected the shelf and the secret compartment where I had stashed a metal army ammo case and a hollow book in which I kept items safe from prying eyes.

I tuned the radio as closely as I could to the Beaumont station where the Byrds were singing "Turn, Turn, Turn" but was unable to avoid the competing Woodville signal from bleeding in occasionally with "Whiskey River." Then I settled back against the trunk rising through the middle of the tree house and carefully flipped the browned, brittle pages to the first chapter. It was set at the turn of the century, about the same time as Sherlock Holmes.

Pastor Henry Maxwell is interrupted while preparing his sermon by a tramp asking for a job. He turns the tramp away. The following Sunday the tramp walks into the church—a very classy, respectable church—at the end of the sermon—a very polished and ornate sermon about following the example of Jesus. He asks the crowd how a guy who is willing to work can starve in a town full of churches and Christians following the example of Jesus. Then he collapses.

Maxwell takes the tramp home. The man lingers on for a week and finally dies early Sunday morning. Maxwell is shaken. The sermon he preaches a few hours later is very different from the exquisite oratory from the week before. He very plainly asks the same question the tramp asked: "What does following Jesus mean?" He offers a proposition: "I want volunteers from the First Church who will pledge themselves, earnestly and honestly for an entire year, not to do anything without first asking the question 'What would Jesus do?' And after asking that question, each one will follow Jesus as exactly as he knows how, no matter what the result may be."

Of course, since this is a very classy society church, most of the folks think Maxwell has taken the Magic Bus to Maggie's Farm, but fifty people take him up on it, including a newspaper editor, a railroad shop superintendent, a college president, a department store owner, a surgeon, a novelist, an heiress, and an operatic soprano. The rest of the book followed the stories of this group for the next year. Some made it, some didn't.

I finished the book Saturday night. It got a bit sappy in spots, especially when the author, who was a pastor, couldn't hold back any longer and had to clear off a spot and preach for a few paragraphs in the grandiloquent style of nineteenth-century preachers and politicians.

And I had some problems with the things people decided Jesus would do. Turns out that if Jesus were a soprano, He would not accept an offer to tour with an opera company. He would also use His position as a college president to get involved in local politics. If Jesus were a newspaper editor, He would not print an account of the prizefight on the sports page, and He also wouldn't produce a Sunday paper, even though all the work is done on Saturday. They never mentioned if Jesus would work on Sunday to get out the Monday paper. I figured He probably would because the Sabbath was over on Saturday night anyway.

But this was nitpicking. I couldn't deny that the question was seductive. What would Jesus do? It seemed like a simple enough question, easily answered. But it was hard to say, in my estimation. What would Jesus do if He were a skinny teenage preacher's kid marooned in a one-blink East Texas town? First I had to get past the obstacle of imagining Jesus as a skinny teenage preacher's kid marooned in a one-blink East Texas town. I never made it past the first step.

I figured I could be a hit on fishing trips. The few I had endured were exercises in tedium, waiting hours for a fish to commit suicide on the hook I dangled in the water. Just think if I could stay on the shore and point to a side of the boat and have Ralph reel in a few hundred bass, perch, and catfish. I would be the most popular guy in school, even if I would have to wear Groucho glasses to disguise myself from the game warden.

I decided to pose the question to the Sunday school class and see what they could make of it. We had pretty much beat to death the parable of the guy who went out to hire laborers four times during the day and paid each a penny, regardless of whether they worked twelve hours or only one, and then told the ones who worked longest to quit grumbling. Proving, I suppose, that Jesus would not have supported collective bargaining.

The genders had reconvened for the wrap-up and things were winding down, so I cut through the chatter and told the class about the book. Then I posed the question that I could not answer. "What would Jesus do if He was one of us? You know, a teenager in Texas in 1972."

Hannah let out a loud breath. "But He wasn't a teenager in Texas in 1972. How could we know what He would do?"

"You have to pretend a little."

"Do I also have to pretend He was a girl?"

"You might have to actually use your brain. But don't hurt yourself." Hannah threw a quarterly at me. "Like, do you think He would wear makeup? Or a miniskirt?"

"You should be careful—" Scooter began.

"I think He would try to stop world hunger," Squeaky said.

Scooter considered the possibility, his mouth frozen in the middle of his sentence.

Bubba spoke up. "For ye have the poor always with you." Squeaky stuck her tongue out at him.

"I think He would close down that liquor store across the county line," Heidi said.

"The Son of man is come eating and drinking; and ye say, Behold a gluttonous man, and a winebibber." By now everyone was used to Bubba spouting off verses, but this one got a few looks. A winebibber? What the heck was that?

"Well, that's just what I think," Heidi said. "You don't have to agree, I don't guess."

Scooter took control of the discussion. "Well, we know what He did. He worked with His father as a carpenter."

Ralph reacted quickly. "Wait a minute. First I have to give away my dirt bike; now I have to go work for my dad at the refinery?"

"No, I'm just sayin' He did somethin' useful, helped support the household, and honored His parents." Scooter leaned back. "You can all do that. It's pretty simple."

"Well," Bubba said slowly. "Where does it say in the Bible that Jesus was a carpenter?" I was shocked. It was the first thing I had heard him say all day that wasn't a verse.

"It's in there somewheres. I don't know the exact address of the verse."

"I don't think it does. It says Joseph was a carpenter."

"Yeah, right, so He probably was one too."

"Could be. But we don't *know* He was. We only 'spect He was."

Bubba looked steadily at Scooter, who looked back like he wished he could promote Bubba to the singles department immediately. I was erasing large sections of the mental blackboard I had filled out for Bubba.

Scooter dismissed the ripple of doubt with a shake of his head. "It only makes sense."

"Might could be, but we still don't *know* it. The only thang we know He did as a kid was to stay behind when His family left Jerusalem. And when they got onto Him about it, He pretty much told them off. And then when His mother tried to get Him to do somethin' about them runnin' out of wine at a weddin', He told her, 'Woman, what have I to do with thee?' If I said that to my mama, she'd slap me."

Dang! I knew all that stuff, but I had never put it together like that. Jolene was looking at Bubba with a mixture of shock and pride. The entire class seemed to be leaning forward in its collective seat. I half expected Ralph to jump up and throw down his cowboy hat and declare, "Let's just take this out back and settle it right now."

Scooter elected to squash the incipient rebellion with sarcasm. "So you're sayin' the answer to the question 'What would Jesus do' is that Jesus would sass His mama?"

"Nope. I'm sayin' we don't know what Jesus done 'til He was thirty. But whatever it was He done, it probably weren't somethin' we would expect. He seemed to always be doin' thangs that surprised or rankled folks. Especially religious folks."

Scooter seemed about to holler, "Them's fightin' words!" He started three sentences, one on top of the other, but the buzzer rang and the room cleared. Not even a showdown could keep anybody in the Sunday school room a minute longer than required.

CHAPTER FIVE With the inevitability of rain at a picnic, the school year arrived. The chaos of the first week blew past like a summer squall, leaving behind the slow drizzle of the school year. I found myself baking in the afternoon sun in the home bleachers. The PA blared "The Horse," and I watched Becky Tuttle go through the half-time routine with the rest of the twirlers. There had been no significant interaction between us since the day that I had been on the brink of leaping into the chasm by declaring my love for her and she had jerked me back from the edge with the dreaded word *friend*.

But that was almost a year ago. Since then I had faced death with Darnell on the Roller Coaster and undergone my private trial-by-ordeal on a three-week trip to California. I was a changed man, using the term loosely. I was changed at any rate.

Or was I? I thought I was, but the changes seemed to remain below the surface, like one of those Disney movies where people exchange personalities but look the same. Others seemed very changed indeed, like Parker and Sonia. And Bubba.

I watched Becky twirl her baton over her head, behind her back, between her legs, throw it in the air, do the splits, and catch it on the way back up, all without missing a beat with her chewing gum. It was kind of like a cat taunting a dog behind a chain-link fence. I thought of Vernon's comments. "Funny how they learn that without nobody teachin' 'em." Seemed to me the baton was passed on from one generation to the next. I was right there in the laboratory watching the training. Heck, I was one of the lab rats. One that never got the cheese.

I was startled from my ruminations by Jolene's elbow in my ribs. I jerked reflexively and knocked the mouthpiece out of my trumpet. It clattered on the bleachers and fell through the slats into a wilderness of dirt, weeds, soda cans, cigarette butts, tobacco pouches, and candy bar wrappers.

I looked at Jolene. "Thanks."

"You plannin' on takin' up twirlin'?" The perennial sparkle lit her black eyes like a subterranean stream casting ripples of light on the roof of a cave.

"What?"

"Ya seem to be studyin' those moves mighty close. Or maybe it's just a certain person yer studyin'."

Leave it to Jolene to take the shortcut to the most embarrassing topic. "Oh. I was just thinking, that's all."

"I bet. Thinkin' of askin' somebody out, I 'spect."

"No!" I said quickly. Too quickly.

I looked back at Becky. The song was ending and she was wobbling in her final pose, the baton horizontal behind her head. She had grown her brown hair out over the summer. It was pulled back in a ponytail that hung across the baton. She was taller. She seemed confident, very at ease with herself. She fit in.

As the metallic echo of the final notes faded, she broke her stance and glanced back at the football field. The team was breaking up practice to let us take the field. She smiled and waved at one of the players. Number 68. He was limping to the bench, his pads bulking him up into an unnatural robotic shape. He nodded in her direction, sweat dripping from his hair, too exhausted to even offer a smile, and grabbed a handful of salt tablets from a jar. I envied him the detachment born from total involvement. It was not a studied nonchalance. He was immersed in something too consuming to allow him to indulge his pleasures. I looked back at Becky. She bounced to the other twirlers and chattered excitedly. This was no place for one such as I. I hadn't changed that much.

"No." I turned back to Jolene. "I was just thinking about something else, that's all. About an old man I met on my paper route." I hoped this detail would lend my diversion an air of verisimilitude.

She studied me for a fraction of a second and dismissed my excuse. "Don't act shy with me, Toddy Raymer. I was there the first time ya saw Becky." She continued to scrutinize me for a sign of weakness.

I looked back at her as blankly as I could. But nobody could stare at Jolene for long without being distracted. It was like looking at the sun. Look too long and you're in trouble. When it came to looks, Jolene was as fresh as a newly minted quarter. Jet black hair, jet black eyes crowned with full black eyebrows and a complexion as smooth as Elmer's glue. Her lips seemed to be begging for someone to kiss them.

I was again amazed that I was sitting this close, actually having a conversation with a girl who would have been on the cover of a fashion magazine if she had been born anywhere else. But I also knew that she was an enemy of the male ego, that she enjoyed squashing it without remorse, like stepping on a cockroach and listening with satisfaction to the juicy crunch. Consequently she remained unencumbered by romantic involvement, a freedom that, in contrast to her peers, she seemed to enjoy.

One could not flutter in the light of such a beauty without the sound of what-if echoing in the void. Like many times before, I pushed the thought aside in the interest of self-preservation.

"Think whatever you like," I said in what I hoped was a mysterious tone. Then I left to rescue my mouthpiece from the bowels of corruption.

———

At lunch C. J. Hecker plopped his tray down next to mine. He nodded to a spot across the table, and a black guy I hadn't seen before dropped his tray in front of me. Like most schools in East Texas, Warren was integrated. And like most schools in East Texas, self-segregation was the natural order of things. There wasn't a significant amount of racial tension, evidently because blacks and whites were content to maintain their own separate-but-equal social circles. The Supreme Court may have overturned Jim Crow laws, but the Supreme Court was irrelevant to East Texas teen culture, which answered to a different court.

C. J. got a pass on this faux pas. He was from Houston and unaware of the unspoken Mason-Dixon Line that ran through the school. Ralph, Bubba, and the others at the table registered a controlled astonishment. They were surprised, perhaps even dismayed, but a higher social law dictated that they remain impassive.

"Mark, Elrick. Elrick, Mark," C. J. mumbled through a biscuit. "Elrick is from Dallas. Coach asked me to show him around."

I nodded at Elrick. "Hey."

"What it is," he said and held his hand up over the table, palm down.

I reached out and tried to shake Elrick's hand.

He pulled his hand back. "Naw, man, that's not it. Give me some skin."

"Huh?"

"Don't you ever hang wit' the brothers? Gimme five."

"Uhhh . . ."

I looked at him, then at C. J., who held his hand out, palm up. Elrick slapped it and held out his hand, palm up. C. J. slapped it and then slid his hand off Elrick's palm until only their fingers overlapped. Then they turned their hands vertical, curled their fingers until they were locked like boxcars in a train, reached up with their left hands and tapped the back of the other's hand three times with their knuckles.

I looked at C. J. "What, did you join the Masons or something?"

Elrick laughed and C. J. said, "Hey, get with it, man." He shoved mashed potatoes in his mouth. "You'll have to cut Mark some slack; he's a preacher's kid."

"Don't give him a bad rap on that," he said to C. J. "I'm a PK too."

C. J. smiled around the mashed potatoes. "Then you two should be like twin brothers or something."

"Different mamas, then," Elrick said and dug into his lunch. I did an inventory while cutting up my steak. His skin was ebony, his face broad, his nose flat. He wasn't slender and he wasn't stocky. He was over-dressed for the occasion—black slacks, black vest, white long-sleeved shirt, and a silver cross on a thick chain hanging in the dark V at his throat. His hair was close cropped in contrast to prevailing fashion. He didn't seem the least self-conscious sitting among the white boys while all the other black students were gathered very loudly at the other end of the lunchroom.

I leaned toward C. J. "Coach asked *you* to show him around?"

"Yeah," he said between gargantuan bites. "He's a sophomore, but he was a quarterback in Dallas; looks like he'll be a running back here."

I glanced at the other guys. They were very studiously staying out of the conversation, but they seemed to be relieved to hear this information. It made no difference to me. I had a vague idea what a quarterback did. I didn't know what a running back did, but I figured it had to do with running forward, the name notwithstanding.

The last time I had spent time with a black guy was four years before in Ohio. I had yet to find a companion to compare with Marcus Malcom Marshall, known to most as M. I had restricted my search to the white population. Perhaps that had been a mistake. It could be that I would finally find a true companion in this new arrival. I didn't consider the fact that four years of gradual assimilation into the culture rendered me indistinguishable from the aborigines around me.

"So, you're a PK, huh?"

"Yep."

"Move around a lot?"

Elrick stopped eating and looked at me. "Oh yeah. Worse than an army brat."

"Yeah, I know what you mean."

"Gotta start over on every team. Can't say how many times I worked my way up from JV."

I had no idea what it meant to work your way up from JV, or why anyone would want to.

"Why in the world would anybody move from Dallas to Warren?" C. J. asked.

"Papa got the call."

"The call?" C. J. paused in his efforts to set a record at clearing a plate of chicken-fried steak with all the fixings. His delay probably cost him the regional title. "What call? Who called him?"

"God called him."

C. J. looked at Elrick, who kept eating without further explanation. He turned his puzzlement in my direction. "The call?"

"The call? You don't know about the call?" I looked at C. J. and dropped my jaw. "Hey, man, he doesn't know about the call."

Elrick looked up, I held up my hand and we did the little handshake thingy. "You'll have to cut C. J. some slack; he's a heathen."

"Very funny. Now, what's this about the call?"

I nodded to Elrick. "A preacher's got to listen to God to see what he's supposed to do. When God wants him to go somewhere, He calls him to that place."

Bubba jumped in. "And after he had seen the vision, immediately we endeavored to go into Macedonia, assuredly gathering that the Lord had called us for to preach the gospel unto them."

Everyone looked at Bubba, who looked like the guy who let a cuss word slip out during dinner with the curate. "I heard that somewhere," he said.

"'Xactly," Elrick said, looking at Bubba as if he were a talking horse.

Bubba asked, "So yer sayin' that when a preacher says he's called someplace, he's sayin' that's what he thinks God wants him to do."

"'Xactly."

Bubba looked at me. "Maybe you could ask him yer question."

"What question?"

"The one you asked Sunday. What would Jesus do?"

"Oh." Since Elrick and C. J. were both looking at me expectantly, I had to say something. I told them about the book and the Question.

Elrick frowned. "What would Jesus do? He would do what He did."

"No. That's a cop-out. If Jesus was here, in this situation, what would He do?"

"About what?"

"About anything. Like, would Jesus play football?"

Suddenly I had the attention of the entire table, white and black.

"Why not?" Elrick asked.

"Well, it's violent. Didn't Jesus come to bring peace?"

"Think not that I am come to send peace on earth: I came not to send peace, but a sword." Everyone looked at Bubba again, but he looked back with a little more confidence. "Jesus said that," he said.

"Jesus would hang with the brothers," Elrick announced. "He would probably push for justice, like Brother Jesse Jackson."

"Who?" C. J. and I both said together. I took the floor. "Why would He do that?"

"He came to free the captives, to relieve the oppressed."

Bubba nodded his head. "Yep, he said that too. 'To preach deliverance to the captives,' and 'to set at liberty them that are bruised.'"

Elrick looked at Bubba while nodding his head. Everyone else looked at Bubba while shaking their heads, wondering what had come over him.

C. J. joined in. "Jesus would be a hippie if He came back now."

Even Ralph was shocked into a reaction. "How do ya figure?"

"It's a no-brainer. Haven't you heard the new album *Jesus Was a Capricorn?* He wore sandals, He had a beard and long hair, He talked

35

about peace, He didn't have any money, He lived in a commune, He talked about overthrowing the government. And the chicks all dug Him, like that Mary Magdalene babe. Didn't you ever hear that song 'I Don't Know How to Love Him'?" He looked at us like we were hopelessly out of it.

I silently worked on my chicken-fried steak and considered the multitude of opinions. It seemed that every person who answered the question had a different idea. An idea that conveniently fit their predisposition. Was Jesus the religious Rorschach figure that caused people to see what they wanted to see? I wondered what M would say. He would probably tell me Jesus was black. And talked a lot like Malcom X. Or Marcus Garvey, or Thurgood Marshall.

But the Question remained. It loomed before me, mocking me, taunting me. Was I tough enough to do what Jesus would do? Or would I wimp out? Maybe Jesus was counterculture after all. He did say some revolutionary stuff. But He also went to the synagogue. It was very confusing, and there were no simple or obvious answers.

I thought back to the night in Barstow, California, when I found myself at a crossroads. It seemed to me that to turn back from this tough question now was to betray the stake I had driven into the ground then.

At that moment Bubba's voice cut through the din that served as a background for my deliberations, in answer to some point: "But whosoever shall deny me before men, him will I also deny before my Father which is in heaven."

That seemed like a clear sign. What more did I want, a singing telegram? I decided I would accept Henry Maxwell's challenge. What the heck would Jesus do anyway?

CHAPTER SIX A few weeks later I was sprawled in the Fortress of Solitude, listening to the strains of Schubert's "Unfinished Symphony" occasionally fading into Homer and Jethro's "Does the Spearmint Lose Its Flavor on the Bedpost Overnight?" and reviewing my pilgrimage to popularity.

It had been four years since I had arrived in Fred wearing bell-bottomed hip-huggers; now I wore jeans. I had known nothing about the area. Now I had intimate knowledge of dozens of dirt roads and trails in a five-mile radius. I used to talk normal; now I talked more like the locals. I had welded iron, built birdhouses, memorized cow anatomies, analyzed soil content, and castrated pigs.

Then I had counted it all as loss for the excellency of the enlightenment that awaited in California. But here I was, back in Fred, not a bit more cool, hip, or enlightened, and still decidedly an outsider. I was accepted at school, but I wasn't invited to hang with the gang. Not counting C. J., but he was an outsider too. There were a few of the locals, like Ralph, who traded invitations to stay overnight, but I was dimly aware of gatherings, particularly on weekends, for which I was never given the opportunity to RSVP.

Was there anything more I could do? A few ideas suggested themselves, but I vetoed them instantly. I did have some standards after all. I definitely was not going to trade in Alice Cooper for Tammy Wynette or Iron Butterfly for George Jones. I couldn't imagine getting that lonely.

As I pondered my social dilemma, I had a brainstorm. Hunting! These weekend gatherings must be hunting parties. Since I had never shown an interest in hunting, doubtless it never occurred to them to invite me. I would take up hunting and be a part of the gang.

Then I realized that I had never shown an interest in hunting because I didn't *have* an interest in hunting. Shooting guns was fun enough, but if you shot an animal, you had to skin it and cut it up, a messy job that didn't appeal to me. Plus, a few Boy Scout camping trips had convinced me my bed at home was infinitely more comfortable than a sleeping bag on the ground.

Just how much was I willing to sacrifice to gain acceptance? It couldn't be any worse than raising pigs, and I'd already done that. Pigs last for months; hunting only lasts for the weekend. I realized I'd come too far not to take the final steps.

The first step was to get a gun. Nobody in my family had an interest in hunting, so we kept as many guns around the house as we kept rhinoceri. I assessed my financial resources: $12.58. Then I scanned the mail-order catalogs. The cheapest gun was a single-shot .22 for $49.95. At $5 a week for cleaning the church, it would take me two months to gather that kind of capital—maybe a little faster if my *Grit* sales improved. I checked the pawn shops in Silsbee and found one for $30.

In an attempt to accelerate the process, I applied for a loan against anticipated *Grit* revenue. It was going smoothly until the secondary loan officer, Mom, inquired into the object of the loan. I believe her words were, "What on earth do you want with a gun?"

"Deer season opens in a month."

"Deer season?" She turned to Dad. "Deer season?"

Dad took a slow sip of his coffee and deliberately placed it on the kitchen table. "Why, I'd completely forgotten. Honey, could you get my hunting jacket out of the mothballs? I'll go clean out the blunderbuss. Mark, you go make sure the powder is dry."

Mom regarded him without amusement and turned back to me. "You're going to shoot Bambi?"

"No, you can't shoot Bambi. That's illegal."

"You're going to shoot his father and leave Bambi a poor orphan!"

"Don't forget to set the forest fire so you can take out Bambi's mother too," Dad added.

I played my trump card. "If you remember the movie, Bambi turned out just fine."

"No thanks to you," Mom muttered over her cup of tea.

Dad put his hand on Mom's shoulder. "It appears we have a budding Nimrod on our hands. This may be a good thing. You remember the venison steak we had at Uncle Hub's last year? I thought you enjoyed it."

Nimrod? Did he just call me a nimrod?

"Yes, but the whole time I couldn't help but see those big weepy deer eyes looking woefully down the barrel of a gun."

"Excuse me. Nimrod?"

"Son of Cush. 'He was a mighty hunter before the LORD: wherefore it is said, Even as Nimrod the mighty hunter before the LORD.'" Dad picked up his cup. "Let's just hope you turn out better than he did."

"What happened to him?"

"He built the tower of Babel."

Mom sniffed in a Very Significant Manner and sipped her tea.

Without the benefit of the loan, three weeks later I was behind the house, practicing with my new rifle. Well, almost new. The stock was a bit loose, and the sights weren't set properly. I had to aim up and to the left to hit the target. But Dad knew even less than I did about guns, and I didn't want to admit to the gang that I didn't know what I was doing, so I just compensated.

The next week Ralph Mull, Bubba Culpepper, Darnell Ray, and Jimbo Perkins were standing by the back door of the Ag building when

I mentioned that I was anxious for deer season to open. They all stared at me in disbelief, except for Ralph, who choked on his snuff and had a coughing fit, which made him drop his spit cup on his boots.

"Yeah," I said nonchalantly, hitching up my pants in the sophisticated manner of Barney Fife. "I picked up a new gun at the pawn shop the other day, and I'm hankerin' ta try her out." Everyone suddenly became interested in Ralph's attempt to soak up the spit by kicking dirt on his boots. This was no time for subtlety. "So, you goin huntin' this weekend, Ralph?"

"Heck, yeah. You kiddin'? Deer season opens tomorrow, doll. Yer daddy'll be there." He rubbed a boot against the back of his pants leg, polishing it up a bit.

"Ya got room for one more?" I asked point-blank.

Ralph stopped and glanced at me. Then he looked around hesitantly. "Well . . . I guess so . . . I mean, sure, why not?" The response from the others was less than enthusiastic. Muted, I would say. I decided to play my hand to the hilt.

"That is, if y'all don't mind." I scanned the group.

"Oh, sure. Right. No problem," they all chimed in, except Jimbo, who just grunted and stared.

Jimbo never had had much use for me, but an incident in 1969 had served to solidify his indifference into hostility.

It was during the summer while we were in junior high. I was alone, as usual, out in the woods, up in a tree working on an experiment, when Ralph and Jimbo came walking up the path with BB guns. This particular experiment was a crude time bomb, and they were walking directly into its path. I kept silent, hoping they would pass before it went off. I wanted to keep it a secret so I would have the element of surprise if I used it in the future.

However, they noticed the lean-to I had built as a target and stopped right in front of it. I nervously watched the sun's progress, checking my watch and the setting of my little contraption. It was a magnifying glass secured in a sequence of nuts and bolts that were mounted to a wooden base lashed to a tree branch. The nuts were marked with a punch in ten-degree intervals and the whole arrangement allowed me to position the plane of the magnifying glass at any angle I wanted. I checked my watch again.

"Hey, you guys," I called from my perch in the tree. They both jumped, almost knocking down the lean-to, and peered into the branches. "It's me. I'm up here." I couldn't move around because I didn't want to disturb the position of my contraption. "Any minute now a log is going to come swinging across the trail and wipe out that lean-to. You might want to get out of the way."

Ralph and Jimbo hopped in opposite directions, looking a bit like Tweedledee and Tweedledum singing "The Walrus and the Carpenter." Then they strolled up to the base of the tree in which I was perched, trying to regain their composure.

"Mark," Ralph called. "Whatcha doin' up there?"

"Oh, I'm just trying a little experiment."

"What kinda experiment?"

"It's a sort of time-release battering ram. It's kind of hard to explain."

"Try me."

"Well, you see that rope tied to that branch above the lean-to?" I pointed to a pine limb about twenty feet above the lean-to.

"Yeah."

"Well, if you follow it down you'll see it's tied to the end of this log right here." I pointed to the log hanging above me. Ralph's eye followed the angle of the rope as it crossed the path to the tree where I was perched.

"Yeah."

"OK. That log is secured to this tree by a thread. You probably can't see it from down there. Anyway, I've got a magnifying glass set so when the sun hits that opening in the leaves, it will focus on that thread, burn it in two, and release the log, which will swing across and smash the lean-to."

Jimbo spat, shook his head, and wandered off, evidently disgusted. Ralph squinted up at me for a minute. "How do ya know how ta turn it so it'll be focused?"

I hesitated, reluctant to reveal my secret. In the end, my pride won out. "Well, we know at this time of year the sun advances one degree vertically every four minutes and one degree horizontally every twelve minutes. So, I focused the glass when the sun hit that hole." I pointed up higher and Ralph craned his neck, his mouth gaping open like a chick waiting to be fed. "Then I figured how many degrees it was vertically to the next hole and turned the glass accordingly, compensating for the proper number of degrees horizontally at the same time," I concluded, triumphantly.

"So, this really works?"

"Sure."

"Ya mean ya done knocked down that lean-to with this contraption?"

"Well . . . not yet," I admitted. "But I'm sure it'll work this time."

He snorted.

"I'd move if I were you." I checked my watch again. "Should be any second." Just then the sun cleared the hole in the leaves. "Here it comes!" The beam from the glass focused on the thread and wisps of smoke curled up. Then, suddenly, the thread was gone. I heard the rope creaking as the log swished through the leaves. "There it goes!" I cried and looked up in time to see Jimbo turn in surprise just before the log knocked him into the lean-to.

I hollered, "Watch out!" but by that time Jimbo was already flat on his back. The log swung slowly above him like a divining rod pointing out water.

"Hey! Are you OK?" Ralph yelled. But before he could render any aid, Jimbo shoved the log aside, jumped up, grabbed his BB gun, and started taking pot shots in my direction.

I scrambled behind the tree, looking for branches that would support a better defensive posture. "Hey!" I heard a BB ripping through the leaves nearby. "I warned you!" A scrap of bark was torn from the tree and dropped on my shoulder. "It's not my fault."

Ralph tackled Jimbo, wrested the BB gun from his hands, and lured him away with it. "Yer just lucky," Ralph hollered as he ran down the trail. "I think that log messed up his aim. He usually hits ever'thin' he aims at."

I waited for a long time before I climbed down. Jimbo's attitude toward me for the next few years was less than cordial.

Friday afternoon I was ready with an arsenal of borrowed camping gear. I was just buttoning up a thick plaid hunting shirt over a work shirt over a T-shirt when Darnell skidded up to the garage in his beat-up '52 pickup. "Toss 'er in, doll," he drawled, a faceless voice booming from a cloud of dust. I suppressed several coughs as the dust cleared to reveal the classic Darnell pose, right hand clutching the knob at the top of the steering wheel, sunburned left elbow jutting out of the window, a silly grin on his face, and a cap jammed on his head at an angle with the inscription "I'm not a trucker, I just found the hat."

Darnell's truck was in a permanent transition phase. No one was sure of the original color, not even Darnell. I claimed it was brown, based on the dashboard, but there was some speculation that even the dash wasn't original equipment. Dominant in the color scheme were Bondo red and primer gray, with various other colors making an occasional appearance. On the whole, it looked like it had been camouflaged for Mars.

I tossed my gear in the back and climbed in. I would have buckled the seat belt if there had been one. I was acquainted with Darnell's reputation as Terror of the Back Roads from firsthand experience.

"Where's ever'body else?" I yelled over the radio that was blaring "Drop Kick Me, Jesus" when it wasn't blaring "Jesus Is Just All Right with Me."

"We're meetin' 'em there."

"Fine," I said through gritted teeth and settled down to the serious business of staying in my seat as Darnell tore out of the driveway and rattled down the road. Riding with Darnell took concentration and a certain amount of prayer.

We arrived at the campsite by a circuitous route down dirt roads, twin-rut tracks, and dried-out creek beds. With a minimum of assistance I set up my tent and installed the sleeping bag. Then we gathered firewood and grilled wieners, shivering and drawing close to the fire as night descended and the temperature dropped quickly.

After supper we sat on logs under the looming pines, poked the fire with sticks, and told stories. The other guys crammed tobacco into their mouths in various forms and spit into the fire. I contented myself with spitting into the fire occasionally. Smokeless tobacco shared the same category as country music in my value system.

Darnell started off with a story about a ghost truck that picked up hitchhikers. Everyone groaned.

"Come on," Ralph said, "we heard that one so many times we could all say it together."

"But I like that one."

"Forget it."

"Wait a minute. Mark hasn't heard it before." He turned to me. "You want ta hear it, don't ya?"

"Sure, why not?" After all, the guy gave me a ride. I owed him something.

Darnell started in on a story about a ghost truck that drops hitch-hikers off at a certain truck stop, giving them a quarter for a cup of coffee. When the hitchhiker tells the waitress "Joe Bob sent me," he finds out that the trucker was killed ten years before in a big wreck right outside the truck stop. It was typical fireside ghost-story stuff, but Darnell loved it. While he was telling the story, the other guys disappeared into the bushes to take a leak. They stayed gone a good while and came back belching clouds of white breath into the November night.

When Darnell finally finished, Jimbo belched a few more times and then told twelve of the dirtiest jokes I had ever heard, back to back. They were so crude that they lost any vestige of humor. Ralph glanced at me nervously. Bubba shrugged his shoulders and shook his head. When Jimbo told a joke, you felt obligated to laugh. Since elementary school he had undergone a metamorphosis from a hick version of the Pillsbury doughboy to a redneck Jolly Green Giant. It was as if somebody had kissed a bullfrog and turned it into an ox. He was more than six feet tall, 210 pounds, and all muscle. Few people called him Jumbo anymore and lived to tell about it. Although the jokes were painfully obscene, I managed a chuckle or two for appearance.

This got Bubba started on a rather long and convoluted story involving a Canadian, an airplane, a herd of sheep, a vacuum cleaner, and a brick. I don't have the faintest idea what it was about. I listened all the way through because Bubba had such a strong accent it was entertaining just to hear him talk. He also had a way of talking that made you think he was just on the verge of saying the one thing that would explain it all.

Unfortunately, he never said that one thing, so I never knew the point of the story. But I did notice everyone else disappeared at least once during Bubba's story.

Based on the competition, I figured I could clean up on storytelling, so when Bubba finally sputtered to a halt, I jumped in and began one of my favorites—the broccoli story. The mysterious rash of bathroom visits continued during the broccoli story as well. I decided something was going on, and I determined to take a peek myself and find out what it was.

I got up and dusted off my jeans. "Well, I guess I'll go take a whiz," I commented casually.

Before I made it out of the firelight, Ralph called me back. "No! Wait. Don't do that."

"Why not?"

"I just don't thank it's a good idea."

"I do. Otherwise I'm going to drown out the campfire."

"Well, then you oughtta go over there." He pointed to the other side of the camp.

"Why should I do that?"

"When I was out on that side, I heard a noise like a arrow, and I don't have ta tell ya what that means."

"Yes you do."

"That means," he lowered his voice, "Jake Crowley could be out there." He shuddered, and the other guys looked around nervously.

"Who's Jake Crowley?" I hollered back.

They all jumped. *"SHHHH!"* Ralph hissed like a snake on amphetamines. "If he's out there, he might hear ya." His hoarse stage whisper carried like a shout.

"So?"

"Look. Just shut up and come back over here and I'll tell ya about Jake Crowley." He gestured wildly. "But ya gotta promise ta keep your voice down when ya say his name."

I went back. I didn't really need to take a leak. I just wanted to know why they were disappearing into the bushes.

CHAPTER SEVEN Ralph squatted down next to the fire and leaned into it. "Jake Crowley was raised out here on the Neches River bottom," he breathed in a voice so low we were obliged to crouch around the fire just to hear him, "and he spent his life huntin' and fishin'. He only went ta school up ta third grade, til he could read and write. He never set foot out a Fred before 1969, when he got his draft notice, and before he knowed it he was headed over ta Vietnam."

The flickering light from the fire illuminated Ralph's face from below, stretching his eyebrows into his hairline and casting the wrinkles on his brow into bold relief. His words came out in white clouds.

"He was green, but they was short on good men, so they set him in charge of a squad and sent him out in the jungle. The first thing he did was ta walk right through a mine field, only he never knowed it because he didn't hit a one. But when his squad follered, they was all cut ta shreds, and he just had ta stand there and watch." The contours of Ralph's burr haircut blended with the darkness behind him, which made his face seem to be detached and floating in space above the fire.

"Well, ever'body told him how lucky he was ta be alive, and they sent him out again with a new squad. They was creepin' through a clearin' when all a sudden they found theirselves in the middle of a mess a snipers in the trees." Ralph leaned back his head and looked around at the trees surrounding us. "When the noise ended, Jake was standin' alone in the middle of the clearin' without a scratch on 'im."

"Well, ever'body told him again how lucky he was ta be alive, except some started talkin' bout how he was jinxed and they was scared ta be in his unit. But he was a good fighter, so they sent him out again, this time at the back of the squad. They was sneakin' through a swamp when the next thing he knowed they was all sinkin' in the mud. He runned up ta pull 'em out, but he couldn't get a holt on 'em, and they all sunk. He decided he wanted ta die, so he walked in the same place, but he wouldn't sink." The shadow from Ralph's big curved nose danced on the left side of his face, obscuring his eye, which glimmered occasionally when it caught a stray beam of light. I glanced without turning my head. We were crouched around the fire in a tight circle, close enough to singe our eyebrows.

"After that, Jake just disappeared. Nobody ever seen him back in Vietnam. But a few years ago, somebody saw traces of a feller livin' back in these here woods, and then somebody else come out with a story of a wild man in camouflage huntin' with a crossbow." I glanced nervously into the darkness beyond the edge of the fire. I noticed everyone else did too. "When they asked his pa about it, he wouldn't say nothin'. When they asked him again, he showed 'em his shotgun and told 'em ta leave. So," Ralph hissed, looking across the fire at me, "wouldn't go out there if I was you."

Everyone sat frozen around the fire. Then Jimbo split the air with a prodigious belch that knocked pinecones from the trees, and I jumped into the fire. Everyone collapsed in laughter as I brushed the ashes off. We banked the fire and crawled into our sleeping bags.

For some reason the comfort of a thin inch of padding between me and the ground failed to lull me into a peaceful slumber. I shivered in the dark and thought about Jake Crowley. At first I was certain Ralph had invented Jake to keep me from whatever was in the bushes. However, while Ralph had many good qualities, imagination wasn't one of them. I doubted he could make up a story like that off the cuff. It might be true. But a crossbow-wielding Vietnam vet roaming the Big Thicket in camouflage? It sounded more like a movie than reality.

Of course. He probably had seen it in a movie. Yeah, that was it. So, I should sneak out and see what was in the bushes. And I would, too, except I was so cold and I was so tired and I really needed the sleep because you have to get up really early to go hunting. Everybody knows that! Otherwise I'd go out there right now, Jake or no Jake. I finally dozed off to a fitful night of dreams haunted by deer in camouflage, ice skating and shooting at me with crossbows.

The next morning I awoke to find Ralph standing over me, giggling. I tried to jump up but I became entangled in the sleeping bag and fell over, to the general hilarity of the entire party. I extricated myself and demanded an explanation.

"I saw ya layin' there with your mouth open, and I wanted ta put some Copenhagen in there real bad. But I didn't want ya ta get sick."

"Get sick! Not likely."

"Oh, yeah. You would definitely get sick, doll."

"Nonsense. If you can do it without getting sick, so can I."

"Oh, but yer daddy got sick the first time." Ralph motioned to the others. "Just ask 'em. They'll tell ya." Bubba, Darnell, and Jimbo nodded their heads like gooney birds in a mating dance.

"You guys might have gotten sick, but I can assure you it will have no such affect on me." When I was defensive, my acquired East Texas accent would fall away and my speech would become formal. It merely served to egg the others on.

"OK, then, yer lordship. Let's see ya put yer money where yer mouth is." He groped in his pocket and pulled out a crumpled bill. "Here's five bucks says you get sicker'n a dog."

"Well, I don't have five dollars on me." This revelation was greeted with hoots and cat-calls. "But I have a box of shells I can put up against it."

"Done." Ralph turned to the gallery. "Jimbo, hold the goods." He handed over the money. I turned to get the shells out of my pack. "Hold on a sec, there, Toddy Raymer," Ralph called. "Where do ya think yer goin'?"

"I was going to get the shells."

"First the Copenhagen; then the shells." He handed me the tin and instructed me to insert a pinch between the cheek and gum. It stung like a jalapeno. My eyes watered, but I maintained a stony facade.

"Just be sure not ta swaller any juice." Ralph winked at the others. "The more ya swaller, the sicker ya get." He chuckled in anticipation. "See me in forty-five minutes to pay up."

"OK." I made a mental note to not swallow and retrieved the shells for Jimbo.

"Hey! These is .22 shells." Jimbo held them up for Ralph to see.

"What am I gonna do with .22 shells?" Ralph demanded.

"Hunt," I replied defensively.

"But we're deer huntin'!"

"Yeah? So?" I suddenly remembered I was supposed to spit. I did so inexpertly and wiped my chin with my sleeve, wondering if I had swallowed without realizing it.

"So, ya don't go deer huntin' with a .22!"

"You may not, but I do," I said as if I had done it all my life.

A silence descended on the camp as they speculated on the depth of my insanity, looking for signs such as foaming at the mouth. Tobacco juice dripped off my chin, but I stood resolute and stared back at them.

Then Darnell sparked to life. "Did ya ever get one?"

"Well . . . not actually . . . I mean, not yet, that is."

Darnell's laughter broke the spell. Ralph shook his head. "Let's get goin'."

Darnell grinned like a voodoo skull. "Not yet. That's a goodun. Not yet. I like that."

Everyone else had already grabbed breakfast. With the snuff in my cheek I wasn't feeling particularly hungry, so we set out in different directions to find some deer. On my way out of the camp, I stumbled across a pile of empty beer cans, discovering the attraction of the night before.

This gave me something to think about besides my queasy stomach as I trudged along. Why would they sneak off to drink the beer? Why not just drink it in the camp? Surely that was what they usually did.

When I realized the answer, it also explained the reluctance to invite me in the first place. I was the preacher's kid. I could change my speech; I could change my wardrobe; I could change my interests. But I couldn't change the fact that I was the preacher's kid. I realized as I stumbled along that unless something drastic happened, I would forever sit on the other side of that wall, peering over at everyone else. Preacher's kid. Holy Joe. Goody Two-shoes.

I returned my attention to the task at hand. I peered around at the brush, wondering where I would hide if I were a deer. In the bushes? By a creek? Staring intently at a suspicious sound in a gully, I ran right into a tree. The snuff had made me dizzy, and I was having trouble walking straight. After an hour I found myself retching what little remained in my stomach, glad that no one was there to see me. I wandered on a quarter mile and collapsed against a sweet gum tree to rest.

I must have dozed off for quite awhile because when I was awakened by a noise, I realized I was feeling much better, almost human. I looked up. About ten yards away stood a deer with an impressive rack, must have been five or six points. He was upwind, looking away from me. Perfect!

I held my breath, slowly raised my rifle, and tried to remember what the hunting book had said. I zeroed in slightly above and to the left of the target and gently squeezed the trigger. Just before the shot went off, I heard a strange twang and fffffft-thud. The deer fell to the ground to reveal a figure standing behind it. A wild figure in tattered camouflage, matted black hair, and mud smeared all over its arms and face. The smudges highlighted the narrow face, hollow cheeks, and hooked nose. It was holding a crossbow in much the same way I was holding the .22. I saw slightly below and to the right of my sights a mirror of my own surprised expression. All this happened in the fraction of a second before my finger squeezed the trigger and the world exploded.

"What have I done?" my mind screamed, but I sat silently frozen in the firing position, leaning against the tree. My eyes were squeezed shut. I slowly opened them. There was the same gaunt face, hovering in the same location. I lowered the gun and let it drop into my lap.

The figure placed a new shaft in the bow in one smooth motion and slowly advanced toward me. I sat immobile and prayed fervently that I didn't look the slightest Asian. Frozen by fear, I watched as the crossbow gradually lowered toward my head. The last thing I heard was the sound of the catch releasing.

Sometime later I jerked to consciousness and, remembering what was happening, I jumped up. I hit my head on a crossbow shaft buried in the tree an inch above me. Rubbing my head, I looked up to see the deer hanging from a limb, field dressed. The wild figure was gone.

This was a remarkable situation. Lacking a precedent, I pondered my next action. After considerable effort I extracted the shaft from the tree and hid it in my jacket. Then I whistled and hollered, and the gang trickled in.

"Whoa," Ralph said as he stepped out of the brush. He looked at me suspiciously. "You did that?" I looked at him and raised my eyebrow. "With a .22?" I smiled confidently. He sniffed the barrel. "Well, it's been fired anyway."

The rest of the gang arrived shortly and were astounded. Darnell slapped me on the back. "Not yet!" he hollered. "Ya sure got me this time."

Jimbo was ready for action. "Let's get this thing cut down and haul 'er back ta camp." He turned to me. "Let's have that knife."

I looked at him blankly. "Knife?"

"Yeah, yeah. The knife. The one ya used ta dress it with."

"Oh, that knife." I patted my jacket pockets, my pants pockets, and looked around in the bushes. "I don't see it." I looked up to see Ralph staring at me. "I wonder where it could have gone."

"Yeah, me too." He kept staring.

"Heck, I got one," Bubba said and stepped up to the rope. Jimbo and Darnell held the deer while Bubba cut it down. Ralph and I carried it back to the camp while the rest returned to the hunt.

I was the only one who got a deer. The rest of the gang were disgusted. They gave up any pretense of going to the bushes that night and dragged the cooler next to the fire. After a few cans, the mood lightened considerably. Jimbo, genetically incapable of recognizing a faux pas, handed me a beer. Ralph froze. Bubba smiled but otherwise gave no indication of his thoughts.

"Here, ya deserve one after today. Ta Mark Crowd, the only man I knowed ta bag a deer with a pop gun." Holding up his can, he belched long and deeply and then leaned on one cheek and passed gas in like manner. Everyone laughed.

I looked at the beer in my hand, all eyes on me. Then I remembered the Question. What would Jesus do? I didn't remember any stories of Jesus going hunting, but He had hung out with fishermen. And He had hung out with prostitutes and embezzlers. And, as Bubba himself had pointed out, He was accused of being a drunkard, which made no sense to me if He didn't drink wine or something. I looked up at Bubba. He held up his can, and I could have sworn I heard him say winebibber.

I gingerly opened the top and sniffed the opening. Whew! It had a delicate bouquet of sour milk mixed with apple juice. I took a trial sip. Hints of rotten tomatoes and decaying logs, with an aftertaste of dirty laundry. A very good year. I grinned bravely and nodded my head, choking down the swallow on a stomach that had barely recovered from the snuff.

Around me they resumed telling stories and emitting superfluous gasses from all available orifices. I made occasional token sipping gestures. After an appropriate time, I excused myself to the bushes where I emptied the can, leaving a little in the bottom. I wanted an excuse not to have another one. Then I came back and watched.

They had finally accepted me. I had scaled the wall, was no longer looking over. I had achieved the end of a four-year struggle for acceptance. And what did that mean? It meant I could now sit in the middle of some God-forsaken wilderness nursing a drink that tasted like a failed chemistry experiment and listen to a litany of profanity and crudity recited to a chorus of eructation and flatulation. I congratulated myself. That's progress, baby!

What would Jesus do? Was I now obligated to sit here enduring cultural torture when I could be home reading Tolkien? For that matter, would Jesus read Tolkien? Why not, Tolkien was a very devout Catholic, wasn't he?

Quietly, I slipped from the fire and gathered up my gear. Jimbo had begun a series of jokes; nobody noticed my absence. I chucked it all into the back of Darnell's truck, figuring it would get home eventually. Taking a last look at the gang hunched around the fire, I started a long, brooding walk home.

CHAPTER EIGHT

After church the next day Dad and Parker talked so long that I decided to walk home rather than wait for a ride. It was warm for the first weekend in November, and I had my jacket slung over my shoulder for the walk across the field, down across the branch, and through the woods to the parsonage.

I was surprised when Jolene caught up with me in back of the church.

"Hey," she said.

"Hey," I said back.

"Whatcha doin'?"

"Going home."

"Oh."

We stood there, me looking at her and her looking at her feet. I frowned.

"Well?"

She looked up. "Well, what?"

"Are you going to say something or what?"

"Uh, yeah. I was wonderin' . . ." She looked back down at her feet, then at the woods, and then suddenly at me. "Would you go with me to the Sadie Hawkins dance Friday?" The words came out all in a rush.

"What?" Was this Jolene? Was she asking me on a date? Was my head on fire?

"The Sadie Hawkins dance. This Friday. At school."

"Me?" A wave of adrenaline coursed through my body as if a dam had burst. Reality struggled to keep its head above the surface like an exhausted swimmer in a flood. The landscape seemed to rush toward me; each individual hair on my head was spinning like a drive shaft. I choked back the thundering echo of what-if that rumbled through my head. Reality gasped out something in the midst of the tumult. It sounded like, "If something seems too good to be true, it probably is." I could barely hear it, but I knew that if I didn't heed the warning I would regret it.

"Is this some kind of joke?" I looked at her, barely able to focus on her reaction.

Her eyes opened wide. "Oh, no." She shook her head; ebony ripples flowed through her hair in the thin winter sunlight. "Really, will you go with me?"

"To the dance." I couldn't process the information. It bore no relation to reality. She might as well have told me to breathe water or walk through a wall. "Not a joke?"

"No, it's not a joke. Mark, nobody else will go with me. You should know that."

"Oh, I see." The world righted itself, my pulse spiraled down toward double digits, and the landscape resumed its natural aspect. Reality, wet and dripping, whispered, "I told you so."

"No, it's not like that. I really would like ta go with ya."

"Right."

"Really!"

"Look, Jolene, I'm . . ." I thought of all the reasons it was not possible that a guy like me could be with a girl like her. The list was long, and most of the reasons were so personal I couldn't say them out loud, not even when I was alone.

Her face fell. "Oh, yer goin' with someone else?"

"No, I'm not going at all." I was suddenly angry at her, at the world, at all the reasons why I would never date a girl like Jolene. "Dang it, I don't know how to dance. I'm a Baptist preacher's kid, for crying out loud! Where would I learn how to dance?"

"Oh, is that all? I could teach ya how ta dance real easy. Nobody else knows how either. They just move around."

I knew that. It was just an easy way to deflect the blow. I threw out another, very real, objection.

"You think I'm going to volunteer to be the straight man in front of the whole school for your little jokes? Jolene, have you ever had a date you didn't embarrass?"

She said quietly, "Have I ever asked anyone out before?"

I had expected the usual snappy retort. I wasn't prepared for the serious face looking back at me.

"You're really serious, aren't you?" I whispered.

"What?" She leaned toward me, her hair swinging down in black curtains. I looked at her eyebrows, full, almost bushy, like a black cat. My hand twitched.

"You really mean it?" I stumbled backward. "You're asking me to the dance, seriously."

She put her hands on her hips. "Mark Cloud, are you stupid or what? Yes, I am askin' you to the Sadie Hawkins dance for this Friday. I done asked about five times. Do ya want me ta write it down fer ya?"

"And you're not doing it to play jokes on me?"

"No, I am not." She glared at me. "Any other stupid questions?"

"Uhh. What time is it?"

She glanced at her watch. "It's 12:17."

"No, I mean what time is the dance?"

"Seven o'clock."

"OK."

"OK?"

"OK. I'll go. Does this mean you're driving, seeing as how it's a Sadie Hawkins thing?"

"Yeah, I'll drive. I'll pick ya up at yer house at 6:30."

"OK."

"All right, so it's settled. See ya tomorrow." She nodded at me and strode back around the church. I watched her, unable to move. At the corner she turned back. "Oh and there's a contest, so dress like Li'l Abner." Then she was gone. After a few minutes I regained some measure of consciousness and stumbled home.

The next day at lunch Bubba told the rest of the gang about the date.

C. J. slapped me on the back. "Dude! Gimme five!" I slapped his hand absently.

Ralph looked at me like I had suggested he hunt deer with a .22. "Son, have ya lost yer mind? Bubba, talk ta the man, will ya?"

"He's old enough to know better."

It was time to defend my sanity. "I do know better. Look, you all know what has happened to every guy who has dated Jolene." Ralph snorted. C. J. sighed. Darnell and Jimbo looked on with sympathy. "So do I. I'm just doing her a favor. She can't get anybody to go with her, that's all."

"She's like a Doberman, doll. She could turn on ya at any minute. Believe me, I been there."

"Yes, I remember." I couldn't suppress a smile as I recalled Ralph's face the morning after. Hiding the car was classic; hiding the distributor cap in the glove box was genius.

"Laugh if ya want, but I guarantee ya won't be laughin' Friday night. Bubba, tell 'im."

"He goeth after her straightway, as an ox goeth to the slaughter, or as a fool to the correction of the stocks."

Nobody had anything to say after that. We ate our rice with chicken gravy in silence.

The week passed as weeks do, no more remarkable than those that had preceded it. Jolene and I chatted in band practice as usual. But I couldn't stop what-if from reverberating in the back of my mind.

For years I had served as her personal eunuch, engaged in verbal sparring matches, listened to tales of the tortures she had visited upon those in the male population foolish enough to ask her on a date. I had even served as reluctant accomplice on a few occasions, although this was not public knowledge. There had never been a hint that she might have the slightest romantic interest in me. Or in anyone else, for that matter, but we're talking about me right now. Forget those other guys.

I played the conversation over in my mind until it wore a rut in my brain. Why was she so shy at first? The Jolene I knew would come right out and ask in a matter-of-fact tone. And cheerfully argue me into submission, like she always did. But she had been shy, and then angry in the face of my objections. Maybe she did hide a secret love. Didn't Mac once tell me that he would have never known Peggy liked him if she had not asked him to the Sadie Hawkins dance?

I alternately shivered at the possibility and quaked at the impossibility of it. I cursed myself for daring to hope; then I cursed myself for spurning the possibility it was true. What if it was true and I walked away because I was too timid or too obsessed with self-preservation or too incredulous? What if it wasn't true and I set myself up for humiliation? What if? What if? I went insane a dozen times that week.

On Friday afternoon Hannah plopped down in the seat next to me on the bus. "What's this I hear about you having a date tonight?"

"What's it to you?"

"This is a rare event, like an eclipse or something. I'm surprised it wasn't in the paper."

"I'm just doing Jolene a favor. She couldn't find a date to the dance."

"Mom and Dad are letting you go to a dance?"

"I told them it was a square dance." For some unexplained reason, a square dance was less odious than the regular round kind.

60

Hannah considered this in silence, no doubt memorizing the detail in anticipation of her sixteenth birthday when she would navigate the tortuous path of taboos and culture.

"Well, Genie says she has a pair of elevator shoes if you need them." She glanced over her shoulder at her friends. They were huddled together, glancing up front and giggling.

I looked at Genie. She collapsed behind the seat in a seizure of giggles. "Your concern is heartwarming. Please thank Genie for her kind offer. If I can repay it with any small kindness, like shooting her dog, tell her not to hesitate to ask."

"OK," Hannah said and bounced back to her friends.

In keeping with the Sadie Hawkins theme, there was a contest for the best Li'l Abner and Daisy Mae. Decency ruled out an actual Sadie Hawkins prize. Besides, Thelma Perkins, recognized in three counties for having taken homeliness to heights heretofore unknown in Fred, had an unfair advantage.

Despite my having shot Bambi's father, Mom agreed to transform me from a scrawny egghead to a muscled bumpkin. That I waited to ask until Friday afternoon didn't faze her. Armed with a copy of the Sunday funnies, she marshaled her resources.

"It's too late for us to dye your hair black, although that would have been better. We'll have to settle for a big cowlick. Lucky you haven't had a haircut in awhile." She took another look at the comic. "Heidi, get the Dippity-do. Mark, put on overalls, a white T-shirt, and two layers of thick socks. Hannah, don't you have an old red flannel shirt that is coming apart?"

"Yes, ma'am."

"Bring it here. I'll get Dad's work boots."

"Wait a minute," I said. "I'm going to wear Hannah's shirt? It'll be way too small."

"That's the point, dear. You have to be bursting out of a shirt, and you will hardly burst out of your own. Now run along and get dressed."

Hannah smirked over her shoulder on the way out of the room. "If you'd grow some muscles, you wouldn't have to wear girl's clothes to make it look like you had some."

I almost caught up with her, but she had timed her head start well. On my way back to the living room, I found the shirt hanging on her bedroom door, which was locked.

At 6:30 I was standing in the driveway checking my watch for the seventh time. I looked at my reflection once more in the side window of the Galaxy. Despite Mom's best efforts, I looked less like Li'l Abner and more like Joe Btfsplk, the scrawny guy in the cartoon who was always accompanied by a dark cloud.

I was making adjustments to my jelled cowlick when I heard the sound of an eggbeater behind me. Bubba's red 1966 Corvair convertible pulled into the driveway. Marianne McCullough was riding shotgun, and Jolene was in the back.

"Son," Bubba hollered. "Ya got yer Sunday-go-to-meetins on fer sure."

"Uh, yeah." I had expected just Jolene, but it made sense they would double. They were twins, after all.

"Hop on in the back."

I wanted to suavely vault into the backseat, but I would probably kick Marianne in the head or split my pants, so I awkwardly crawled into the car. I looked over at Jolene. Daisy Mae would have given both her eyeteeth to look like Jolene. She was wearing black shorts cut off somewhere around her elbows and a red blouse with white polka dots, pulled down off her shoulders. Her outfit echoed the colors of her creamy white complexion, her raven black hair, and the maddening red of her lips. I had the distinct impression that I was violating some law of nature by being seen within a five-mile radius of her.

"Hey," I said.

"Hey."

"Nice outfit."

"Thanks. You too."

Then we hit the highway, making conversation difficult over the wind and road noise. Just as well. What would I say?

In the buffeting silence, Dusty Springfield sang "The Son of a Preacher Man" on the radio. I had grown to hate the song with its worldly-wise PK and a seemingly grateful woman who had learned about love in his arms. But when I looked at Jolene, she raised an eyebrow and smiled in a manner I found difficult to interpret. Was she trying to tell me something? I studied her face for additional clues, without enlightenment. It gave me something to think about for the rest of the drive.

The gym was filled with guys in overalls and girls in cutoffs milling around. Squeaky was there with Ralph, Bertha with Darnell, and a girl I hadn't seen before was dragging Jimbo around by his nose. C. J. was dressed as Arlo Guthrie; the girl who had brought him looked disgusted. Becky was there with Number 68, but I tried to aim my back toward their part of the room. I even saw Elrick playing attendance on some queen of the Nile. He had the clothes and the biceps to match, and his mate made a better Daisy Mae than any of the blondes in the room.

We stood around the punch bowl until the festivities commenced. The faculty chaperones lined the couples up in twin rows, guys on one side, girls on the other. Each in turn, we strolled through the gauntlet and past the faculty judges. I tried to stretch as much as possible to look the masculine Li'l Abner next to Jolene's Daisy Mae. That she was half a foot taller was a handicap. I felt at once proud and ridiculous.

After the procession the dance began, featuring bluegrass and cornpone country records over the tinny PA in the gym. Jolene was right;

these folks didn't know how to dance. Jimbo lumbered around like a dancing bear. Darnell looked like he was being electrocuted. Ralph ambled around like a guy looking for the bathroom. Or maybe he really was looking for the bathroom. Bubba had learned his dance moves from a spastic chicken. The line dance for "Cotton-Eyed Joe" looked more like a comic samba line in a Marx Brothers movie.

I ducked into the bathroom, afraid to embarrass myself in front of Jolene. When I returned, she dragged me into the crowd. For a rare moment I was transformed from an observer into a participant. The first few moments of heightened self-consciousness gave way to experimentation. Nobody was looking at me. They were too busy with their own steps.

I closed my eyes and listened to the music and began moving around. After a few seconds I opened my eyes and realized I was dancing with Jolene. Or at least I was dancing in her vicinity. It occurred to me that all I had to do was keep moving somewhere near the beat and this phenomenon would continue. I did and it did.

Time didn't stop; it evaporated. The music played; we moved to it. The universe reversed gear and shrank to a space just large enough to hold Jolene and me. Nothing else existed but me trying to remember to move and Jolene dancing in front of me. I was in one of those dreams where if I stepped off a chair just right, with just the right amount of indefinable finesse, I would float. I had finessed the step; I was floating.

I scarcely noticed as one song blurred into the next. Then the music stopped and they were announcing the winners of the contest. I was amazed that the gym was still there. I hadn't seen it for quite some time. Then I heard cheers and clapping and felt Jolene dragging me by the loose suspender. I wasn't sure why until we stumbled onto the stage and they sat us on wooden chairs.

We had won the contest. I doubted my biceps had much to do with it. And after the ride in the convertible, my jelled cowlick now made me look like an albino Buckwheat. I was obviously riding on Jolene's coattails. The principal made a speech and asked us to come forward to be crowned with a garland of daisies. When I stepped forward, I felt a drag on my left foot. My left bootlace was looped around the leg of the chair. The left leg. The one next to where Jolene was sitting. Surely not.

There was a smattering of chuckles. I stopped and looked at Jolene. The internal debate awakened in a foul mood.

She stopped and looked back at me. "What?"

I looked down at the chair. She impatiently pulled it from my bootlace and grabbed my arm so I could escort her to the front where we received our crowns. I was stunned; she was smiling.

The chuckles increased. The annual staff photographer went down on one knee in front of us. From the corner of my eye I saw Ralph gesturing wildly. He stage whispered, "XYZ! XYZ!" and pointed to his crotch. The international distress signal that your fly is open. Then a flash blinded me. It took all the self-control I could muster to resist the urge to look down. Instead, I accepted my crown and waited for the return to the throne. As I leaned over to put the chair back, I saw that my fly was indeed open, the red shirttail sticking out like I was taunting a bull. I shoved the chair into place, turned away from Jolene and the crowd, and rectified the situation. Then I sat down.

A long ways down. There was no chair. The crash on the plywood stage reverberated through the gym, and the crowed erupted in laughter. I jumped up and glared at Jolene. She shrugged her shoulders and attempted a half smile, which infuriated me more. With a face glowing redder than my shirt, I threw the crown at her and stormed off the stage and out of the gym.

Once outside, I disappeared quickly into the shadows in the parking lot. I watched as Jolene came out and called for me. She looked around for awhile and went back inside.

I wandered through the cars until I found Ralph's dad's pickup and shivered in the bed until the dance was over. Ralph gave me a ride home although it was plain neither he nor Squeaky welcomed my company.

CHAPTER NINE The next day I left the house as soon as I emerged from the cave of my bedroom. I had seen no one when I came in the night before and made my exit through the back in the morning. Not wishing to be seen, I used the method that had rendered me invisible for years. I hit the *Grit* route, avoiding the homes of my classmates, especially one particular classmate. I didn't even stop at the gazebo, now painted and surrounded with a flowerbed, on the off chance Parker or Sonia had heard about the cataclysm.

The temperature had dropped considerably overnight. I started out wearing a jacket, but I pedaled furiously through the sand roads, fueled by rage, and soon the jacket was tied to the handlebars. I took every track off the main road, no matter how pointless it seemed. As the sun sank lower, I went deeper into the river bottom. By late afternoon I rounded a familiar corner and saw a green Pontiac, a tendril of smoke rising from the driver's window. I looked across the road. Smoke rose from the chimney, but the porch swing was empty.

I tossed a paper in the backseat. Vernon nodded and held out a dollar and a Coke. He had a shiner on his left eye. I studied it for a second until I saw he noticed. I looked away, shoved the dollar in my shirt pocket, and took several gulps of Coke. We sat in silence for a long time. I was the first one to break it.

"She's not out there." I tilted the Coke toward the porch swing.

"Nope. It's a might cool." He took a sip of his Coke. And whatever else. The smell was pretty strong. "Ain't seen her in a spell. Don't know if it's the cold or if she's runned off." He contemplated it for a few seconds, then shrugged.

"What was it you said about girls? About them knowing without being taught?"

"Oh, that." He slapped his left hand across his face and took a drag on his cigarette. "What makes ya ask?"

I was reluctant to relive my humiliation in my own mind, much less tell someone else. "You know the Culpeppers?"

"Yeah, sure, I know the old man pretty good."

I hesitated. Vernon turned his broad face toward me speculatively, the black eye making him look like an Eskimo raccoon. Then the wrinkles on his face adjusted very slightly, just enough to suggest the echo of a smile somewhere within. "Ah," he breathed, smoke blooming out between us. "The girl. What's her name?"

"Jolene," I forced out between gritted teeth.

"Yes, Jolene." He considered the sinking sun for a few moments. "But she's quite a looker, ain't she?"

"More than somewhat."

"I hear she has a bit of a giddy streak to 'er. Not quite right in the head as I hear it."

I laughed. "I guess that's one way of looking at it." I told him of her escapades, including the story of Turner McCullough and the Brakeman's Daughter, leaving out the detail that I played the part with the shotgun. No sense in that getting out; I could get lynched.

Vernon enjoyed the stories. As much as it annoyed me to acknowledge it, so did I.

"So, where do you figure in?"

I hesitated again, then spilled the whole sorry story, from her asking me out and my objections (at least, the ones I said out loud to Jolene; not the others) to my ride home with somebody else.

"So, this was last night?"

"Yep. I mean, yessir."

"I see. Well, Mark boy, it's like this." He reached under the car seat and pulled out a silver flask, expertly refilled his Coke can with the amber liquid, and put it back under the seat. He held the can up toward me and said, "Salute," but it sounded like "sal-you-tay." I held up my Coke and nodded, and we both drank.

"I recall a feller from New York I spent a bit of time with back some thirty years ago. We had a drink or two in our time. And a talk or two. He said it is writ somewheres that a woman will hanker after her husband and he will rule over her. That's as may be, but from where I sit, I see a good bit of the tail waggin' the dog. I don't deny that it can start out that way. A woman hankerin' after a man, I'm sayin'. But once she's got 'im, it's a bit murky which is rulin' who.

"It's a rare man as can do without a woman. Them Catholic fathers do it, I hear, but it's bound to be a powerful strain on 'em. And I don't know many women as can do without a man. But this here Jolene might be one of 'em. She's strange enough in other ways, that's sure enough."

I held up my Coke and said, "Sal-you-tay." Vernon dipped his can toward me and took a healthy drink.

"I do know one thang. Ya can't let yerself be fooled by how a woman looks. Beauty and cruelty are like as not ta be joined at the hip. A homely woman ain't got room ta be overly proud, but a looker don't usually grow up with any natural predators. She's at the top of the food chain." He took a long drink from the can and lit another cigarette.

"Like that 'un over there." He waved the lighter toward the house as he set it back on the dash. "Her fool of a old man probably doted on 'er when she were a cute little squirt, wouldn't let 'er ma lay a hand on 'er. Ever'where she went she was probably pet on and cooed over and never told no 'til it was too late."

He looked over at me very deliberately. His eyes were rheumy and bloodshot, flushed redder by the sunset. "Then some poor young fool sees 'er all built like a brick outhouse and his head turns ta mush and he marries her expectin' a life of paradise. And maybe he gets it fer a few weeks or a few months."

I stared back at him, trapped by the deadly seriousness in his eyes.

"Then she molts her skin like a snake, and the she-devil that her pa and ever'body else has been makin' all these years turns that paradise into a hellhole." He looked away and took a long drink. "It might take awhile, maybe even a few years, if he's lucky, but there ain't no undoin' what's been bred in the bone."

I was willing to elect Jolene as She-devil of the Year, even open a campaign office in Beaumont and hire a staff. But this seemed to be laying it on a bit thick.

As if he sensed my doubt, Vernon muttered, "I seen it many a time. All over the world. Mark my words."

A change of subject was in order; it was time to trade confidences. "So, how'd you get the shiner?"

"This?" He pointed the cigarette and his half fingers at his left eye. "In my line of work I sometimes have ta settle a score or two. Sometimes it gets rough. But I give more'n I git when it comes to that."

"What line of work is that, exactly?" I had no idea what he did when he wasn't leering at the sunset and the local she-devils.

He looked at me sharply for a few seconds, or as sharply as he could. He was starting to get a little blurry around the edges. "I'm a kind of broker. I connect people who want stuff with stuff people want."

I waited for more details. None came. "OK."

The sun had gone down. Vernon was pouring himself another dose. Not a good sign.

I opened the door to turn on the dome light. "Say, how about if I throw my bike in the back and drive you home? I need to get going anyway."

Vernon looked at me with his broad, blank face. "Guess I'm not quite fit ta drive tonight, am I? Yeah, go ahead and drive. Or else I'll have ta sleep here fer a few hours, and it's a bit cold fer that tonight."

I threw my bike in the back while Vernon stepped gingerly around the car with one hand on the hood to steady himself. As I pulled up to the road, a car came around the curve from the left. I waited for it to pass, surprised. This area was pretty remote; not many cars came out this way. It slowed as the lights caught the Pontiac and stopped with the brights shining in my face. I squinted and held up my hand to block the glare but couldn't make anything out. Then an arm reached out of the driver's window and waved me on.

I turned right and drove Vernon home, brights from the mystery car in my mirror the whole way. When I pulled into Vernon's drive, the car slowed to a stop. As I got out, it pulled away. It was a black LTD, the windows up. It looked familiar. I shrugged, gave the keys to Vernon, and pulled out my bike.

The door of the trailer opened, throwing a rectangle of yellow light across the cinder-block steps and weeds next to the dirt drive. The woman came out and set a broom against the trailer. She was wearing an apron over a nice dress about twenty years out of style. This time her hair wasn't pulled back; it hung down to her shoulders. She had a dark complexion, and despite a thin nose that hooked like an eagle's beak, she was quite attractive. For an old lady, I mean.

Vernon looked at her and smiled. "Gianna, I don't recall if'n ya met Mark boy, here." He grabbed my shoulder and pushed me toward her.

She pushed me aside without a glance and held Vernon's face toward the light with both hands. "Oh Vernon, how I am being sorry for that eye. I don't know what happened, how I was upset so I never think." She kissed his eye, then his lips.

She had an accent I couldn't place, probably European. But what did I know? I met some Romanian refugees once, and a family from Hungary, but that was the extent of my education on European accents. That and television.

Vernon pushed her back by the shoulders and turned her toward me. "Gina, don't worry about that. Say hello to Mark boy. He's the one who brings me the newspapers."

Gina smiled. "How do you do, Mark boy?" She held out a thin, almost dainty hand. I held out my hand, and she wrapped her hand around my fingers, not the palm. Her little bones squeezed until I thought my fingers would snap. I suppressed a wince.

"Hello, ma'am."

She smiled at me again and stepped back to Vernon, sliding her arm through his in much the same way Jolene had through mine the night before.

"Well, I better get home. See ya."

They nodded and waved, and I rode off into the falling dark. I was almost to the highway when I noticed a glow in the sky. As I approached, the tree line fell away and I saw a huge bonfire in the front yard of the Walker estate. Parker stood in the yard in his shirtsleeves, watching the gazebo burn.

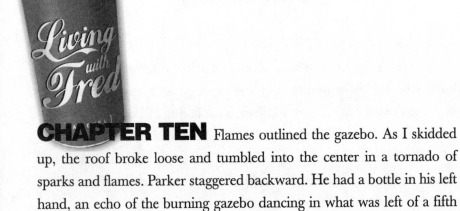

CHAPTER TEN

Flames outlined the gazebo. As I skidded up, the roof broke loose and tumbled into the center in a tornado of sparks and flames. Parker staggered backward. He had a bottle in his left hand, an echo of the burning gazebo dancing in what was left of a fifth of Jack Daniels, like a volcano burning in a deep auburn sea.

"What happened?" I didn't know if I meant the fire or the whiskey.

He turned toward me, his good eye toward the fire, red and glinting in the light. "She left me. Again."

"What?"

"But I didn't lay a hand on 'er." He thrust his finger toward me as if I had contradicted him. "Not a finger."

I nodded.

"Not a finger. I just watched 'er go. Sat and watched 'er."

I looked at the house. The truck was gone.

"Then I walked the four miles to the county line and back and sat out here fer a spell." He swung the bottle out toward the gazebo and stared at the fire for awhile.

"Lucky fer me this time she left me my boots. I was wearin' 'em, and I weren't passed out, so it would'a been awkward fer her to pull 'em off, I guess." He smiled to himself.

"So I sat and I thought. And what I thought was it seemed a little cold around the house these days. Figured we could use a fire."

One of the pillars fell into the conflagration. Parker held both arms out toward the gazebo like a man presenting a masterpiece.

"So I built a fire. How do you like it?" He turned back to me, still holding out his right hand toward the fire. "Now that"–he waved his hand–"that is a fire!"

"Yessir."

"Some things need burnin'. And when they do, somebody's got ta burn 'em." He unscrewed the cap, took a slug, and twisted the cap back on. "I ain't never shrinked back from what had ta be done."

He looked at me. The scar snaked down from his hairline, across his left eyebrow, under the patch, and out across his cheek to his jaw. It was turned a pale pink against his ruddy face by the firelight. "Remember that."

"Yessir."

"Never hold back when ya got ta do somethin'. Just step up and take yer medicine like a man."

"Yessir."

Parker fell silent and stared into the fire. I felt awkward standing there, but it seemed more awkward to say "See you later" and pedal away. I inched closer to the fire to take the edge off the chill of the November night air. Another pillar collapsed, falling toward me, half out into the lawn. I jerked back and almost fell off the bike. Parker stepped up, dug one boot under it, shoved it into the fire, and stomped out the flames in the grass, grinding the heel of his boot into the dirt.

"Ya know why she left me?" He squinted at me with the one eye, still twisting his heel back and forth.

"Nosir."

"I'm a religious nut." He cocked his head sideways like the dog in the Victrola ads. "Did ya know that? I'm a religious fanatic. A Holy Joe."

I was often called similar names. Being a PK, it was an understandable, if mistaken, assessment. But for Parker to be called a religious fanatic, this was madness.

"Kinda takes ya by surprise, don't it? She snuck up on me with that one. Blindsided me, ya might say." He chuckled. "What would my pa say?

"'Yer always prayin',' she says. 'Always readin' that Bible,' she says. 'It's always Pastor Matt this and Pastor Matt that,' she says. 'We don't never go nowhere but church; sometimes I just want ta go out and have some fun,' she says. Well she went out all right. I guess she's out havin' fun."

He swung up the bottle and unscrewed the cap in a single motion. He took a good long hit and held it toward me. "But she messed up. The party is right here. We're havin' fun right here."

He slowly lowered the bottle, put the cap back on, and hunkered in front of the fire, leaning back on his heels. "How do ya figure it, preacher boy? She leaves me 'cause I beat 'er too much. So I get religion and quit beatin' 'er. Then she leaves me 'cause I ain't beatin' 'er enough, I guess." He tapped the bottle against the steel toecap on his boot. "I guess I should'a learned to beat 'er just the right amount." He spit into the fire. "Probably takes a little practice ta learn the proper mix."

I decided this was a good time to make an exit. I cleared my throat. Parker ignored me and threw pieces of gravel in the fire, one after another.

"Well, I guess I'd better be going home," I said.

Parker threw the whole handful of gravel into the fire and stood up.

"Devil take 'er, I say. I ain't gonna twist this way and the next just ta suit 'er fancy. I'll do as I please, and she can do the same. Either way, I won't be needin' that anymore." He kicked gravel toward the ruins of the gazebo. "I just did it fer her, anyway, and she ain't here no more."

"OK, well I have to go home now. I'll see you later." I nodded at him and spun the bike around on the back tire.

"You can tell yer pa that I'm through with it."

"Yessir."

"No need him askin' after me. I won't be up ta the church tomorrow."

"Yessir."

"Now get out a here."

"Yessir." I pedaled off. Parker turned back to the fire and twisted the cap off the bottle. The volunteer fire truck passed me as I turned onto the highway.

———

It was past suppertime when I got home. Mom, Heidi, and Hannah were watching Bob Newhart. The remains of the meal and one empty plate were on the table, but I went straight to the study. Dad was sitting in my grandmother's armchair in a corner under the floor lamp, his feet on the ottoman, a Bible in his lap, and reference books scattered about. He looked up when I came in.

"You missed dinner."

"Yes, sir. I was kind of delayed." I realized I was still wearing the *Grit* bag. I took it off. "I was passing Parker's house and saw the gazebo on fire."

Dad pulled his feet from the ottoman and sat up. A Strong's concordance fell to the floor. "What?"

"Parker burned it down. Doused it with gasoline and burned it. He was drunk."

"How do you know he was drunk?"

"I saw him drinking. The bottle was almost empty. Jack Daniels."

Dad sunk back in his chair, set his elbow on the arm, leaned his forehead against his hand, and sighed.

"And Sonia left. That was why he did it. She complained he was too religious and not fun anymore, so she left, and he walked to the county line and bought the whiskey and got drunk and burned down the gazebo."

Dad looked thoughtful and, for a reason I couldn't fathom, less depressed. The phone rang twice and stopped. Our ring.

"Oh, and he told me to tell you he wouldn't be coming back to church and not to ask about him."

Mom called from the kitchen. "Honey, Deacon Fry for you."

"I'll get it back here." Dad set the books aside and went to his desk. "Hello. Yes. No, I was just doing some studying. Yes. He's right here." He looked over at me. I reviewed the past few days for potential infractions, an automatic reflex to the guilt prompted by Dad's look. In my haste to disappear I had not cleaned the church today. But how would Deacon Fry know that? He never went to the church on Saturdays.

Dad was silent for a long time, but his face got harder as the monologue progressed, like Quick Set concrete. It was a good time to get something to eat, but as I turned to the door, Dad froze me in place with one finger as if he were a wizard. I retreated to the armchair and organized the papers in my bag, barely hearing the rest of the conversation.

I was skimming the stories on the back page when Dad hung up. I looked up. He looked at me for a long time.

"It seems Parker isn't the only one who has been drinking."

"What?" Talk about being blindsided.

"Deacon Fry tells me you were drinking on that hunting trip you took last weekend."

"How would he know that?"

"So it's true."

"No! I mean, yes. Well, sort of."

"Would you care to clarify your statement? I'm interested to know how one 'sort of' drinks."

"I took one sip of beer. I poured out the rest of it when nobody was looking."

"And why did you take the one sip?"

"Well, I was sitting there with everyone and . . . ," I cleared my throat. "Well, uh, I was . . . uhm. Have you ever read a book called *In His Steps?*"

Dad frowned. "Yes. And?"

"I read that book this summer, and it talked about asking yourself what would Jesus do in a situation, and then doing that. So, I was out there with Ralph and Bubba and everybody else, and Jimbo wanted to congratulate me for getting that deer, so he gave me a can of beer to celebrate, and I wondered what would Jesus do."

"And you decided Jesus would knock back a cold one?"

"Well, that sounds different than how it sounded to me at the time. I thought about how Jesus hung out with some rough folks, like fishermen and tax collectors and prostitutes and all, instead of religious people. And the Pharisees accused Him of being a drunk, and I didn't see how they could get any mileage out of it if He didn't drink something, otherwise they would know it couldn't stick. I mean, they were jerks, but they weren't stupid. The Pharisees, I mean."

"OK. We shall defer for the nonce the question of what it was that Jesus drank. Instead, allow me to ask Gamaliel a few questions."

I waited, figuring he would start making sense eventually.

"How old are you?"

"Sixteen."

"And how old was Jesus when He was accused of drinking?"

"Uh, somewhere between thirty and thirty-three."

"Correct on both counts. So, assuming there were drinking laws two thousand years ago, do you think Jesus was of legal drinking age?"

Uh-oh. Here was an angle I hadn't considered. "Yes," I admitted glumly.

"I see you have anticipated my next question. I will close with Romans 13:2 that says those who disobey the laws of the land disobey God. Checkmate."

I grunted, ungracious in defeat.

"Deacon Fry also tells me that tonight you were seen driving a drunken man around and going to his house. And not just any drunken man but a known bootlegger."

"Oh, so that's what he meant."

"That's what who meant?"

"Vernon. Crowley."

"And what did he mean?"

"I asked him what was his line of work, and he said he connected people who wanted stuff with the stuff they wanted. I was wondering about all the bottles in his trunk."

Dad snagged the ottoman with his foot and leaned back in his chair with his feet up. "And how do you come to know so much about Vernon Crowley and what is in his trunk?"

"Oh, that's no big deal, really. He's on my paper route. He parks out on a hill on the river road and watches the sunset, and I bring him a paper and he gives me a Coke, and we talk about stuff. Or just sit and watch the sunset."

"And you were driving his car because . . . ?"

"Because he sometimes gets a little too much of the other stuff in his Coke and can't drive home."

"The other stuff?"

"He keeps a flask under the seat and spikes the Coke with it. Sometimes he sort of overdoes it on the spiking."

"And your Coke?"

"Oh, it's just Coke. He doesn't open it before I get there, and he never offers me anything."

"Let me see if I have this straight. Today you went out selling *Grit,* and you stopped at Mr. Crowley's car around sunset to have a Coke. You drove him home because he was drunk, then rode your bike past the Walker's place and saw Parker drunk and burning down the gazebo."

"Yep. I mean, yes, sir."

"Sounds like a busy schedule. When did you eat?"

"I didn't. I haven't had anything since breakfast. Besides a Coke."

"Then perhaps you should get some dinner."

"Yessir!" I jumped past Dad toward the door.

"And, son," Dad said without turning in his chair.

I stopped. "Yes?"

"Be careful of Deacon Fry. He is the head of the deacons."

"Careful of what?"

"Just be careful. Abstain from all appearance of evil. Paul said that for a good reason."

I turned back. "What I don't understand is, Deacon Fry lives out on the highway. What was he doing out at Vernon's place? There is nothing past his house but shacks and the river."

Dad swiveled the chair toward me. "How do you know he was there?"

"I saw his car. He was following me when I drove Vernon home. He stopped in front of the house when I parked, but he took off when I got out."

"I see. Well, you should not worry your pretty little head about Deacon Fry's nocturnal peregrinations."

"Why is it any of his business if I drive Vernon home? I wasn't breaking any laws. Drinking laws or driving laws. I have a license. And all I drank was Coke." I was flushed with the righteous indignation of the smugly innocent.

Dad looked at me for a long moment, then motioned me to the armchair. "Have a seat. You've fasted for ten hours; ten more minutes won't enervate you."

I plopped down. He put his feet back up on the ottoman.

"Remember your question about what Jesus would do?"

"Yes."

"Do you remember what happened to Jesus?"

"You mean at the end?"

"Exactamente."

"He died."

Dad waited.

"Uhh, He was killed."

"Exactamente. Killed by whom?"

"The Romans."

"Yes, they pulled the trigger, but who put them up to it?"

"The Pharisees."

"Who were . . . ?"

"The religious leaders."

"More precisely, the legalistic religious leaders."

"Are you saying Deacon Fry is a Pharisee?"

"I'm saying abstain from all appearance of evil, especially in the immediate proximity of Deacon Fry or anyone related to him or anyone who might talk to anyone related to him."

Great. That was the entire county and probably a few neighboring counties as well. My temper flared at the injustice. "How is being friends with Vernon Crowley and driving him home when he's had too much to drink an appearance of evil? Don't you think that is what Jesus would do?"

"Perhaps. But we have already established what happened to Jesus when He did the things He would do."

"So, you're saying I shouldn't try to do what Jesus did? Because Deacon Fry might have me killed?" My voice had squeaked up an octave. I cleared my throat.

Dad smiled, but there was sadness and fatigue in the smile. "No, unlike the Pharisees, Deacon Fry doesn't have the power of life and death. Yet, at any rate."

"Then what are you saying?"

"He may not have the power of life and death, but he has the power of hire and fire."

"He would fire you because I gave Vernon Crowley a ride?"

"No, but it's just another brick in the wall he would like to build. Like the beer you had on the hunting trip."

I sat up in the chair. "Deacon Fry wants to fire you? Why?"

Dad looked at me for a long while, considering what to tell me. "Your mother and I haven't discussed this in front of you or the girls because we didn't want you to be unduly alarmed. There is a contingent of old-timers who have been in this church for generations. They are not pleased that I want to change some things, to reach out to people who don't come to church. Like Parker and Sonia, for example. Deacon Fry is the foremost among his brethren in this regard."

"But, but, but . . ." It wasn't fair. I agreed with Squeaky. Life might not be fair, but God should be. We were talking about the church, after all.

"Yes, my little motorboat?"

"But that's what the gospel is all about."

"Perhaps, but as they say these days, it is not what Deacon Fry is all about. He does not approve of certain people. For example, he was careful to point out to me that, in addition to being a bootlegger, Mr. Crowley has committed the offense of marrying a heeb wop."

"A what?"

"In the common tongue, that would be a Jewish Italian person."

"Heeb?"

"Hebrew."

"Wop?"

"It comes from a sign on Ellis Island that read 'With Out Passport.'"

Where did he come up with this stuff? It was amazing that there was room in his head for anything useful, like remembering the names of his kids.

I was outraged at the suggestion that my behavior should be governed by some hick deacon bigot with an obsession for power.

"So, you're saying that the question I should be asking is what would Deacon Fry do. Is that what you do, follow the gospel of Deacon Fry?"

As soon as I said it I wished I hadn't. I wanted to snatch it out of the air before the sound waves reached him. But sound travels more than a thousand feet per second. I just wasn't that fast.

Dad flushed red, grabbed the arms of the swivel chair, pulled his feet under him, and leaned forward, speaking in a rush. "Life is not as simple as it looks when you're sixteen. It's not a true-false test with one right answer and one wrong answer. You don't–"

He bit off the rest of the sentence and leaned back in the chair with great effort, took a deep breath, and let it out noisily through his nose. His head was tilted toward me, and he looked at me silently from under his eyebrows.

I held his stare as long as I could. I regretted saying it, but my face burned with the passion of idealism and self-righteousness. I didn't want to back down, but as his breathing calmed and his glare softened, I found I could no longer look him in the eye. I looked down at the *Grit* bag and fumbled with the papers.

"Mark, it would be nice if everything was that black-and-white, but as you see more of it, you will discover that life is more complicated than any of us would prefer. What I'm saying is that you should be wise as serpents and harmless as doves."

"What?"

"You should use discretion because what you do will get around and will have consequences."

"I thought it was more important to follow Jesus than the opinion of man."

Dad leaned forward in his chair, his elbows on his legs, his hands clasped between his knees. He looked at me very seriously. "Mark, you should always follow Jesus rather than man. But it is a dangerous thing to follow Jesus if you hold anything else in your life dear. If you choose

83

that road, nothing could give me more joy. But you had better know the cost. Because it will cost you. It will cost you everything."

I nodded silently. He stood up and stepped aside. I walked to the door as he returned to the armchair and pulled the Bible back in his lap. But he didn't seem to be looking at it, or anything really, as I left the room.

CHAPTER ELEVEN Sunday morning I took my accustomed seat in the Sunday school class. When Jolene came in and sat next to me as usual, I got up and moved to the other side of the room without a word. I could feel her looking at me. I looked studiously out the window with my chair angled against the puke-green wall, aware of pity from the rest of the class. It increased my anger. I was grateful when the class started, giving them something else to look at.

Scooter chose me as the victim to read the first set of verses from Matthew 18. I flipped to the page in the quarterly and read in a monotone. "Then came Peter to him, and said, Lord, how oft shall my brother sin against me, and I forgive him? till seven times? Jesus saith unto him, I say not unto thee, Until seven times: but, Until seventy times seven."

Scooter looked around the room. "Everybody got that? How many times should you forgive somebody when they mess up?"

"Four hundred and ninety," Squeaky answered.

"That's stupid," Ralph said. "Who's gonna keep track of that?"

"I think that's the point," Scooter said. "You don't keep track. You just forgive 'em."

I snorted, still looking out of the window. Fat chance.

Following the usual boy-girl pattern, Brenda picked Jolene to read the next section. It was one of those "the kingdom of heaven is like" things. A king had a servant who owed him more than a million dollars and couldn't pay it. He was about to be sold into slavery with his wife and kids and station wagon when he fell on the ground and begged for mercy and time to pay. The king not only let him off; he cancelled the debt.

"Thoughts?" Scooter asked. The usual awkward silence followed, broken by Ralph.

"What I want ta know is how did a servant end up borrowin' a million dollars? Didn't they do credit checks back then? I mean, what servant is gonna have a million dollars worth of stuff fer collateral? Gee whiz!"

"Jesus isn't talkin' about an actual servant. When He says, 'a certain king' it means He's tellin' a parable. It's just a story to make a point."

"Then He should try to make 'em a little more believable. I mean, a million dollars!"

"Ralph, be careful how you go to criticizin' the Bible, especially in this class. Why don't you read the next section?"

Ralph repented of having opened his mouth and flipped to the next section. With the cluelessness that marks jerks the world over, the servant went out and hunted down a buddy who owed him a few dollars and had him thrown into prison for nonpayment.

"Well, the nerve," Squeaky said. "Talk about bein' ungrateful!"

"Exactly," Scooter said. "Why don't you read the next section?"

Turns out the other servants ratted him out and the king was upset. He had the guy thrown into prison to be tortured until he paid off the million dollars. Which would be never, the best I could figure, since he was in prison and couldn't work it off.

"Serves him right," Squeaky said after she finished. Scooter had Bubba read the last verse.

"So likewise shall my heavenly Father do also unto you, if ye from your hearts forgive not every one his brother their trespasses."

Scooter closed his Bible. "It's kinda like the Lord's Prayer. Forgive us our trespasses as we forgive those who trespass against us. In the same way we forgive others, that's how God forgives us."

Squeaky declared this arrangement to pass her fairness standard. Ralph had other ideas.

"But what if they do something really bad? Really wrong? I still have ta forgive 'em?"

"They killed Jesus, but He still forgave 'em."

Bubba couldn't stay out of the action for long. "Father, forgive them; for they know not what they do."

This one hit me wrong. I was hoping for something on the order of smiting mine enemies and let not the evil man prosper and so forth. This lesson was taking a wrong line. Let him who is without humiliation at the hands of Jolene Culpepper shut up was the way I saw it. Violating a longstanding policy, I volunteered an opinion on the lesson.

"It says. 'For they know not what they do.' What about if they know what they do, and do it anyway? You mean they can do wrong on purpose and I still have to forgive them? I don't think so."

"But God commendeth his love toward us, in that, while we were yet sinners, Christ died for us." I nailed Bubba with my glare. He looked apologetic but didn't take it back.

Scooter didn't thank him for providing an answer, but he did take the ball. "God forgave us when we were His enemies. It's kinda like that question ya asked awhile back. What would Jesus do? He would forgive. He done did."

That was asking a bit much. During the chaos of splitting the girls from the boys and pulling the partition into place, I slipped out and looked for a place to duke it out. Behind the church I leaned against the wall just below the window to the library, which was usually deserted. Here I was unlikely to be disturbed. I put on my boxing gloves.

Did God really expect me to forgive Jolene? Surely He wasn't that cruel. As Squeaky said, the idea of getting the same kind of forgiveness you gave seemed fair, and I was willing to forgive as I was forgiven. Those who are forgiven much may love much, but perhaps those who sin a little need only a little forgiveness. I doubted I would ever need forgiveness of that magnitude because I couldn't imagine ever committing such a crime.

After all, look at what she had done! In front of the entire school. Tying my shoelace to the chair, pulling the chair out from under me. And the zipper. I didn't know how she did it, but I was certain that somehow she was responsible. And thanks to the overeager school photographer, I would be immortalized in the 1973 annual with a red shirttail jutting from my fly. It was inhuman to demand I forgive that.

But the Question kept coming back. What would Jesus do? Back in the summer it had seduced me into abstract speculation. I had been fascinated with it, but now I hated it. I wished I had never read that infernal book. I wished I had never heard the Question. It was fine to sit up in a tree house and theorize on what Jesus would do. It was quite another thing to have it thrown in your face when the answer ran counter to every instinct.

I would not do it. It was asking too much. I swore it with such vehemence that I almost said it out loud. Then two thoughts came unbidden into my defiant brain. The first was an image of a kid in a trailer park in the California desert, choosing between an angelically perfect Stranger who preached a rational gospel of physics and chance and despair, and a broken God-become-man who forgave those who visited upon Him unimaginable humiliation, torture, and death. The second was an image of a middle-aged preacher telling a smugly self-righteous kid to count the cost. It hadn't even been twenty-four hours.

Because it will cost you. It will cost you everything. My brain shouted back at the thoughts. No, You can't ask this of me. The answer came back. But I do ask it of you.

But it's not fair, I complained. True, the answer returned. Forgiveness isn't fair. I wasn't being fair when I forgave you. Do you really want Me to give you what you deserve?

I was reeling from that punch when my boxing match was interrupted by voices from the window.

"Mac, ya just don't know what it's like ta live with him these days."

"It should be a lot better than it was."

"I know. I don't know why I can't be grateful. I am grateful. But I've gone from bein' scared to bein' bored. He's always prayin' and readin' the Bible. We don't never go out and have fun like we used ta." There was a silence. "Remember how we all used ta go out, all four of us?"

"Yeah."

"That's what I mean. How come we can't do that anymore?"

Mac cleared his throat. "There's not four of us anymore."

"Oh, Mac, I'm sorry, I don't know what I'm sayin' anymore. It's just got me so I can't think straight."

"Don't apologize. It's not yer fault. I should be able to get on with it, but I can't. I don't hold nothin' against Parker, but it's not the same anymore, is it? I can't pretend like it is. Nothin' will be the same, I don't think."

More silence. "But I just don't understand why he has ta get so religious all of a sudden. Ya know?"

"No."

"Well, look at you. How long you been goin' ta church?"

"All my life."

"Right, see? And yer not so religious. Yer just like regular folk. Why can't Parker be more like that? It's like he's either got ta be a devil or a angel. Can't he just be a regular person?"

"Parker always done things his own way. He ain't never been like me, and he's not like ta be."

"Then he should be. It would be an improvement."

"I'm not so sure about that."

"Mac, don't be so modest. Of course it would. I remember how nice you were back when . . . You remember we used ta have some good times ourselves."

"That was before you dumped me for him."

"Yer not gonna hold that against me forever, are ya? I was just a silly school girl."

"I'm not holdin' it against ya; just remindin' ya. You picked him fer a reason, probably cause he was a bit of a devil. He's the same Parker he was then, takin' things ta the extreme. That's what you chose."

"He's not the same Parker. That's what I'm tellin' ya. He's a fanatic."

"Well, I don't see him here today."

"He will be. I'm just not there ta wake him up. He'll make it to church, and he'll be on the front row hangin' on ever' word Pastor Matt says."

The buzzer drowned out Mac's answer, and their voices faded. I got up, dusted off my pants, turned around, and ran right into Jolene. We both fell back and rubbed our heads. I looked at her. She spoke first.

"Mark, I wanted to tell ya I was sorry. I came lookin' for ya Friday night, but I couldn't find ya."

"Yeah, I saw you."

"I'm sorry. I really am. I just . . . well . . ." she looked away, her eyes misty.

My eyes were a little misty too. "I forgive you."

"What?" She looked back at me.

"I forgive you."

"You do?"

"Yes. I don't want to, but I have to. I gave my word."

"What? Ta who?"

"I just want to know why you did it, is all. After you told me no jokes."

Her china complexion colored, and she seemed genuinely embarrassed. "I didn't plan it, honest. I meant what I said about no jokes. But then, when ya got yer bootlace stuck in the chair, and then the thing with yer zipper, well, I just got carried away. Force of habit, I guess." She looked down at her feet, glanced up at my face, and shrugged.

"What? You mean you didn't tie my bootlace to the chair?"

"How could I do that without ya noticin'? And those shorts were too tight fer me ta bend over that far."

"You didn't do the zipper?"

"No!" She became indignant. "Mark Cloud, you don't seriously think I would—"

"I couldn't figure out how you did it."

"I didn't. You did. It was that way when you came back from the bathroom. I just didn't tell you is all."

"Thanks."

"Don't mention it. All I did was pull the chair back when ya went ta sit down. You did the rest ta yerself."

I had the entire church service to think it over. But on the way to the sanctuary I checked my fly.

Before church started Hannah sat in the pew behind me and leaned forward. "Hey."

"Hey." I didn't turn around.

"I heard about Friday night."

"Great. You and your friends have a good laugh?"

"No." She put a hand on my shoulder. I glanced down at it. "Mark, I'm sorry that happened to you."

I continued to stare forward. "Take a number."

She jerked her hand back. "I guess I'll have to. Looks like you already got number one." She stormed into the aisle.

I turned around. "Hey."

She jerked back toward me. "What?"

I looked at her deep blue eyes. I imagined what they had looked like when she put her hand on my shoulder. Now they flashed with anger. "Thanks," I said quietly.

Her eyes softened. She said, "You're welcome," and went back to her friends. They all looked at me mournfully. I couldn't stand it. I turned back around.

Two rows ahead, Deacon Fry's bald head looked sinister to me now. After the revelations of the previous night, I was unable to look at him with simple distaste. I found myself despising him and his basso profundo glissando on "It Is Well with My Soul." When I discovered Dad's sermon was on forgiveness, I distracted myself from what I considered divine overkill by reflecting on my loathing for Deacon Fry.

Parker was not on the front row.

CHAPTER TWELVE

Right after lunch Dad grabbed his keys and said, "Come on." I didn't ask where we were going. In Fred, only suckers asked questions. You either knew or you figured it out. To ask a question was to reveal a weakness.

It didn't take long to find out. Parker's house was only three miles away. We parked next to the ruins of the gazebo. Dad banged on the door under the carport. Hard. We waited. He banged again and stepped back a few feet. There was some noise from inside. Things knocking about and footsteps. The door opened a foot. Parker squinted out, looking like death on a Popsicle stick. With knobs on.

"Glad to find you home, Parker. You don't mind if we come in, do you?" Dad surprised Parker and me by shoving the door open, putting plenty of weight behind it. Parker was caught off balance and muttered an oath as he stumbled back into the kitchen, against the bar that separated it from the breakfast nook.

"I didn't ask you in," he growled, grabbing the counter for support.

Dad walked past Parker to the table, pulled out a chair, and sat down. I walked in cautiously and nodded at Parker, closing the door behind me. He wasn't wearing the patch. I looked quickly away from the pale sunken eyelid.

It was cool and dark in the room. Dad leaned back and flipped a light switch on. Parker winced and shielded his eye with his hand. His hair looked like the dustbin at a barbershop. His face was so pale the scar was barely visible. Stubble dotted his jaws and neck. He was wearing a rumpled white T-shirt and jeans. No shoes or socks.

"Ya can go back out the way ya came in."

I stood by the door, my hand on the knob.

"I will in a couple of minutes," Dad said. "First, come in here and sit down. Mark, why don't you make us some coffee?"

I had never made coffee in my life. Dad saw my look of bewilderment turning to panic.

"Just look around until you find what you need. It's not hard. The coffee pot is right there." He pointed to a percolator next to the toaster. Great.

Parker swiped his hand across the counter, clearing it of a considerable amount of junk and dishes. And the coffee pot. The toaster hung halfway to the floor, suspended by the power cord. Black crumbs trickled to the white linoleum.

"What do ya think yer doin' here? This is still my house, and I can throw ya out if I want ta."

"Of course you can," Dad said. "And after we talk for a spell, you can throw us out as many times as you like." He kicked a chair back from the table. "Now come over here and sit down while Mark makes us some coffee."

Parker was in no condition to put up an extended resistance against Dad's calm siege tactics. He slouched to the table and collapsed into the chair. I began picking up the junk from the floor.

"I see there was some difficulty with your gazebo."

"No difficulty. It went up like dry pine straw on a hot day." *Touché,* I thought as I collected the scattered percolator pieces.

"Missed you this morning."

"That's 'cause I didn't go this mornin'. Or any other mornin' from here on out."

"Because?"

"Because it don't work. She left me same as if I was still beatin' her."

I had assembled a coffee pot; a lid with a black knob in the middle; a long, thin metal tube; and a round metal basket with a bunch of little holes in the bottom and a big round hole in the center. I looked down in

94

the pot. There was a hole in the middle about the same diameter as the tube.

"I know back in June you came to the church to find your wife. Did you come to Jesus to get your wife back? Was that it?"

Parker sat there for awhile, elbow on the table, head in hand, massaging his temples. I put the tube through the hole in the basket and into the hole in the pot. It all seemed to fit. I dug around the cabinets for coffee.

"No."

"Then why did you come to Jesus?"

The slamming of cabinet doors echoed in the silence. I found a one-pound can of Seaport next to the flour. I pulled the lid off and poured it into the basket, filling it. Then I realized I needed water.

"It's hard ta say, really."

"Give it a shot."

I pulled the basket out of the pot and held it in one hand while I ran some water in the pot with the other hand. I dropped the basket back in, spilling some coffee into the pot in the process. Whatever. I slapped the lid on and plugged it in, then leaned on the counter and watched Dad and Parker.

"For a second I thought maybe it was true. Maybe somebody could see somethin' of use even in somebody like me. It seemed like it might could be true, fer awhile."

"When did it quit being true?"

"When she left again. If I really was a new man and she was a new woman, then it would work out. We wouldn't still be fightin' same as we was before. And she would still be here."

"That's it? That's all it took for you to bail out?"

Parker glared at Dad.

"God doesn't come along with a magic wand and levitate us into a second Eden. Staying married is hard work, even with God's help. It's probably harder without it. I wouldn't know; I never tried it that way. But you never struck me as a man who gave up just because things get a little hard."

The percolator belched in the stillness as Parker stared at Dad. I checked the coffee. How would I know when it was done?

"I talked to Sonia, and she seems to have her reasons for leaving. I don't know what really happened, and I didn't come here to find out. I'm sure there's blame enough to go around for everybody. But her decision doesn't change anything about what happened between you and Jesus."

"It don't matter. It's over. I'm done with it. You seen what I done last night. Probably heard about it too," he said, glancing over his shoulder at me. I pulled back and my foot hit something. It seemed to be a part of the percolator, a lid to the inner basket. Oh well. I set it on the counter.

Parker reached into his back pocket and pulled out a half-empty Jack Daniels flask and slammed it on the table in front of Dad.

"Parker, that bottle doesn't scare me now anymore than it did five months ago. And it doesn't scare Jesus."

"I ain't worthy. I done put my hand to the plow and then turned back." Dad raised an eyebrow. "Yeah, I been doin' some readin'. I ain't the ignorant heathern you met back in June. Them that put their hand to the plow and then turn back ain't worthy of the kingdom."

"I'll keep that in mind. Mark, how's that coffee coming along?"

"Oh!" I shuffled around and found some mugs, poured two cups, and took them to the table. Dad took one and blew in it.

"Parker, a mistake isn't fatal. It's not like skydiving. You don't just get one shot. It's like breaking a horse. It's a long slow process, and when you get thrown off, you get back on."

He took a sip of the coffee. A convulsion shuddered across his face and through his frame, and then he looked the same as he had before. He set the cup down slowly.

Parker looked at him strangely and tried his coffee. He spit it back into the cup and turned on me. "What did ya put in here? Motor oil?"

"Is there something wrong with it?"

"Wrong with it? You could blacktop my driveway with this!"

"I just used water and coffee."

"How much coffee?"

"I filled up the metal basket thing."

"Dang, kid. How much water?"

"Oh, about half a pot, I guess."

Dad smiled. There were little black flecks sticking to his teeth. "Mark, how many times have you made coffee before?"

"Counting this time?"

"Yes."

"One."

"We will give you another chance. This is the day of second chances. You willing to try again?"

"I guess so." It wasn't my coffee. And I sure wasn't going to drink any.

"What brand of coffee is this?"

"Seaport."

"Pour all this out and rinse everything out. Then try about two cups of water and four scoops of coffee. If you have any left."

"Yessir."

"So, Parker, you think you're man enough to get back on the horse that threw you?"

"I ain't sure it's worth it."

Dad looked around the breakfast nook and the den. It looked like the FBI had ransacked it. "Well, it's certainly an improvement over the last five months."

"I've been keepin' my nose clean fer five months and what has it got me? I go up ta the church and folks look down their nose at me. I read the Bible and pray and my wife leaves me. I don't see a lot of difference from before." He looked around. "Except the house was cleaner."

"Parker, you're not going to get a medal pinned on you for following Jesus. He kept His nose clean for longer than five months, and look what He got. One week the crowd loved Him. The next week they killed Him. You don't do it for what you can get. You do it for what you can give back."

"I'm tired of givin'."

"You don't sell your truck just because you hit a few speed bumps. We all get tired. But just think of what He did for you. Think of what He brought you out of. Then it might not seem like so much to do."

Dad got up. "I think we'll get on back to the house. Maybe this next pot of coffee will be more to your liking. And I recommend you get rid of that." He pointed at the JD. "It's not going to help you out, no matter what you decide to do."

"Preacher, yer wastin' yer time."

"It wouldn't be the first time. We'll just go out the way we came in. I expect to see you around."

"Don't hold yer breath."

CHAPTER THIRTEEN

On Parker's advice, I didn't hold my breath. Good thing. We didn't see him again at church. Not for the Thanksgiving harvest service. Not for the Christmas Eve candlelight service. Not for Easter, the day when just about everybody came, including known heathens.

I tried to be as wise as a serpent. I still sold papers to Vernon, still watched the sunset while sipping a Coke. But if it appeared he was mixing his Coke a bit strong, I took my leave before he required a driver. And I also ceased to entertain romantic notions about Jolene. Not that she asked me out again or anything.

I sold Parker a paper when I saw him outside, usually working on his truck, but otherwise I had no contact with him. The charred circle in the yard remained undisturbed through a rare winter ice storm that laid white frosting over the ruins. The usual April showers were followed by May flowers sprouting through the blackened bones of the gazebo.

Sonia had not returned from the Harmons whither she had fled. Their initial reluctance faded when the story of the drunken bonfire was circulated. She tooled around Fred in a brown Dodge Dart. Some said Parker bought it for her. I figured she was making payments on it from her new hair-styling job in Silsbee. And the Mary Kay sticker on the back window indicated she finally found a way to turn her obsession with makeup into a profit center.

Near the end of the school year I was wandering around after lunch bored, singing "Mercedes Benz" loudly. I got to the part about Dialing for Dollars as I walked into the library. Miss Thermopolis whipped around and silenced me with a withering glare over her cat-eye half glasses. I meekly skulked to the magazine table to reread the latest issue of *Spiderman*. Elrick and Bubba were sprawled in the orange and black armchairs. They looked up as I plopped down on the orange couch.

"See, that's what I been tellin' ya," Elrick said, nodding his head toward me. "No soul. Got no soul at all. Can't have decent church without no soul."

I stopped with my hand halfway to the comic book. "What?"

Bubba looked at me speculatively; Elrick ignored me. "You heard 'im when he come in. The only soul he got is on the bottom of his shoe." Bubba nodded his head slowly.

"Wait a minute. Are you talking about me?"

"Yeah."

"I don't have a soul? What am I, some kind of zombie?"

"Everybody got a soul, even animals. But not everybody got soul. And you can't have proper church without soul."

"Are you saying I don't have soul?" Who did this guy think he was? I had eaten chitlins and collard greens, for crying out loud. I used to have a Nehru jacket and love beads. I was cool. I was just disguised as a hick geek, like the prince dressed as the pauper to avoid attention.

"Yep."

"Hey! I have as much soul as the next guy."

"Maybe. If the next guy is Howdy Doody."

I sputtered and turned red. "Hey! We have church. Don't we, Bubba?"

I felt the steely stare of Miss Thermopolis rake across me like a Martian Heat-Ray. I leaned forward and blustered in a stage whisper, "Bubba, tell him. We have church."

"Not to hear him tell it. And he might could be right."

I was speechless at this treason. Elrick wasn't. "OK, tell me about how ya have church."

"We have music, announcements, special music, and a sermon."

"Everybody has that. But what kind of music?"

"Hymns." Was this guy stupid?

"But do they sound like *The Beverly Hillbillies* or *Soul Train?*"

"Neither! They sound like hymns." This guy *was* stupid.

"Who plays the music?"

"My mom plays the organ; Judy plays the piano."

"That's it? Two old white ladies playin' keys?"

"They're not that old! Judy's not even married yet. And of course they're white. It's a white church."

"Does anybody clap?"

"No."

"Dance?"

"No!" Hey, we were talking about a Baptist church. What was he thinking?

Elrick leaned back in his chair and spread his hands. "When ya want ta see proper church, let me know."

I looked at Bubba. He shrugged. "Mark, think about it fer a second. We sit there and watch Harlan wave his hand around and sing funeral songs. Then we all sit there and try ta stay awake while yer Dad reads some verses and talks usin' a bunch of big words nobody knows."

"I know them." It wasn't much of a rebuttal, but it was all I had. He was right about everything else. I glared at Elrick. "So, what do you think real church is?"

He smiled from his orange throne. "Tell ya what. Come on down Sunday and you'll see."

———

The next Sunday night Bubba met me at the church in his ragtop eggbeater, and we drove into the setting sun. I had received a special dispensation from Dad to skip Training Union and the Sunday night service. Once we hit Warren I was the navigator, reading the directions Elrick had scratched on the *Sixteen* magazine subscription card as we made turns from highway to side street to back road to dirt road into a section of Warren neither of us had ever seen. We passed brick houses and shacks, well-kept lawns and dirt yards, picket fences, barbed wire fences, hound dogs, mongrels, free-range chickens, cows, goats. And people who watched us pass by without expression. Not even curiosity.

At sunset we reached our destination—a white frame building with a manicured lawn and dirt parking lot. Unlike our church on Sunday nights, this parking lot was full. There were even cars on the road and behind the church. Two guys in black suits directed traffic. We were allotted a space near the front entrance. Bubba put the top up, and we locked the doors.

On the front steps we were greeted by a tall skinny woman with large hands and feet and a red hat with a black feather in it. She extracted our names and turned to a short, wide woman standing in the doorway in a purple dress with large yellow flowers.

"This here's Bubba and Mark. They done been asked here by Brother Elrick."

The yellow-flower woman shook my hand with both of her hands, her short fat fingers wrapped in white gloves. "y'all just wait right here." She disappeared through the inside doors. In a few seconds she opened the doors and waved us in.

Elrick was inside, dressed in a blue double-breasted pinstripe three-piece suit. I looked around. The room was almost full of people dressed like they were going to the president's funeral. If our pale skin wasn't enough to set us off, our jeans and plaid shirts made it plain that we were not regulars.

"Nice suit," Bubba said.

Elrick flashed a smile and walked down the center aisle. We followed him to the second row on the left side, where he installed us and vanished. I looked at Bubba. He looked at me. He looked nervous. I looked away before he made me more nervous. All around us well-dressed black people were visiting and finding seats and settling in.

Directly in front of us, reading from left to right, was a skeletal man with large knuckles at a Hammond organ, a very large man with a black Fender bass, a guy with an Afro behind a red Pearl drum set, and an unbelievably short guy with an absurdly large red Gretch hollow-body electric guitar. There were two short benches with two guys each sitting on them and a piano on the right. Behind them were three rows of choir. I caught a glimpse of Elrick on the back row just as a slender man in a maroon suit on the left bench stood up. He looked at the organ player, who snapped his fingers four times. Music exploded from the front of the church.

The band broke into a groove that would have made James Brown's backbone slip, even if his hand wasn't on his hip. The choir immediately started clapping on the back beat. The people behind us did the same. Bubba and I sat there. The maroon guy strutted back and forth in the front and yelled things like "Come on wit it" and "We're gonna have church tonight" in the open spaces of the groove. Then he sang, "What can wash away my sin?" and the choir answered back, "Nothing but the blood of Jesus" in that fat half-song half-yell sound I had heard on black gospel records.

This was a song I had heard all my life but never like this. Hymns at our church were fairly solemn affairs. No one had ever felt the need to supplement the piano with a rhythm section. Harlan Johnson would stand in one place and mark out the four beats with his right hand moving in a vague cross, the choir somewhat audible from behind a barrier of hymnals. Thin soprano voices would slice through the melody while Deacon Fry would scoop the bass, Uncle Herbert's piercing tenor soaring above everything else in the room.

But this. This was music that didn't make any excuses or take any prisoners. They didn't do this because it was time for music on an order of service. They meant it. I felt my pulse beating with the groove as they segued into "Soon and Very Soon." I recognized this song from Mom's Andre Crouch songbook. But compared to this arrangement, Mom, bless her heart, might as well have been playing the typewriter. Something made me look back. Everyone in the place was standing. I poked Bubba with my elbow and nodded. He looked back, looked at me, and we stood up too.

By the time they had moved on to "This Train," I could feel the beat infecting me. The drums and bass played like they had been chained together since birth. The organ had a Leslie cabinet, and Mr. Bones wasn't afraid to use it. When he would speed up the vibrato and then slow it down, it felt like he was pulling my soul out like taffy. The guitar had a thin sound that caused me to ignore it for several songs. Then my conscious mind awakened to the exotic jumble of chords and riffs that belied his sloppy style. The pianist threw in choppy staccato chords in counterpoint to the rhythm section.

I felt my foot tapping inside my sneakers and my knee keeping the beat invisibly under my jeans. I realized that I wanted to clap and dance around like everyone else. But it was something I had never done before. I would look completely ridiculous if I tried. So I stood there mute, chained to the mast of my self-consciousness.

Bubba, however, seemed unable to resist the siren call. He began clapping his hands, swinging his elbows back between beats so far that they almost touched behind him. Soon he appeared to be perfecting the spastic chicken moves he had displayed at the Sadie Hawkins dance. When the maroon guy hollered out, "Are you ready for a miracle?" Bubba hollered back, "Ready as I can be!" along with the choir and everybody else. I was both amused and dismayed. You couldn't look at him without at least smiling, but I was afraid his enthusiasm might be mistaken for mockery and get us lynched.

After forty-five minutes, the music stopped without us experiencing bodily harm, except the time Bubba impaled me with an errant elbow and I folded into the pew for several verses. The maroon guy flopped onto his bench with a handkerchief, and a big guy in a blue suit stood up. He made several announcements about prayer breakfasts and mission lunches and dinner on the grounds and clean-up day and so on. Then he announced a collection to replace the roof on Widow Franklin's house.

Two hefty guys came down the center aisle, each with a large wicker basket that both Bubba and I could have fit into, set them in front of the left and right sections, and stood next to them with their hands clasped in front like bodyguards. As the maroon guy led the choir in "The Lord's Prayer" in an arrangement unknown to George Beverly Shea, people filed out of their pews, passed by the baskets, dropped money in, and returned to their seats.

When the last person had passed by, the blue guy nodded to the hefty guys. They dumped the baskets onto the table in front and counted the money. One wrote on a piece of paper and handed it to the blue guy. He read it, shook his head, and said, "That ain't enough. We needs three hundred dollars." He turned to the maroon guy. "Do it again."

The choir sang "The Lord's Prayer" again and the crowd filed past the baskets again. The money was counted again; the note passed again. The blue guy shook his head again.

"We still needs fifty dollars. You know Widow Franklin's son be over at the war and can't help out his mama. Now Brother Walker volunteered his time free ta do the job; all we're buyin' is materials." He looked to the back of the church. "Brother Walker, how you be fixed for a crew?"

I heard a familiar voice reply, "I could use a couple more hands." I jerked around. Parker Walker stood in the back pew. His right eye looked back at me without expression.

"OK. You heard him. We're gonna do it again. If you can't put in cash money, then put in a paper wit your name and phone number and

Brother Walker will be callin' you." This time the result was satisfactory, and the maroon guy got up again. After thirty more minutes of music during which he shed his maroon jacket, revealing a sweat-soaked pink shirt, he collapsed back onto his bench.

A broad, solemn-looking man wearing a black suit and wire-frame glasses got up, dropped a large black Bible on the pulpit, and looked out at the crowd. He spoke slowly in a low rumble, reading from the Bible. He paused again, sizing up the crowd, and began speaking. He started out deliberately with one point: be the same Christian on Monday as you are on Sunday. But that one point was covered thoroughly. As he built layer upon layer, his volume and pace increased until he was pacing past the pulpit shouting hoarsely, with organ riffs punctuating the dramatic pauses. By the end of an hour he had shed his coat and was wiping sweat from his face with a folded white handkerchief.

He nodded to the maroon guy and asked folks who meant business with God to come to the front. We all stood and the choir began singing "My Tribute," another song from the Andre Crouch book. The song had a power that survived even Mom's IBM Selectric interpretation. I had often felt an inner stirring while listening to this song, stronger than the surge of feeling when hearing the national anthem on Independence Day. This version was practically overwhelming. I struggled to keep back the tears. Bubba swayed back and forth, eyes closed, cheeks wet with tears.

People filled the front, praying, raising their hands, singing, swaying. The choir sang "Jesus on the Mainline," and a guy in a white suit danced so ecstatically that he shook out of his jacket and ended up quivering on the floor. Another guy picked up his jacket, folded it neatly, and set it on the front pew. When the service ended, I eyed the white suit guy as he calmly got up, put on his jacket, and walked out, greeting folks as he went. Elrick introduced us to his dad. I asked the question that had plagued me for half the service.

"How long has Parker been coming here?"

"Brother Walker has been fellowshippin' with us since Christmas. Thank you, Lord. There's many in the church that has been blessed. He fixes cars, houses, plumbin', electricity, anything that is broke. Don't ask a penny, but he gets plenty a produce and home-cooked soul food, you can be sure."

On the way out, Elrick gloated over the undeniable triumph of soul. He declared Bubba to possess a surprising amount of soul, which caused Bubba to duck his head and blush, but I saw he smiled with pride.

I received no such praise.

CHAPTER FOURTEEN

At the end of the school year Heidi returned from her first year of college. One afternoon we went to the mall in Beaumont. I was looking for decent albums in the cutout rack. She was looking for a new swimsuit. We parted ways at the parking lot and reconvened at the '64 Falcon two hours later. I tossed my copy of Bruce Cockburn's *Sunwheel Dance* in the backseat and took the keys. We had a deal. She drove down; I drove back up.

Around Lumberton I broke into her monologue. "So, let's see the swimsuit." Heidi held up a bikini top. "Whoa! What happened to the rest of it?" She held up a bikini bottom. "That's it? That's the whole thing?"

"Yes." She seemed self-conscious as she pushed it back in the bag.

"What's Dad going to say about that?"

"It doesn't matter. He's not going to wear it."

"The question is, will he let you wear it?"

"I'm an adult. I can do as I please." I evaluated her from the corner of my eye as I passed a log truck. "Besides, he won't know. He's not going swimming with me."

"What about when he asks to see what you bought?" She held up a "Don't Mess with Texas" T-shirt. "That's not a swimsuit."

"I didn't tell him I was buying a swimsuit." Nice tactic. I filed it away for future reference. "So, I hear you had a date with Jolene."

I glanced at her, gauging how much she knew. "Yeah. Wasn't a big deal. She needed a date to the Sadie Hawkins dance, so I went with her."

"OK," she said slowly and looked at me for awhile. "Whatever happened to Becky?"

"Nothing. She's still around."

"You never told her of your passionate devotion?"

"Nope."

"Why not?"

"It never came up."

"Mark, I specifically told you what to do. I can't go do it for you too."

"Look, I was ready to tell her. Then she used the F-word."

"What? She cussed you out?"

"No, even worse. She called me her friend."

"Oh." Heidi was uncharacteristically quiet for awhile.

"That's OK. After next year you'll be going to college. I can introduce you to some girls."

The prospect didn't set me aquiver with anticipation. I had seen her friends.

―――――――――

The summer gave me more time for my financial ventures. On a Wednesday, June 6, I set out to sell some *Grit*. At sunset I joined Vernon for a well-deserved Coke. The day was dying of fever. I was practically in a delirium myself after miles of burning sand roads in the open sun. Even Vernon seemed flushed with a dementia of his own.

Inside the Pontiac it felt like a sauna. The slightly sweet smell of whiskey was absent. In its place I detected the faint aroma of Drano. I scanned the car for signs of a cleaning, but it looked the same as always.

I pushed the door open with my foot as an invitation for an errant breeze to make itself at home and sucked on ice retrieved from the cooler. The swing across the road was empty.

I raised my Coke toward Vernon. "To D-Day."

He closed his eyes for a few seconds, raised his Coke can toward me, and drank deeply.

We sat in silence for a long time. Vernon lit a cigarette. I got tired of the silence.

"So, did you get drafted or what?"

"What?" Vernon turned his head slowly toward me.

"WWII. Did you get drafted?"

"When the Japs hit Pearl Harbor, I was seventeen. I hitched a ride down ta Beaumont and volunteered."

"Seventeen?"

"I knew some who joined at sixteen. If ya looked the part and was willin' ta tell 'em yer eighteen, they were willin' ta write it down."

I had watched the draft lottery for the past few years. I got a high number the year before Nixon signed the peace treaty. I spent a lot of time wondering what I would do when I turned eighteen. Run? Fight? Get killed? I didn't know anyone who had gone to Vietnam. I certainly didn't know anyone who had volunteered.

"Back then it weren't nuthin' ta see whole towns volunteer. Not like it is today with fellers runnin' off ta Canada. Not that I blame 'em one bit." He looked at me. "How old are ya, Mark boy?"

"Seventeen."

"Are ya now? I would a figured fifteen, sixteen tops." He shook a cigarette out of the pack and tapped it against the lid.

"Thanks." I scowled at him and took another sip of Coke.

"In a year, ya need money ta get to Canada, you tell me, ya hear?" The lighter snapped open and sparked to life.

"They signed the peace treaty six months ago."

"It's a shame. I would a even took ya. Ain't never seen Canada."

"It's not much to look at. Like Minnesota." A draft-dodging flight to Canada with Fred's most notorious bootlegger. What would Deacon Fry say?

Vernon blew out a stream of smoke and tossed the lighter back on the dash.

"They shaved my head and poked me full a holes and sent me on a bus ta Camp Wolters out by Mineral Wells. We was run through trainin' like a grinder crankin' out sausage." Vernon nodded at the square medal with diagonal blue and white stripes hanging from the rearview mirror. "Third Infantry Division under Patton, Fifteenth Regiment, Audie's unit, but different company. You know Audie Murphy, don't ya?"

"I've heard the name." I wasn't big on war movies, but I didn't mention that to Vernon.

"The most decorated soldier in WWII. He was a little runt, shorter'n you and just as skinny. Died a few years back in a plane crash. Same age as me.

"Well, they balled us up and threw us at the Krauts in Africa like waddin' up a dishrag and throwin' it at a rattlesnake. It don't hurt the snake none, but it slows him down and makes him madder'n a wet hen. It was the Brits that pulled us through that one, but I'll call ya a liar if ya tell anyone I said it.

"Once we run 'em out a Tunisia, we had ta turn around and run 'em out a Sicily. Then we follered 'em over ta Italy. They almost pushed us back into the ocean at Salerno, but we beat 'em like a rented mule, and they finally turned tail and run. By the time we got ta Naples, there weren't much left of it. The Fifth Army kept chasin' the Krauts up into the mountains, but they dug in like a badger and we couldn't blast 'em out."

He pulled the flask from under the seat and refilled his can. He started to put it back under the seat but thought better of it and set it on the seat between us.

"So they sent us up around the back of 'em, ta Anzio. A beach that'd make Galveston jealous. But we weren't doin' any swimmin'. They was hundreds a boats with men and tanks and trucks all comin' up on the beach. Normandy was even bigger, but I weren't there ta see that one."

He stopped and stared as the sun approached the tree line. "No, I weren't there for that one." He took a drink like a man taking medicine.

"We got in there and threw the Krauts out of town. We was rarin' ta go chase 'em right up the highway, but the general, he didn't want ta get caught with his pants down like in Salerno, so he had us stay put fer a week while they got all the gear and supplies ashore. Then we set out ta give 'em what for.

"That's when we found out they done the same thing. First we tried ta take the town of Cisterna. Colonel Darby took his famous Rangers ta infiltrate the area at night, but when the sun come up, they found out the Huns had brung up Panzers the night before and cut 'em ta pieces. Went out with 767 men, and six come back.

"Ever'where we pushed, they pushed back. We was trapped on a strip a beach about five miles deep and ten miles long. With ol' Anzio Annie, a German railroad gun blastin' ever'thing within twenty miles ta powder."

He hit his hand against the side mirror to knock off the ash.

"We was supposed to create a subversion for them poor fellers gettin' the sand pounded out a them down in Cassino, and here we was, gettin' the sand pounded out a us. The Krauts had their best troops down there in Italy. Not the picked-over hand-me-downs we run through in Germany at the end. These fellers was tougher'n a overcooked boot and twice as nasty.

"We spent most a month tryin' ta bust out. Killed a lot of fellers on both sides. Then they spent most a month trying ta push us back into the ocean and killed even more fellers on both sides. Then we both fell back, plumb exhausted, and tried ta figure out what the other was up to.

"We set there three months. We was supposed ta be marchin' into Rome, and it no further off than from here ta Beaumont, but we was crouched in foxholes, starin' a hundred yards across a muddy field at

Krauts starin' back at us. And it was just as bad on them. They was just fellers who been drivin' cabs or unloadin' trucks or sellin' corsets or what not, and now they was hunkered down in a muddy hole fer hours, and if they stood up ta get a little circulation, they would get their hair parted with a bullet. They was just fellers, just like us."

He took a long pull from his Coke can. I did the same.

"It's not hard ta throw a grenade at a feller killin' dozens a yer buddies with a machine gun. But when ya can't dig more'n a foot'n a half afore ya hit marsh water, and ya lay in that shallow ditch fer hours and days and weeks and ya look across at another guy just as wet and tired and miserable cramped up as you, it's different. If he stretches a bit and shows some skin, that's a different kind a killin' ta shoot 'im down."

That didn't make sense to me. "But he would shoot you if you did the same thing. Just because he's not shooting at you right at that moment doesn't mean he won't if he gets the chance."

"How many men you shot, Mark boy?"

"None."

"Why ain't you killed none?" He blew a stream of smoke impatiently, like he was expecting a lame excuse that he would rather not have to listen to.

"I've never been in a war. It's not the same thing as murder. You're supposed to kill the enemy in a war. It's not wrong. It's self-defense."

"Tell that ta yer trigger finger when ya got some poor German farm boy who needs ta take a pee lined up in yer sights. When he takes off that helmet and ya see a pale blond kid lookin' about like you do right now, and yer front sight lined up between his blue eyes, then tell yerself it ain't murder."

He went to refill his can from the flask, but it was empty. He muttered under his breath, rolled himself from behind the wheel, and opened the back door. He dragged the cooler out, pulled up the backseat, and extracted a frosted wine bottle half full of a white liquid. He refilled the flask, put everything back, and dropped heavily into the front seat. That should have been my cue to slither out of there like a wise serpent.

He lit another cigarette. "One night after we been there about four months, a bunch of us was back in town on relief. It weren't really like leavin' the front; it was only a few miles back, and it got shelled as much as the line. But it was nice ta get out of the mud and sit in a real chair and eat hot food and take a bath.

"Somebody found some whiskey in one a the houses that was half gone. We sat on what was left of a rock wall in the dark 'cause it were a new moon and looked at the stars and got drunker'n Cooter Brown. I started diggin' around in the closets. I found a top hat, you know, one of them tall black hats like Abe Lincoln wore?"

"Right."

"It almost fit me. I wore it ta one side like Jeff in the Mutt and Jeff cartoons. I wandered around the town wearin' the hat and headed out into the woods and walked right into a Kraut camp. They was as surprised as I was, and they jumped up and grabbed their guns, but they didn't shoot. I just stood and looked at 'em with my hands in plain sight.

"One of 'em came up ta me and seen I was drunk. I probably smelled like a busted still. He laughed and told ever'body, and they all laughed. He swapped my hat with his helmet. It fit him a lot better'n me. He bowed ta me and ever'body laughed. Then he turned me around, said 'Good luck' in English, and pushed me back the way I come.

"Seein' those Krauts sobered me up pretty good. I didn't get too far afore I realized I had come up right through a mine field, one of ours. I did it fine drunk, but I weren't takin' no chances sober, so I cut around aimin' ta outflank it. I outflanked it so good I got lost as a ball in tall weeds. I kept walkin' 'til I couldn't walk anymore. Then I found a gully with some cover and got some shuteye. In the middle of the night I heard some guns, but I couldn't see anything from where I was and it stopped, so I fell back ta sleep."

Living with Fred

CHAPTER FIFTEEN "The sound a planes woke me up, feelin' like a pile of catfish heads left out in the sun. It was gray and rainin'. I could hear bombs a few miles away. It sounded like the whole beachhead was explodin' all at once. I had wandered out a the house without my M-1. All I had was a sidearm. I begun creepin' through the woods. My one aim was ta get back on the right side, but ever' time I headed west, I run into the backside of Huns fightin' a terrible fight, so I doubled back and tried a new tack. By the end a the day I doubled back so much I run across a highway, which I figured was the Highway 7 I seen on the maps.

"That was bad news. I was two miles behind the line and half the Huns in Italy was between me and my company and fightin' mad as hornets. I was sittin' on a rise on the east side a the highway, watchin' the sun set over my buddies, and doin' some cipherin' on my odds on gettin' back when a convoy with swastikas come up, and I rolled back behind the rise and made a noise like a rock.

"I did some figurin' and figured the best idea was ta get some distance between me and the Krauts, so I headed east toward the mountains to find some cover. By night I found some woods and a deserted farmhouse.

"I spent the night in the barn and most of the next day, only goin' out ta scavenge food from the house. I didn't risk a fire. I listened ta the fightin' a few miles off and had cheese and bread and wine and was glad ta get it, since I had gone a day without a bite.

"I settled in that night, purty snug and wishin' the fellers luck. Between the Allieds and the Krauts they was more people down there then they was in Beaumont, and they was all trying ta kill each other.

Didn't seem like one more feller gettin' hisself killed was gonna change things much.

"Seemed like I had just fell asleep when I woke up. It was darker than half a foot up a bear, but I heard somethin' movin' around too big fer a varmint. I grabbed the helmet. I didn't have ta grab the gun; I was sleepin' with it. I seen the door open and somebody go out. Out!"

Vernon looked at me to make sure I caught that detail. I nodded.

"Weren't much of a moon, just a fingernail shavin', but it was enough ta see the outline of a woman. She made fer the house and I follered her. I found a oil lamp in the front room and picked it up but didn't light it. I come up on her in the kitchen, diggin' around in the dark.

"When she seen my outline in the door, she froze, and I heard her breath rattlin' in and out. I set the lamp on the table and lit it. She stifled back a scream, and I seen her starin' at my head. Then I realized I was wearin' a Kraut helmet, so I took it off and pointed at my patches and said 'American.' That settled her down some but only a little. I holstered the gun and that seemed ta help.

"She was young and cute as a bug's ear, a dark lookin' girl with hair as dark as night and wearin' a black dress and barefoot and shakin' like a leaf. I fixed her up some bread and cheese and poured us some wine. She knew a little English, which was good since I didn't know but four or five words in Italian, and as I already knew where the bathroom was, they weren't much help.

"I don't remember what all we talked about. It only seemed like a few minutes, and then the sun was comin' up. We decided it was best ta get back ta the barn, so we took the bottle with us and settled back in the hay and talked some more.

"Her name was Sarah, and she was from Rome but had gone hidin' when the Krauts showed up. She was a Jew, and the Krauts didn't like Jews for some reason she didn't explain, so when they come and started shippin' Jews out a town in cattle trains, her family paid a lot of money to get smuggled out a the country. But the feller got even more money from the Krauts to turn 'em over, so when she showed up late, she seen 'em haulin' off her family, and she was the only one that got away.

"She was livin' with a family in the farmhouse until the bombin' started and the family left. She didn't go with 'em 'cause if they was caught with her, they would all get hauled away along with her. So she hid in the barn, and then I showed up.

"We got purty friendly. I was nineteen, and fer the past two years I had seen more camels than women. She was young and scared and lonely. When she looked at me with those eyes that looked like two black rocks in a artesian spring and said, 'The enemy of my enemy is my friend,' I didn't need my pa there ta tell me what ta do.

"After that I weren't in such a hurry ta get back ta Anzio. The fightin' died down and nobody come lookin' fer me. After a few days, I weren't in a hurry ta get back ta Fred neither. Nobody knew where I was. They would figure I died in the battle. After a week I shucked off my fatigues and tried out some clothes from the house. They fit close enough.

"We worked around the place, and I started ta thinkin' I might just up and settle there. I had the love of a good woman, and I figured when the family come back, they would welcome an extry hand ta help out around the place.

"One day we set down and tried ta figure out what day it was. Come ta find out it was my birthday, June 6. I done been there a week and a half."

"Today is your birthday?"

"Mark boy, don't interrupt. Who's milkin' this duck?"

"What?"

"Just shut up and drink yer Coke. It was my birthday. She decided ta make a cake, and I went off ta find some scotch in another deserted house. It took half the day. I didn't find any scotch, but I found some grappa. It weren't as smooth, but I figured it might grow some hair on my chest.

"When I come back at sunset, the door was open. I didn't see anything else irregular, so I went inside slowlike, keepin' my eyes open. The first thing I seen was a dead Kraut on his back on the floor in the front room. He had a hole in his chest, and there was a ocean a blood. It was sticky. I could see he done been there a hour or two.

"I looked around carefullike and listened, but there was nothin'. I took the Luger from the dead Kraut and moved like a cat ta the next room. There was another Kraut face down on the table, as still as a picture. A trail of blood went out the back door."

Vernon stopped and the night closed in around us, the sound of crickets throbbing so loud I wondered how I had heard the story over them. The sun had long since gone down although I hadn't noticed it. The night had brought no relief from the heat. A blanket of humidity hugged us. There was not even the hint of a breeze. My shirt was plastered to my skeletal body.

I looked at Vernon. The waning quarter moon glistened on the sheen of sweat on his face. His watery eyes glowed from behind a thin veil of cigarette smoke. He no longer held the Coke can. He was drinking straight from the flask. He took a hit and grimaced as he swallowed. He didn't seem to be looking at anything in particular. Or maybe at one thing in particular. One thing that wasn't here in Fred in 1973. Something that I couldn't see but that he saw as clearly as the house silvered in moonlight across the road. He began talking again in a monotone, like a man under hypnosis answering questions.

"I follerd the trail ta the barn, the Luger in front. I got ta the door and a burp gun opened up on me from behind. A mess a rounds dug into the barn door next ta me, and I shoved it open and rolled inside. When I come up inside, I was starin' straight at a Kraut helmet. I pulled off three rounds from the Luger afore I took another breath.

"It took a few seconds fer my eyes ta see in the dark a the barn. Under the helmet I saw a dark face cute as a bug's ear and long hair black as night. It was Sarah."

He paused for a few seconds and then resumed. His voice remained as emotionless as a Berlitz tape.

"I didn't kill 'er. She was already dead, had been fer awhile. The Kraut with the burp gun must a winged 'er before she made it ta the barn."

He fell silent again. The only motion he made was to take another hit from the flask. His left hand was on the steering wheel. Smoke from his forgotten cigarette snaked up through the humid air and spread across the windshield.

"So who shot at you?"

Vernon jerked like he'd been slapped. "What?" The tower of ash on the cigarette crumbled and stuck in gray clumps to the sweat on his knuckles.

"The burp gun outside the barn. Who shot at you?"

"Oh, that. It was the third Kraut. I went out the back way and got his gun without a fight. He was hit in the spot no man wants ta get shot and couldn't walk. He was lyin' against the hedge, bleedin' ta death. He knew some English. I got two glasses from the house and sat next ta him. We drank grappa and talked.

"He was a young kid like me. Lived in a small town in Germany, liked ta hunt and fish. But he was good with the books and was up ta the university in Berlin when he got called down. Before he died he told me the Americans pushed through from Cassino all the way ta Rome. They got separated durin' the retreat and was tryin' ta get past Rome ta the front line. They come ta the farmhouse lookin' fer food, and Sarah opened up on 'em with my sidearm when they come in the door. They weren't after anything more than food."

"So how did you get out?"

"I hiked back ta Highway 7 and walked ta Rome."

"And the fingers?"

He looked at me without comprehension. I pointed to the half hand holding the cigarette.

"Your left hand? How did you lose your fingers."

"Oh, that." He held up his left hand and looked at it as if it belonged to someone else. "I was swimmin' in the Nile and a crocodile bit it off." He smiled. A very sad, drunk smile.

"How about I drive you home, Vernon?"

"How 'bout ya do that, Mark boy."

Once more we performed our ritual, and I handed him the keys in front of his house. For once, Gina didn't come out. Didn't even open the door.

"Yer too good ta me, Mark boy." He reached up and tousled my hair like some B movie from the '40s. "Ya know, not many folks have ever heard that story. As a matter of fact, I only told one other soul besides you."

"Hey, what if—" I started, then stopped.

He was fiddling with his keys. He pulled something from the ring and held it out to me. "Yer sixteen; ya must have a key ring. Hang this on it fer good luck."

It looked like a bullet on a chain. Not a bullet, really, just the shell casing. "What is it?"

"It's a shell from the Luger. Kept me out a danger the rest a the war. I used it ta cut cigars, but I don't never smoke cigars anymore. Only Lucky Strikes."

"Are you sure? Isn't this kind of special?"

"Yep. But I made three of 'em. I got one left in the house."

"OK. Thanks." I shoved it into my pocket.

"So, what was you goin' ta ask me?"

"Nothing. Just if you wanted to come to church Sunday. That's all."

"Why would I want ta do that?"

"I don't know. I just thought to mention it. It starts at ten if you do."

"That's mighty early fer a old feller like me."

"OK. I have to go. It's way late, and I'm probably going to catch it."

"Good night, Mark boy."

"Good night, Vernon."

I pedaled at a furious pace all the way home through the blanket of the humid night.

CHAPTER SIXTEEN The next Sunday morning I walked into church and discovered a stranger sitting in my regular spot. I took a disgruntled perch behind him and gave him the once-over during the opening prayer. He was tall and slim but not thin. He had close-cut, curly black hair that made him look like a Roman statue. I visualized him standing on the podium wearing a wreath around his head and a toga. All he needed was white circles for eyes. Then he would have looked exactly like the statue. Or maybe like Little Orphan Annie.

We sang a few songs, and Harlan Johnson asked if there were any visitors. Velma Jowett stood up. She was in the row in front of the stranger.

"My nephew Buddy is visiting from Buna." She motioned at the stranger. "Buddy, stand up." Buddy unfolded himself from the pew the way some tall guys seem to stand up, like a Swiss Army knife being opened. He nodded at Dad and turned around to nod at everyone else. He suddenly froze. He looked as if he'd been pole-axed between the eyes. Thoughts of aunts seemed to fade from his mind. I followed his stricken gaze to where Jolene was whispering something to Squeaky on the other side of the aisle.

"Ever'body be sure to welcome Buddy while you greet each other," Harlan said. He stepped back from the podium and looked to Judy Graham to play "I'm So Glad I'm a Part of the Family of God."

Dad stood up while holding up a hand toward Judy. "Wait." He stepped to the microphone. "We have another new face, there on the back row."

Harlan tried to signal something to Dad, but he was oblivious. Everyone turned around to look at the back row. I didn't bother until I saw Deacon Fry's face harden. I heard a voice I had heard many times but never in church.

"I'm Vernon Crowley, from right here in Fred. I ain't been here afore, but I reckon enough folks know me just the same."

I spun around. Vernon winked at me from the back row.

Dad smiled. "Vernon, we're happy to have you here. Let's all greet each other. And be sure to make Vernon feel welcome." He nodded to Judy.

I nodded at Vernon when he looked my way, but in the interest of being as wise as a serpent, declined to walk back and make him feel welcome. Deacon Fry evidently pursued the same policy.

I did greet Buddy, but he scarcely seemed to notice me. I didn't take offense. It was a natural reaction upon seeing Jolene for the first time. He spent the next several hymns staring at her. Eventually I took pity on him and decided to spare him some pain. During the offering I leaned forward and whispered, "Forget it."

"Why? Does she have a boyfriend?" he asked without moving his eyes from her.

"No, it's worse than that." In subdued tones I began to explain the special case of Jolene Culpepper.

I told him about the guy who came back from the bathroom at the drive-in to find all four tires flat. His dazed look changed to surprise. I told him about the guy who tried to get a good-night kiss and found a goldfish in his mouth. Surprise changed to amusement. I told him about the guy who cussed during the whole date and found the suds on his beer had turned to soap suds. Amusement changed to affection. I told him about the guy with the reputation for always scoring on the first date who found his shirt sewed to the car seat halfway through the drive-in movie. Affection changed to respect.

By the time the sermon was over, I could see that instead of discouraging him I had presented him with a challenge. After the benediction he hastened to Jolene's pew like a horse scenting water.

Ralph stepped up and leaned his head in their direction.

I smiled. "I think Jolene has found a new victim."

Ralph grinned and sat down to watch. Imagine a guy who has just flattened his nose trying to walk through a locked door who, instead of unlocking the door, stands back to watch somebody else make the same mistake. That was Ralph.

I shook my head and wandered outside, leaving Buddy to his fate. Vernon was shaking hands with Dad.

"Ya got yerself a mighty fine boy, Reverend. He's been a good listener and a great comfort ta me at one time or another."

"Thanks. He also makes a mean cup of coffee." Dad smiled over Vernon's shoulder at me as I stood in the shade of one of the columns. "Maybe we could get together for a cup sometime and talk."

Vernon looked wary. "About?"

Dad's smile got bigger. "Just get to know each other. Maybe think of ways we can work together to help out the community."

Vernon looked at Dad for several seconds. "Maybe we'll do that one day, Reverend. Maybe we will." He turned and walked to his Pontiac, nodding at me as he passed. I smiled as I noticed he was parked next to Deacon Fry's LTD.

Deacon Fry stepped up. "What was he doin' here?"

"He didn't say. Good morning." Dad held out his hand.

Deacon Fry looked at it for a second, then shook it quickly. "I hope you discouraged him from comin' back. We don't need his kind here. We have a reputation to think of."

Dad smiled. "I absolutely agree." My head jerked around so fast I had thoughts of chiropractors. "We do have a reputation to think of. To which reputation were you referring?"

"Holiness, Pastor Matt. Righteousness. To be beyond reproach."

"Ah, but if you are reproached for the name of Christ, you are blessed. I was thinking more of the reputation Jesus Himself said we would have, that all men would know that we are His disciples by our love for one another."

"For one another, Pastor Matt, for one another. He's not one of us."

"Not yet, but I prefer to think that this is just his pre-Christian state. It is good to remember that at one time all of us were in a pre-Christian state."

Deacon Fry snorted and left. I declined to speculate on Deacon Fry's pre-Christian state. Probably would induce nightmares.

Bubba Culpepper was in the parking lot, leaning against a telephone pole and lusting in his heart over a metal-flake blue Chevrolet C-10 short-wheelbase pickup with a twin exhaust, genuine simulated-leather interior, and mud grips.

"Who belongs to this thang?"

"Beats me, but I bet he'll want you to wipe off the drool before he leaves. Might ruin the finish." I saw the Buna Bobcats ribbon hanging from the mirror. "Ah. This truck belongs to the future victim of your sister. He's just inside now, stretching his neck across the stump."

"What?"

"If I'm not mistaken, the guy who owns this truck is at this very moment asking your sister out on a date."

"Oh." He grinned. "Maybe if he don't survive the date, I can keep the truck!"

"I'd get it in writing before, if I were you."

I was crazy with curiosity, but I wasn't going to break down and actually ask. As it turned out, I didn't have to. Waiting for the bus Monday morning, Jolene brought up the subject for me.

"Do you think he's cute?"

"Oh, yeah! I was just going to ask him out myself, but you beat me to it."

"Seriously, Mark. Do you think he's cute?"

"Seriously, Jolene. I don't think he's cute. I don't think any guy is cute. And don't ask me questions like that!"

"Well, I think he's cute." She smiled and reawakened the echoes of what-if in my mind. I immediately suppressed them. Thus we retain our sanity, one day at a time.

"So, does this mean an end to the cold war?"

"Of course not!" Her eyes flashed with anticipation. "He gets the full first-date treatment next Saturday night."

Despite my latent longings, I didn't envy Buddy the experience. I had done my duty. He had the advantage of an advance briefing from an inside source. I heard the details of their first date the following Sunday.

Buddy, evidently an astute planner, took Jolene to Pizza Inn in Silsbee. They sat down and ordered two salads and a pizza. Buddy even had the waiter light the candle with his Bic butane blowtorch. The sudden silence after the waiter left seemed to grow. Jolene took a bottle of fingernail polish from her purse and tried to open it. Then they both suddenly talked at once.

"So, I hear you're in the band," Buddy started out, just as Jolene held out the bottle and asked, "Could you open this for me?"

"Sure." Buddy took it and opened it. "Here." He handed it back with a smile.

Reaching quickly, Jolene hit his hand and polish spilled all over him. "Oops!" she exclaimed. "I'm so sorry."

"No problem," Buddy said, still smiling. "It could happen to anyone. I'll just go rinse it out in the bathroom." He returned a few minutes later, his jeans a mass of water splotches and smeared polish. "I think I got most of it out," he said in obvious contradiction to the evidence.

While he was putting sugar in his tea, the salad arrived. "Great," he said and picked up the salt. On the first shake the lid came off and dumped a mound of salt atop his salad like a sand dune. He froze for a second or two, still holding the shaker above the plate. Then he recovered.

"Oops, I guess I shook it too hard." Eating a tomato that was only half buried in the mound, he noticed that it tasted mysteriously sweet, like it was coated with sugar. His mind racing to the obvious, he tried his tea. Definitely salty.

"How's your tea?" Jolene asked sweetly.

"Oh, just fine." Buddy smiled back at her. When the pizza arrived, he discretely screwed the lid back on the Parmesan cheese before he used it. Other than getting a slice of pizza dumped in his lap, the meal ended without incident.

Jolene was impressed. He had kept his cool at every trick, something that had never happened before. She didn't know that I had given him a peek at her résumé, but that wouldn't have made much difference. The guys in Fred knew her reputation; they just figured it wouldn't happen to them. Maybe they thought their masculine charms would overwhelm her. Instead, her feminine charms beguiled them into a state of vulnerability, and her sense of humor had done the rest.

Buddy and Jolene left the restaurant and drove back in silence. The whine of mud grips on the highway and the hypnotic flashing of the center line put Jolene in a reflective mood. She thought back on past dates and all the grief she had visited on unsuspecting Don Juans. Those jokes had been entertaining, but they had also served a purpose. She remained free from messy emotional entanglements with unsuitable partners.

But she was forced to wonder if maybe she had gone too far. How did she know they were unsuitable? Just because they couldn't take a joke? Was that an adequate measure of suitability? Perhaps.

It was true that they all seemed to be walking on a paper-thin veneer of ego. One crack in the ice and the whole thing collapsed, not with a wallop but a gurgle, as Langston Hughes might have said if he were from Fred.

She had found the male of the species to be a strange specimen. It would submit to grueling cruelties at the hands of its fellows in order to gain a place on the football team. It would endure primeval hardships—vicissitudes of cold and heat, ice and rain, beast and vermin—in order to mount a multipointed extension of deer skull bones on the wall of the den. It would sit motionless for hours in a flat wasteland of water, grilled by the sun and plagued by the relentless nagging of gnats and the nibbling of mosquitoes, in order to mount the laminated remains of a fish next to the deer.

But let one girl tie its shoelaces together and laugh when it fell, and it lost all composure. It collapsed in a fit of indignation, like a balloon blustering its way noisily around the room to disappear behind the couch, limp and lifeless.

Jolene wanted someone who could stand up for himself, and her, without sputtering and sulking. Someone with confidence and perseverance, someone who couldn't be distracted from his true goal by a practical joke or a silly jab at an exaggerated sense of honor. But it didn't look like she was going to get what she wanted. She had even begun to doubt whether such a creature existed at all. She worried that she might be expecting too much, that maybe the male ego was incapable of such objectivity.

She was summoned from her reflections by the bumping of the truck. Buddy had turned off the highway onto a dirt road and from the dirt road onto a two-rut track. He maneuvered the truck to a secluded spot, romantically hidden behind a capped natural gas well. He rolled down the window. The sound of crickets and frogs wafted in along with the smell of pine trees. And a hint of sulfur.

Jolene turned her head to the passenger window and slid a set of Groucho glasses from her purse. He may have withstood the ordeal of the meal, but she was confident this denouement would signal his demise. Surely his ego could only take so much. He was, after all, the male of the species, susceptible to its noted inability to endure taunting. She had read in science somewhere, and taken as her motto, that the female of the species is more deadly.

She quickly put on the glasses and turned dramatically, as a praying mantis might turn with a cold smile to her unsuspecting mate.

Only to see Buddy's eyes staring back at her from behind an identical set of Groucho glasses. Seeing them framed by the bulging plastic nose and bushy eyebrows, she noticed for the first time how incredibly blue they were. Hypnotically blue. Impossibly blue.

"Oh," she exclaimed softly as he leaned across the seat with a smirk, took her gently by the shoulders, and kissed her, Groucho glasses and all. The big plastic noses got in the way, and before long they dissolved into laughter.

She pulled away and leaned against the door of the truck, looking at him curiously. For the first time her date had made her laugh, not because of what she had done to him but quite the opposite. He sat up, draped his left arm across the steering wheel, and looked back. They stared at each other for a long time with a mixture of amusement and appreciation.

The date ended with them strolling hand-in-hand to the door of the local sheriff, placing a flaming bag of cow manure on the porch, and ringing the doorbell.

CHAPTER SEVENTEEN

The next night after church Jolene was already planning her retaliation. We sat on the hood of Bubba's Corvair and discussed the situation.

"I can't believe I let him off that easy!" I saw a familiar gleam in her eye, like the reflection of burning warships on the sea. "This calls for somethin' big."

"What? I thought you liked the guy."

"I do. That's why I have to come up with something big."

"Hey, I'm lost here. Could you explain how if you like this guy then you have to pull a joke on him? I thought that was what you did to the guys you didn't like."

"There's no use trying ta explain it to ya. You're a guy. Look, just ferget it. Right now I need ya ta help me come up with a plan."

"Oh, no." I jumped off the car. "I'm not getting pulled into this again. Once was enough."

Jolene grabbed my shirt and pulled me back. "That's it! We'll do the shotgun thing again. Great idea."

"I don't think so, Jolene." While I had enjoyed the joke at the time, I lived in fear that Jolene's many victims might discover my treachery.

It was the one time I had actually aided and abetted the enemy. She had been forced into a truce in desperate circumstances on a double-date with Bubba and Marianne. Afterward she was looking for a way to deal with Turner McCullough, the one date who had escaped unscathed and was encouraged to pursue the hottest girl in Fred.

I had told her of "The Brakeman's Daughter," the story by Damon Runyon, where False Face loved to play jokes on people, particularly this joke. He would get a guy worked up about a girl but would tell him

terrible stories about how jealous her old man was and how he shot at
the guys who tried to date her up. They could only go when the old
man was gone on his job as a brakeman for the railroad. The joke was
that there really was no brakeman or daughter. He would set up a time
to take the sucker out to see her at an empty house way out in the
woods, but when they showed up, somebody would come roaring from
the back of the house shooting a gun in the air, and False Face would
yell, "Watch out, it's the brakeman!" and run off. He would eventually
lose the sucker in the woods and ditch him, leaving him to find his way
back to town.

It was a joke that had worked with eminently satisfying results on
Turner. Jolene used that to her advantage.

"Aw, come on. Remember the look on Turner's face when you called
him a egg-suckin' somethin'-or-other. What was that again?"

"You mean that no-good, mealy-mouthed son of a motherless, flea-
bitten, egg-suckin' cur?" I boomed in my Mr. Culpepper voice. Then I
realized where I was. I looked around the church lawn. Several groups
of stragglers were still standing around talking. Or at least they had been
talking. Now they were all looking at me. Bubba turned from his conversation with Ralph and looked at me thoughtfully. I waved meekly and
turned back to Jolene. The phrase had called back to my mind the sight
of Turner diving through his car window and the ecstasy of laughter that
followed. I could do worse on a Friday night.

"Well, maybe one more time."

Once more the scam was afoot. Jolene set out preparing the ground
by pumping Buddy with stories of how mean, ornery, and jealous her
daddy was and how he particularly despised Buddy. Since he lived in
Buna, there was little danger of him meeting Mr. Culpepper and discovering the truth. Jolene set the next date for a weekend when everyone
was going fishing. After the date Buddy was supposed to take her out to
her family at the lake.

Finally the day arrived, and I parked the '64 Falcon behind the barn as before, donned Mr. Culpepper's big, black cowboy hat and the over-sized coat, and positioned myself on the side of the house between the Culpepper's two hounds. They had not improved their hygiene since last year. This time I laid the shotgun on the ground, knowing I would have to restrain the dogs until I got the signal.

Buddy was running late. I shook my head and talked to the dogs. "What is it with these guys? Does nobody show up for a date on time around here?" In response, one of the dogs released an aroma that obliterated plant life for a fifty-yard radius. I gagged and pulled out my shirt-tail, trying to use it as a mask to filter out the fumes. It didn't work.

Just as I saw a pair of headlights turn off the highway, rough hands grabbed me from behind and covered my mouth. I couldn't breathe, which was a small blessing. I struggled briefly but ineffectively as I was dragged to the back porch by someone very large.

A voice rumbled in my ear. "I'm gonna take my hand off yer mouth. If ya make a sound, I'll squeeze yer neck so hard you'll look like a ostrich. Understand?"

I nodded vigorously and my mouth was released. The hat and coat were pulled off me. I turned around to see Mr. Culpepper putting them on. He opened the back door and pushed me in. I ran into Bubba.

I tried to ask what was going on, but Bubba grabbed my shirt and held his finger to his lips with an expression of such ferocity that I immediately clamped my mouth shut. I allowed myself to be led to a corner bedroom with windows facing the side and the front of the house.

As the headlights approached the house, I saw Mr. Culpepper pick up the shotgun and switch out the shells.

Buddy pulled up in a cloud of dust, jumped out of his truck, and strolled up the walk. Right on cue, Jolene burst out of the front door and exclaimed, as convincingly as ever, "Watch out! Daddy's come back!"

I watched from the bedroom window, powerless to stop the events that had been set into motion.

BOOM! A shot rang out according to plan, but the real Mr. Culpepper came storming around the house, roaring, "Where is that no-good, mealy-mouthed son of a motherless, flea-bitten, egg-suckin' cur?" Or something very like it. *BOOM!*

Buddy skidded to a stop on the walk with the dogs dancing all around him like dolphins around a schooner. His head bobbed back and forth like he was at a tennis match as he looked from Jolene to Mr. Culpepper. However, Jolene didn't seem to see Buddy at all. She was standing, white-faced, staring at her dad as if he had come back from the dead. "Daddy?"

"Son," Mr. Culpepper snarled in a voice that froze my blood, "I'll learn ya ta come foolin' round my daughter." He leveled the shotgun at Buddy and pulled the trigger. *BOOM!*

I jerked like I'd been slapped, but Buddy jerked back like he'd been hit with a bat and fell to the ground, his hand clasped to his chest. Jolene screamed in horror and raced to him, kneeling down at his side.

"Daddy! You shot him!"

"Missy," Mr. Culpepper said. "It was fer your own good. Never trust a boy that drives a Chevrolet."

"What?" Jolene stared at him in disbelief.

I looked at Bubba. He had a grin on his face that was about to split his head in two. "Never trust a boy that drives a Chevrolet?" I grabbed Bubba's shirt and shook him. "He shot him because of his truck?" Bubba just kept grinning. "Have you all lost your minds?" I screamed. He pushed me away and pointed out the window.

Jolene looked from Mr. Culpepper to Buddy in confusion. Buddy slowly pulled himself up on one elbow, looked into Jolene's eyes, and winked. "Gotcha."

Jolene's jaw dropped until I thought it would bounce off the ground. Bubba lost all sense of composure and stumbled out of the door, collapsing on the porch swing and swaying slowly in spasms of laughter. I followed him out. Mr. Culpepper was leaning on the shotgun and chuckling in his low voice, like a rusty pump.

Buddy scrambled to his feet to escape the dogs, which were licking him energetically and slapping each other with their tails. He dusted off his jeans and pulled Jolene up from the pose in which she had frozen. Her mouth slowly changed from a long vertical oval to a horizontal line and then inched even more slowly into a curve as she joined in with the joke.

I was still having problems getting my pulse down to double digits. I had enough surplus adrenaline to roof the barn. "How did you know?" I asked no one in particular.

Bubba was in no condition to talk. He gasped weakly from his perch on the swing and tumbled to the floor. Mr. Culpepper just leaned on his gun and grinned. Buddy supplied the details, a lop-sided grin cutting across his face.

"When Jolene started feedin' me this story about her dad, I figured somethin' was fishy, so I called him. He told me she set a date a few months back when ever'body was gone, and when they come back, she was still here and he noticed the shotgun had been fired. I found out who the date was with and had a little talk with Turner. It took some doin', but I finally got him ta tell me what happened. Especially when he realized what I was plannin'."

No one had noticed the brown Dodge Dart that had pulled up behind Buddy's truck. Sonia got out and looked at the crowd standing around the front porch with momentary confusion. She singled out Jolene and smiled.

"Hey, honey. I just come by ta show ya some of our new stuff."

"New stuff?"

"Mary Kay." Sonia held up a pink bag with the logo on the front. Her smile changed from forced to genuine. "Just wait 'til ya see the new eye shadow. It'll make yer eyes pop out!"

Bubba had a relapse of his laughing fit. He crawled up on the swing and wiped his eyes. I sat down next to him and looked at Sonia's eyes. They didn't look like they were going to pop out. They looked more like they were trapped underneath an explosion of eye shadow and mascara. Alice Cooper would have been jealous. Her customary layer of makeup seemed even thicker than the last time I had seen her. Probably got a discount.

Jolene coughed. "I don't wear makeup."

Sonia gasped. "What? You don't wear makeup?" She rushed to Jolene's side and grabbed her arm. "Well, honey, we can fix that right now. It's never too late ta start. I can teach ya the basics in half a hour."

Jolene stood immovable as Sonia tried to drag her into the house. "Really. I really don't wear makeup."

Sonia stopped like she had run into a wall. She looked back at Jolene for some sign of a smile. After all, Jolene had a reputation. "On purpose?"

"On purpose."

"Oh, honey," she said as if Jolene had just told her she had cancer. She turned on Mr. Culpepper. "What have you done to this poor girl?"

He blinked, stepped back, and muttered a few words.

Sonia turned back to Jolene. "Here honey, it'll be OK. At least take a look at some fingernail polish." She held out her left hand, blood red nails toward Jolene. "See, we got some nice colors, and they're chip resistant."

Jolene looked at the hand as if it were a spider. "No, thanks, Mrs. Walker. I already got some."

"Sonia."

"What?"

"Just call me Sonia."

"OK."

Sonia gave Jolene one last piercing look. "Are ya sure ya don't want ta get maybe a cuticle trimmer or somethin'? We could pluck back them eyebrows, and it would do wonders. Ya got so much fresh material ta work with."

"No, thanks."

Sonia looked around like she had caught us tormenting a cat. "OK, honey. If that's what you want." She gave Mr. Culpepper a meaningful look and stormed back to her car.

Bubba began laughing again. I didn't join him. I was thinking about the light ring of skin I had seen on Sonia's hand when she flashed her fingernails at Jolene. On the fourth finger of her left hand. Where a ring used to be.

CHAPTER EIGHTEEN The Friday after Thanksgiving dawned clear and cool, giving me the perfect excuse to work off some excess poundage with my *Grit* route. After a few hours I no longer felt like a lead zeppelin. Or an iron butterfly, for that matter.

I was working the route like the tortoise of fable and song, slow and steady, hitting all the usual spots. I sold a paper to Parker. He smiled but didn't say anything besides "Keep the change."

On a long thin sandpit disguised as a road, the sound of distant thunder caused me to look up. No clouds. I looked ahead. Nothing. I looked behind. The smudge on the horizon confirmed my fears. Every second counted. As the rumble resolved into a metallic tattoo of rattles, I dove into the ditch on the right, dumped the papers, and covered my head with the *Grit* bag.

As the rattles intensified, the roar of a straight six was introduced, like a basso continuo over a legion of spastic snares. Just when it seemed I would be swallowed in the cacophony, the sound of the engine dropped away. It was replaced by a crescendo of rattles softened by the damping of a cloud of dust. I could hear tires sliding through sand, but I didn't move until the cloud had settled, like a dusting of ash after an eruption.

"Are you through?" I hollered from under the bag.

"Say, doll," Darnell yelled back. "You developin' pictures under there or what?"

"Saying my prayers." I shook the bag out and put papers back in.

"Funny, I never figured you fer the religious type."

I gave him the Cloud glare, the one reserved for the most odious sarcasm. Darnell looked back through greasy Coke-bottle glasses. The driver's window was facing me. While I stood defenseless in the ditch with

only a bag on my head for protection, Darnell had executed a 180-degree
skid five feet away. I had been kidding about the prayers, but I made up
for it now.

"You out peddlin' that magazine again?"

"Newspaper." I picked up the bike and brushed off the seat.

"I ain't doin' nothin' but wastin' gas. Toss that runt bike in the back
'n I'll drive ya around."

I hesitated, ignoring the slight to my classic Spyder bike with chopper handlebars and tiger-skin banana seat. The last time I had accepted
the offer, Darnell had plowed a new row in a cornfield after playing
chicken with a log truck. When I had escaped his evil clutches by bail-
ing out of the truck, he had spun off in a cloud of corn shucks with my
vintage bike still in the back, leaving me stranded miles from civilization.
And a few miles from Fred as well.

"Yer brain got a vapor lock or somethin'?"

"I was just trying to remember if my life insurance is paid up."

"What do you care? You won't be around ta use it if ya need it."

Good point. "Look, I appreciate the offer, but I want to negotiate a
few conditions first."

"It's yer nickel."

"We will not take blind corners sideways."

"Course not."

"We will not play chicken with anything larger than a chicken."

"You got it."

"If at anytime I decide to exit the vehicle, and I use the term loosely,
you will remain stopped until such time as I am able to retrieve my bike
and move at least ten feet from the Hound."

"The hound?"

"The truck."

"Oh. Sure thing, doll."

"You swear on a Chilton manual?"

"A whole stack."

"All right." I threw the bike in the back and climbed in the variegated '52 Ford pickup christened the Hound of Hell by Dad in one of his more charitable moments.

We went through the rest of the route like a dose of salts and arrived at Vernon's hill earlier than usual. He was already there. I caught Darnell's eye and nodded. He skidded head-in on the passenger side of the Pontiac. I hopped out into a cloud of dust.

"I got a ride this time. Got an extra Coke?"

Vernon nodded his head toward the cooler. I took shotgun and retrieved two Cokes, handing one to Darnell as he slid into the back.

"Vernon, this is Darnell Ray. Darnell, Vernon Crowley."

Darnell froze in the middle of popping the top on the Coke. "Crowley?"

"Yep," Vernon said. "I reckon I know yer pa, G. B."

"Yeah, that's him." Darnell looked at me with a strange expression and pulled the ring. "Thanks for the Coke."

Vernon nodded his head and took a long slow drag on his cigarette. "I see you fellers is a little early today. Same here. Had ta get out a the house. That woman talks more'n a feller can listen and don't never say nothin'." He spoke in small puffs of smoke. "I got a full tank and some spendin' money. Maybe we should just up and drive ta Canada."

He looked at me from the corner of his eye.

"I might just go. After I finish this cigarette." He lit a second one from the tail end of the first.

"Hey," Darnell said. "You were in the Third Infantry?" He nodded at the square medal on the mirror, the one with diagonal blue and white stripes.

Vernon turned slowly around and looked steadily at Darnell. "Yep, I was."

"So was my daddy. Korea, Fifteenth Infantry Division."

"WWII, Fifteenth Infantry Division." Vernon turned back and took a sip of his Coke.

"Yer kiddin'! Did ya know Audie Murphy?"

"Not ta speak to. I seen him a few times."

"Wow!" Darnell hit the back of my seat. "You didn't tell me ya knew a war hero."

I wiped the Coke off my face. "Next time I'll wear a sign."

Darnell started pumping Vernon for information about the war. Before long he was telling one story after another about Casablanca, Tunisia, Sicily, Salerno, Anzio, France, Germany, Austria. Must have been the turkey; I had never heard him talk so much. Not even D-Day. I found it a bit annoying. It had taken me months to get Vernon to tell me about his war adventures, and here Darnell was, getting the inside scoop on his first visit.

About the time Vernon was going on about fighting in the rain in France, the two Cokes I had sipped began to make known their desire to be released into the wild. I excused myself and repaired to the woods. As I returned, I heard a car passing on the dirt road. I emerged in time to see the back of a black LTD headed toward the river bottom. I looked at Vernon; he didn't seem to notice. Across the road the sun settled on the chimney of the house. In a fit of gratitude for not being spotted by Deacon Fry, I waved at the girl on the swing. She didn't wave back.

Vernon talked the sun down and the moon up. The temperature had dropped, and we could see our breath when we talked. He was smiling when we told him good-bye.

Darnell was bubbling like a new percolator. "Can you believe it? He killed twenty Germans with his own hands!" He was so excited he violated every stated and implied condition I had negotiated. I had never expected him to comply with them anyway. I held the dash and muttered imprecations under my breath.

141

"I would take that with a block of salt. That was after he had emptied the flask into his Coke can."

"Still, he was in France with Audie Murphy when he won the Congressional Medal of Honor!"

"He was in the same country. He wasn't actually with him in the tank. Not even in the same company."

Darnell drove in silence for awhile. Or what passed for silence in the Hound.

"Another thing ya didn't tell us."

"What?"

He looked at me, his face glowing greenly from the dash light, glasses opaque disks of green, a green fog emerging from his mouth as he spoke. "Crowley. You know . . . Crowley."

"So?"

"Don't that ring a bell?"

"Should it?"

We skidded onto the highway without slowing, a feathery arc of sand turning into the screech of rubber on pavement.

"Jake Crowley."

"Oh!" All these months I had never connected the two names. "Are there a lot of Crowleys around here?"

"Don't know any others. Just those two."

"They don't look anything alike."

Darnell almost drove off the road. "How do you know what Jake looks like?" He looked at me so long I was sure we had drifted across the road into the oncoming lane.

"Watch the road, will ya?" My mind raced. "I saw Jake in an old annual." That sounded good. "In the library," I said, heading off Darnell's next question.

"Why would you do that?"

Yeah, why would I do that? "Uh . . . because I thought Ralph was making it all up, so I wanted to check to see if somebody by that name really did go to school here."

"Ah." Darnell seemed doubtful.

I didn't offer any information. Could it be? Funny, Vernon had never said anything about Jake. Or maybe it wasn't that funny after all. If your kid was Jake Crowley, would you tell anybody?

An hour after I got home, the phone rang. Two long rings. That meant it was for us.

We were watching *The Sound of Music* on the late movie. A bit late for a call. Probably wasn't good news. I did an inventory of my recent past for items that Deacon Fry might see as wise as a dove or as harmless as a serpent. Maybe he had seen me after all.

Dad answered the phone. Then he made some coffee. Ten minutes later the doorbell rang. Dad opened the door and said, "Come on in, Hurst."

Deputy Hurst came in, tall and lanky in his brown sheriff's department outfit. He held his hat in his left hand. His right hand rested on his radio. He was Ralph's uncle, so I had seen him a few times. The girls glanced at Hurst and turned back to the movie. Mom got up.

"Hurst, nice to see you." She saw the coffee pot. "Would you like some coffee?"

"Thanks, ma'am." He and Dad sat down at the table. Bored with the yodeling goatherd puppet show, I abandoned the movie, fixed a Dr Pepper, and joined them while Mom poured three cups of coffee. Then she sat down at the table.

Hurst looked grim. "Well, there ain't no pretty way ta say it. And it sure as h—" He looked at Mom apologetically. "It sure as heck weren't a pretty sight. Gina Crowley is dead. Vernon Crowley called the sheriff's department about a hour ago and said she was shot and we ought ta come out."

"My goodness," Mom said.

Dad said, "I'm sorry to hear that."

I almost dropped my glass.

"When we got there, Vernon was sittin' on the ground out by a hedge holdin' a shotgun in his lap. He didn't make no move ta use it when we come up and didn't do nothin' when I took it. I checked it. Fired recently."

Vernon shot Gina? I had seen her knock him out of the trailer into the drive and him come up and make excuses for her. I couldn't imagine him shooting her, or anyone else. Of course I couldn't imagine him killing twenty Germans either. Maybe talking about the war had worked him up. Maybe he had a flashback.

"He had a glass with some clear liquid in it, moonshine I figured, until I found a bottle and a second glass half full settin' next ta him on the grass. The label of the bottle was all in Spanish or French or some-thin'."

"Grappa?" They looked at me as if they just now noticed I was there.

"Now that you say it, I think it did say that on the bottle. Grappa, yeah."

"Was the bottle kind of frosted looking?"

"Yeah," he said slowly.

It was more of a question than a look Dad shot at me. It drew the answer out of me like a cork from a bottle.

"Back in the summer he told me about drinking grappa on D-Day."

"And the bottle?"

"He had a bottle of clear stuff. I guess it was grappa." I decided to not mention that he also told me he drank it right after he had shot the woman he loved, even though she was already dead. Might confuse matters a little.

"So we have established the suspect has a taste for grappa. Now all we have to do is find out what grappa is."

They looked at me. I shrugged. "Something you get when you're in Italy and you can't find scotch."

"Mark, have you been drinking grappa with Mr. Crowley?" Mom seemed afraid to hear the answer.

"No!"

"Do you know Vernon?" Hurst asked.

"I just sell him newspapers."

"No need to worry, dear; Mark has told me all about Vernon. He just sells him newspapers," Dad said.

Hurst considered the information for a few seconds and resumed his report. "We asked him about the second glass, was there anybody else there. He just shook his head. I asked him where Gina was. He pointed to the trailer. I left Joe with Vernon, tellin' him to keep his eyes peeled fer any other parties, and went into the trailer."

He paused and glanced at Mom before proceeding. "Gina was on the floor, layin' against the wall opposite the door. She had been shot in the head at point-blank range with a shotgun. There was considerable blood. No need ta check fer a pulse."

Dad let out his breath slowly and loudly and shook his head, staring into his coffee. Mom's eyes misted over. In the den the von Trapp girls sang "So Long, Farewell." In the kitchen, things were a little too surreal. I sipped the Dr Pepper.

"No signs of forced entry, no signs of a struggle. We asked Vernon what happened. All he would say is he come home and found her dead. That's it." Hurst took a slow sip of coffee. "I know Vernon has a reputation for bein' a pretty rough customer, sometimes comes into town bruised up like he's been fightin'. He could a been knockin' Gina around fer years and nobody would know. She never leaves the house as far as I can tell. I been a deputy over ten years, and I never seen her once. And of course ever'body knows he's runnin' shine although nobody can find the still. And there's rumors he's got a side business in marijuana."

That one took me by surprise. Dad, too, from the look on his face.

"I recollected that Vernon has been comin' up ta the church on Sundays the last few months or so and thought ya might want ta have a talk with him. He's out in the car right now. You can ride with us ta Woodville if ya like, and I can bring ya back after we book him."

Many times over the years I had vowed never to be a preacher. This was the best reason I had heard so far. What do you say to a notorious bootlegger who just shot his wife at point-blank range with a shotgun? I don't think they have a class on that in seminary.

Dad looked at Mom. A silent communication passed between them. He nodded. "I think I will." He stood up to get his jacket. "You're a good man, Hurst. Thanks for coming by and letting me know. And I'm sure Vernon will appreciate it. If not now, then maybe later."

CHAPTER NINETEEN

Dad got back long after I had gone to bed. Saturday morning we were pruning back the branches from the fruit trees Dad had marked with spray paint back during the summer. He wielded the shears, and I collected the branches in a wheelbarrow. I asked him what had transpired between him and Vernon in the patrol car.

"All he would say about the crime was that he had come home and found Gina already dead."

He clipped a branch and waited for me to retrieve it before moving to the next tree.

"But just before they took him in, he said something strange. Hurst left to take care of something, and I was alone in the car with Vernon. He said something like 'Reverend, I did what I had to do. I'm sorry I can't help you now, but I have listened to your sermons and read the Good Book and I did what I thought was right.'" Dad looked at me. "Does that mean something to you?"

I thought it over and shook my head. "No, sir. How could he think that the Bible said it was right to shoot Gina?"

"That's just it. He keeps saying when he came home she was already dead. But the gun had been fired, the room smelled of powder, and they found shot in the wound and in the wall nearby." I looked at him and waited. "Oh, I stayed around to hear some details from the incident report. Privilege of the clergy, don't you know." He smiled.

"Anything else?"

"The only prints on the gun were from Vernon and Hurst."

"So it's pretty definite Vernon fired the gun."

"Doesn't seem to be much question. But what did he mean that he couldn't help me? I was there to help him."

I didn't have an answer.

The next day at church speculation ran wild. Before and after Sunday school little groups of people buzzed like electric hair clippers. During Sunday school, Scooter had difficulty keeping the class on topic. Opinions ranged from innocent until proven guilty to lynching. When the buzzer went off, Darnell cornered me in the empty classroom.

"Doll, you didn't tell anybody we was with Vernon Friday, did ya?"

"Nobody asked me."

"OK, then let's just keep it that way." He looked around nervously. "I mean, he's a war hero and all, but yer daddy don't want ta get dragged down ta the courthouse and all. I don't want ta rat out a war hero. Plus, my daddy wouldn't like it none ta hear I was associatin' with criminals."

"Rat him out?"

"We seen him drunker'n Cooter Brown. He must a gone right home and shot the old lady while he was drunk."

"Darnell, that's not going to stop the presses. They know he was drunk. He was drinking when the cops got there."

"I'm just sayin' is all. Let's keep it between you and me."

"Between me and you and a dog named Boo."

"I'm not jokin', Mark."

"Ya vohl, Herr Commandant." I shot my hand forward and clicked my heels together. I figured it was fitting since Darnell's greasy blond hair always looked like he had inherited Hitler's barber. He walked off disgusted.

In the service, from my vantage point behind Deacon Fry, it looked as if his head had been left on the red hot setting. If he had ground his teeth any louder when Dad mentioned Vernon in the closing prayer, he would have been fined for violating noise-abatement statutes in Louisiana.

After church I heard him tell Dad the deacons would meet with him in his study. I immediately went to the study and cracked the window enough to allow sound out without being noticeable. Then I ducked around the back side of the church and found a spot under the window. It was warm for Thanksgiving, so I wasn't too uncomfortable waiting outside.

I didn't have to wait long. I heard the door open and the creak of the swivel chair behind the desk. After a short silence Dad said, "Well, gentlemen?"

Fry's voice rattled the glass. He must have been sitting right next to the window. "Pastor Matt, I think we should open with prayer."

"As you wish."

"Our dear heavenly Father," Fry growled, "we beseech Thee today for Thy wisdom which Thou dost so liberally bestow upon them which bother ta ask Thee for it. Dear heavenly Father, we know Thou art a hard Master, reaping where Thou hast not sown, and gathering where Thou hast not strawed. Precious Jesus, Thou hast said we must be perfect as Thou art perfect. Precious Jesus, Thou hast said that unto whomsoever much is given, of him shall be much required: and to whom men have committed much, of him they will ask the more. Your holy Word tells us that Thou wilt judge more severely them that teachest."

Teachest? I had to suppress a snort. I half expected him to follow that with "I thank Thee that I am not like other men," but I was disappointed.

"Father, give Thou us the wisdom to know the right thing ta do, and the will ta do what must be done. Amen."

I was disappointed that I couldn't see Dad. How could he listen to this with a straight face? I had rolled my eyes so many times, they were practically staring out of my ears.

"Pastor Matt, we asked you here ta discuss certain matters that seem ta be comin' up more regular than is proper."

"OK."

"Since you prayed fer that bootlegger, ya know what he done."

"On the contrary, Deacon Fry, I don't know what Vernon has done. And unless you were there with him, neither do you."

"You know what he is charged with."

"Of course I know that. I was there when they booked him."

"So we hear, Pastor Matt. So we hear."

"However, he says that he found Gina already dead when he came home."

Fry erupted. "You would take the word of a—" He choked off the end of the sentence and started over more calmly. "Pastor Matt, we ain't here ta argue the case of the bootlegger. The courts will see ta that. We're here because we're concerned about what is happenin' ta this church since you come here."

"I see. Are you referring to the fact that we are now out of debt for the first time in thirty years or the fact that attendance has doubled three years in a row?"

"I'm referrin' ta the irregular behavior goin' on. I been goin' ta this church all my life. My daddy before me come ta this church, and his daddy before him. There's been a Fry here as long as there's been a church here. And in all that time, we haven't had hussies jumpin' up in funerals and blasphemin' God or drunkards comin' into a service and bustin' whiskey bottles on the altar or bootleggers sittin' next ta honest citizens singin' hymns like one a the saints. Not 'til you come."

"And you're concerned."

"Yes, we are concerned."

"We?"

"We. As head deacon, I am expressin' the feelin' of the deacon board."

"I assume they are permitted to speak as well to confirm their agreement with this feeling?"

A short silence. "Course. But they won't tell ya any different. The good name of this church is bein' disgraced and made a mockery in the community."

"Since you are so certain, you won't object if I ask them myself, will you?"

"Ask 'em."

"Elmer? How say you?"

Elmer's thin voice barely made it out of the room. He was a tall, thin, frail old man who wore his pants three inches below his armpits and had a perpetual case of phlegm. Sometimes he would go outside and snuffle and hawk with great vigor and enthusiasm for several minutes before he successfully dislodged a loogie and spat noisily into the grass. To be inconspicuous, he would go to the side of the church before he got revved up. Unfortunately, that placed him directly beneath the windows next to the last few rows, and the sound of his exertions would ring through the sanctuary, frequently drowning out whatever was happening inside. He cleared his throat a few times before he started.

"Well, Pastor Matt, it do seem a might irregular doins as is goin' on in church the past year. I ain't sayin' as how it might not be a good thing fer the lost sheep ta be brought into the fold, but it's a might irregular all the same."

Dad waited. A snort and a cough signaled that Elmer was done.

"Scooter?"

Scooter! I had forgotten he was a deacon.

"I don't know, Pastor Matt. I know we are ta reach out ta the lost. But we're supposed ta call them out of their sin. Like Pastor Bates said this summer, if ya don't fear God, then you don't feel the fires of hell that are as real as this chair. It doesn't seem right to let sinners sit there pretendin' they're as respectable as the saints."

"How exactly would we enforce this policy? Do we have bouncers at the door with a sin-ometer? Do we have the ushers throw out sinners who accidentally sneak past security?"

"It just doesn't seem right is all I'm sayin'." He sounded apologetic. "If they came to repent, that would be different."

"So we wait until the invitation, and if they don't come down, then we throw them out?"

Scooter didn't say anything.

"And you, Weldon?"

"Sure I'm concerned. I mean, ever'thin' Deacon Fry said is true, ain't it? We got drunkards and murderers comin' here. The Word says that murderers will burn in the lake of fire and drunkards can't inherit the kingdom of God."

"The same verse says that those who slander won't inherit the kingdom of God. Shall we start weeding out those who claim to know that people are guilty before they go to trial?"

Fry broke in. "Pastor Matt, decent people don't want ta come ta church and have ta sit next ta unrepentant sinners."

"The same verse also says thieves will not inherit the kingdom. But Jesus Himself hung between two thieves, one of whom was repentant and one who was not."

"He didn't have any control over who they hung up next ta Him." I could almost hear Dad's eyebrow rising, but he didn't say anything. "Pastor Matt, folks are talkin' about this church, and they ain't talkin' in a good way."

"And as head deacon, I am confident that you caution them with what the Bible has to say about gossip and spreading discord. And slander."

"This is not a jokin' matter, Pastor Matt. I am serious."

"So am I, Deacon Fry. Jesus Himself said, 'The Spirit and the bride say, Come. And let him that heareth say, Come. And let him that is athirst come. And whosoever will, let him take the water of life freely.' The bride, that's you and me, Deacon Fry."

The thought of Deacon Fry as a bride was a horrifying, if somewhat amusing, image. I shuddered.

"The bride, the church, says, 'Let him that is athirst come.' Now why is it that a fifty-year-old bootlegger who has never in his life darkened the door of a church suddenly starts to come? Could it be he's thirsty for something besides moonshine? Jesus says, 'Let him come.' You say 'Get him out of here.' I agree, Deacon Fry. This is not funny at all."

I wanted to jump up and holler "Go get 'em, Dad!" but it would blow my cover. Fry evidently wanted to jump up and holler too.

"Don't you sit there and preach at me like I don't know my Bible. If that bootlegger wants ta come and repent, let him come, I say, and fall on his knees like a repentant sinner. If not, then he should be warned that the church is fer them who are ready ta drink the water of life, not them that want ta trample it full a mud. We just got rid of the drunkard, and now we have a murderer practically on the Sunday school rolls. This all comes of you bein' so lax on sin. And then there's the problem of your boy."

Uh oh. I didn't realize I was on the agenda.

"The problem of my boy? Is he a problem?"

"He is and you know it."

"Are the toilets not clean enough? Did he forget to dust the piano again? Shall we dock his wages? You think five dollars might be over-priced for his services?"

"You know what I'm talkin' about. He's associatin' with that boot-legger."

"I understand that he sells newspapers to Vernon, and they some-times chat."

"It's probably him that's encouragin' him to come ta church."

"I hope so."

"Pastor, I don't think yer hearin' me."

"I'm afraid I'm hearing you just fine, Deacon Fry. Let me ask you a question. You ever go fishing?"

"Of course."

"Catch a lot of small- and medium-sized fish, I guess. Good eatin' as they say?"

"Of course."

"What's the biggest fish you ever caught?"

"What does this have ta do with anything?"

"Just humor me for a second."

"I caught a twenty-pound channel cat once."

"How was that? Fun?"

"Yes. What of it?"

"I've heard stories of a giant catfish up at Dam B as long as Elmer here. Old Granddad I believe they call it."

"I've heard the same tomfool stories."

"Most of the time fishing is catching the pan-fry fish and having a good dinner. But don't you ever wish you could catch the big one. Don't you want to take a shot at catching Old Granddad?"

There was a long silence. I could picture Deacon Fry staring at Dad, Dad looking back with an expression that was almost amusement if it would loosen up just a smidgen, and the other deacons awkwardly waiting to get home to Sunday dinner. I heard a chair creak. Somebody was standing up.

Deacon Fry's voice growled. "Careful you don't get swallered by Old Granddad, Pastor Matt."

Then I heard the sound of boots walking out of the room.

CHAPTER TWENTY

The frenzy of the Christmas season swept in and drove practically everyone to the brink of exhaustion. There was the school Christmas concert, the junior class Christmas party, the band Christmas party, the Sunday school Christmas party, the cantata, the youth Christmas caroling hayride, the Christmas play, and finally, as if there wasn't already enough madness in our lives, the Christmas party that some maniac planned at our house the Friday before Christmas.

Fortunately Heidi was home from college, so the complete burden of the slave labor didn't fall on Hannah and me. The girls were full of Christmas cheer as they decorated the tree and sprayed fake snow on the windows and baked snowman cookies and tastefully arranged Christmas cards about the house. I provided an alternative view on the All Bah-Humbug All the Time channel. I felt I could have taught Scrooge a thing or two. Let those little imps who persecuted him come around me and I would thump them on the head with a Yule log and send them home crying to their mommies.

It was not that I was necessarily a curmudgeon. Well, actually it was. But I had sufficient provocation. No Christmas cookie baking for me. Instead, I was untangling Gordian Knot brand Christmas lights and testing each bulb individually to find the three from a strand of a hundred that didn't work. All nine strands. For the fake garlands I found a private location beyond the prying eyes of those who would like them untangled but would not like to do the untangling themselves. Then I used scissors to remove the knots and wire to join the remaining sections together. I didn't think anybody would notice if our garland resources were diminished by six feet this year. And if they did, I would congratulate them on their keen eye and award them the prize of untangling them the next year. And I would hide the scissors.

The crowd was large, as expected, and there was much wassail and eggnog, nonalcoholic versions, of course, and hot chocolate and singing of Christmas carols for the bzillionth time. Mom played the piano, so we had to sing all the verses. There was a lot of humming after the first verse. I had found some mistletoe and hung it from one of the air conditioning vents in hopes of maneuvering Jolene under it. I figured it was the only safe way to get a kiss, and even then it was high risk.

I aborted the mission when Jolene came in with Buddy. With those two superpowers, the best policy was to stand clear and make a sound like Switzerland. I soon bored with the festivities and opted to climb on top of the garage with Bubba and hunt for the Little Dipper. It was a clear cold night. We donned down-filled jackets and athletic socks for mittens and lay on the shingles.

Star watching is by nature a fairly silent occupation. Beyond the occasional "I think that's the North Star. No, not that one, the brighter one just above that tree. No, not the sweet gum, the magnolia," we didn't have much to say. I suspected Bubba had fallen asleep when a conversation drifted up over the eaves. At first it was hard to tell what they were saying, but when they came out of the garage into the driveway, I heard the crunch of the wheelchair on the gravel and the voices became clear. It was Mac and Sonia.

Bubba had his eyes closed. I leaned up on one elbow and poked him. He jerked and grabbed my shirt. I held my finger to my lips and nodded to the driveway. He let go of my shirt.

"It's just this trip tomorrow," Mac was saying. "I have ta be in Beaumont before eight o'clock in the morning, so I better get home before midnight."

"I could go with ya." There was a long pause. "Ta Beaumont tomorrow, I mean. Keep ya company."

"Oh. No, that's OK. I'll be there until after sundown doin' borin' business stuff."

"I wouldn't mind."

"Nah, I wouldn't feel right havin' ya wait around for me like that."

"If ya don't want me ta go . . ."

"I'd like yer company if I could actually spend the time with ya, but I would ignore ya for over ten hours. We would only get ta visit the hour on the drive each way."

"That's fine with me."

"Nah, Sonia, it's probably not a good idea."

"What do ya mean?"

Another long pause. I rolled to the edge of the roof and peeked over the eaves. They were in the driveway about halfway to Mac's van. Sonia was between Mac and me with her back to me. I could only see the wheels of the chair. I rolled back on the roof and whispered, "It's Mac and Sonia."

Bubba snorted. "Really? What was your first clue?"

"Mac, don't ya ever get lonely all alone in that big house?"

"Yep." You could hear the truth of it in his voice.

"Do ya ever think about . . . you know." Pause. "About tryin' again? With someone new?"

I heard the sound of wheels on gravel. I peeked again. Mac was headed toward the van. "When was the last time ya saw Parker?" he called over his shoulder.

"I don't know. I don't care," she called to him without moving.

"I hear he's quit drinkin'."

"Again? How long do ya think it will last this time?"

Mac reached for the door handle, then stopped and spun the wheelchair around. "Sonia, don't ya think you should give it another try?"

"No." Sonia walked over to the van. At the new angle, I was afraid they might see me. I rolled onto my back and listened. "Mac, why are you sayin' this?"

"Look, I know yer lonely, just like me. And yes, it would be nice if we could get back together like ten years ago. But that just can't happen, Sonia. You have ta quit torturin' yourself. And me."

"Why?" I could hear the tears.

"Because you are a married woman, no matter how much ya try to pretend like yer not."

"No, I'm not."

Mac sighed. I heard the van door open. "Yes, you are," he said in a quiet, tired voice.

"No, I'm not. Well, I won't be pretty soon. I filed fer a divorce."

I looked at Bubba. He raised his eyebrows. I nodded.

The gravel crunched. "On what grounds?"

"Incompatibility or somethin'. The lawyer knows all the legal words."

"Sonia, that don't matter. You remember what Parker said the night he busted into the church and created a scene?"

"He said a lot of things. I try to ferget most of 'em."

"He said you were married in the sight of God, even if you weren't married in the church. He's right. This divorce won't change anything. You are still a married woman and will always be a married woman until one of ya dies."

"Don't say that! Yer startin' ta sound like him."

"Maybe that's what's wrong with me. Maybe I haven't sounded enough like Parker lately."

Sonia made a sound that I could only guess was meant to be a laugh. It didn't sound very funny.

"You never answered my question. When is the last time ya saw him?"

"I ain't seen him since the night I left. Except passin' on the highway.

And even then, when I see his truck, I look the other way. So I ain't really seen him at all."

"I hear he's changed a lot."

"That was the problem. He changed too much."

I heard an engine and the crunch of tires on gravel. A set of headlights flashed across the trees and the house. I moved to the edge and rested my chin on the roof. Bubba crawled next to me. We peeked like the Little Rascals at the foreshortened figures in the driveway.

Mac and Sonia were outlined in the light like two convicts in a prison break. An F-150 rolled to a stop ten yards away. The lights went off and Parker got out.

"I figured I would find y'all here."

I looked at Bubba. The garage light illuminated him from the nose up. The bottom of his face was in shadow. He looked at me and whispered, "Uh oh."

Mac looked at Sonia. "Looks like ya just broke your record."

Sonia was not amused. "What are you doin' here? You don't go ta this church anymore."

"I didn't come here ta go ta church."

"Then why did ya come? Ta drag yer woman off by the hair like a caveman?"

Parker stood without speaking, looking at Sonia and Mac. I started looking for a concealed weapon. I leaned toward Bubba and whispered, "Why don't you go tell somebody Parker's here."

"You go tell 'em," he said without taking his eyes from Parker.

Parker blew out a lungful of air. "No. I come here ta forgive ya."

Sonia jerked backward like she'd been slapped.

Mac squinted his eyes and leaned forward. "Ta forgive who?"

"Both of ya. You and her."

"Me?" Mac almost rose out of his chair. "Me? You come here ta forgive me?"

Parker nodded. He didn't appear to be enjoying his mission.

"What do I need ta be forgiven for?" Mac demanded.

"Yeah," Sonia chimed in. "What do I have ta be forgiven for too?"

Parker took a deep breath. "I'll have ta take ya one at a time." He looked back and forth, and his eyes settled on Mac. "OK. When I come ta the Lord, I figured you would kinda help me along, be like a brother. 'Cause you was so much older in the Lord and it was all new ta me. But ya didn't. Ya acted more like I was invisible. Ya acted like the rest a them up ta the church besides Pastor Matt."

Mac glared defiantly at Parker, evidently finding no pleasure in being forgiven.

"I was bitter about that fer a long time. 'Til a man wiser'n me finally showed me I had ta let it go. That it was hurtin' me more'n it was you and holdin' me back from what God wanted ta do."

"And who was that? Pastor Matt?" Mac asked sarcastically.

"No, it wasn't."

"That's it? You just come and dump that on me and that's it?"

"It's all I got. Fer you anyways."

"So you think it was my job ta be yer big brother? When I can't see yer face without seein' Peggy and Kristen starin' back at me? When it's torture just ta be in the same room with ya? I forgave ya, but that don't mean I can forget what happened. I wish I could forget it. I prayed every night ta forget it."

Mac whipped the chair around and pushed the handle for the hydraulic lift. "No, it's too much ta ask. I forgive ya for killin' my family, but it don't mean I can go on like it never happened. I can't forget. A empty house don't let me forget."

"I know that. That's what I come ta see. Or what Brother Williams brought me ta see. That's why I forgive ya. And that's why I ask ya ta forgive me fer expectin' that from ya."

Mac didn't reply. He got into the van and left.

Bubba said, "Wow," quietly. Neither of us took our eyes off of Parker.

Sonia turned to go back into the house. Parker stepped in front of her.

"I just got ta say this one thing, then ya don't have ta ever see me again. I'll even sign the papers without gettin' a lawyer."

"You got a lot of nerve goin' around forgivin' people, Parker. Can't ya see we don't want yer forgiveness?"

"Please, Sonia. Just hear me out this one last time, then ya won't have ta bother with me ever again."

"I don't have ta bother with ya now!" She stepped around him toward the garage.

He turned to her as she passed and said softly. "Please. Don't eight years count fer nothin'? Can't ya just give me ten minutes?"

Something in his voice must have stopped her. She turned slowly and looked at him. At least I think she looked at him. They were right next to the garage. All Bubba and I could see were the tops of their heads.

"OK," she said quietly but bitterly. "Ya got eight minutes. One fer each year. The clock is tickin'."

"First I have ta tell ya I forgive ya." Sonia snorted and tossed her head like a high-spirited racehorse but said nothing. "I forgive ya fer walkin' out on me when I was tryin' the best I could ta be a proper husband like the Bible told me ta be. I couldn't understand that. You come ta God before I did. I was just tryin' ta do what I thought was the right thing. But ya walked out on me anyway."

"Parker, you go around here tellin' ever'body else what they done wrong—"

"I know, I know, I know," Parker said, shouting her down. "Just let me finish."

Sonia clamped her mouth shut and crossed her arms. She glanced at her left wrist, even though she wasn't wearing a watch.

"I know I'm tellin' folks what they done wrong. And I know folks don't like ta hear that. I know 'cause I don't like ta hear it. But a wise man has showed me that I have ta hear it or I'll be trapped by it."

Parker threw his hands out and let them drop to his side. "Sonia, I know I done things wrong. I'm still doin' things wrong. I might even be doin' this wrong. I don't know. But now I'm tryin' ta do the right thing. That's all this is, me tryin' ta do the right thing. I have ta forgive and ask forgiveness.

"That's two things ta do, and I can't do both of 'em at once. I have ta do one first, then the other. I don't want ta end with tellin' somebody what they done wrong. I want ta end with askin' forgiveness fer the things I done wrong. So I have ta start with forgivin' if I want ta end with askin' forgiveness."

"Yer runnin' out a time."

"Ya don't make it easy on a guy."

"I ain't got no cause to."

"OK, OK. I didn't come here ta get in a fight. I forgive ya fer that 'cause ya really did it. We both has ta face what is and what we really done. Actin' like ya didn't do it don't make it go away. It just traps ya in it.

"But I also have ta face what I done. I didn't think of you; I just thought of me. When ya left me the first time, I only thought of how ya done me wrong. Then I come ta Jesus, and all I could think about was how much I had ta make up for and how I had ta be the thing I ought ta be, and I never even thought about bein' the thing you needed. You tried ta tell me, over and over. But it didn't fit what I thought I was sup-posed ta be doin', so I didn't pay it no mind. So I drove ya away. That's what I done. And I ask ya ta forgive me."

Sonia didn't say anything for a long time. When she finally spoke, I could tell she was crying.

"It's not fair. You can't just waltz in here and say yer sorry and make it all go away. It's too late fer that."

"I didn't think I could. I'm not saying I would object if ya come back, but that's not why I come. Ain't nobody else been in our bed, and I ain't lookin' fer somebody. But I didn't come here ta try ta get ya back. That's not up ta me; it's up ta you. I just come here ta forgive and ask forgiveness."

"It's not that easy, Parker. I can't. Mac couldn't. It's too hard. You ask too much."

"Yep, I reckon I am askin' too much. But it's what I had ta do. And you have ta do what you have ta do." He kicked at the gravel. "I figure my eight minutes is up. Bye."

Sonia didn't say a word or move as he walked back to the truck and left. She stood there for several minutes after he left.

"Bye," she said and went back into the house.

Bubba and I stayed up there for a long time. We didn't say much.

CHAPTER TWENTY-ONE It took them awhile to

indict Vernon. Just his luck for getting booked during the holidays. They say every American has the right to a fair and speedy trial. They also say the wheels of justice grind slowly. Vernon got the slow grind, espresso version.

My *Grit* route was shortened considerably, but I missed staring at the sunset and the girl on the swing while sipping Coke in a Lucky Strike haze.

In December they called the grand jury up and indicted him on murder one. The D.A. didn't get a case like this every day, and he was going for broke. A few years before, the Supreme Court declared all state death penalty laws unconstitutional, and the Texas death row was cleared in March 1973. Lucky for the D.A. the 1973 Texas legislature revised the penal code to get around the Supreme Court's ruling, and the death sentence was back.

A high-profile case like this could make a career. This one was a slam dunk—a bootlegger with a reputation for violence, the wound matching the gun the accused was holding when the officers showed up. Who needed a confession with evidence like this?

At the end of February the case went to trial. I was in school, so I couldn't attend. I kept up with it as best I could with newspapers and radio.

In March, on a Sunday afternoon, I was in the Fortress of Solitude loading film in an Argus C3. Along with a light meter and a flash attachment, it was a birthday present from my folks, used but in great condition. The radio played an uneasy medley of "Hey Joe" on the Beaumont station and "Folsom Prison Blues" on the Woodville station. Johnny Cash finally hung his head and cried, and the news came on, which was lucky for me. If the news had come on just after Jimi went to Mexico, that would mean I was listening to the news in Beaumont, where I wouldn't hear anything about the trial until the verdict came out. In Woodville the trial was big news and received detailed coverage, including a summary of the testimony given for that day.

Unfortunately I only caught it in snatches as Hendrix gave way to Steely Dan. I closed the camera and listened.

". . . the autopsy showed shotgun wounds to the head and . . . *In the mornin' you go gunnin' for the man who stole your water* . . . were additional laceration wounds on the neck from a sharp blade . . . *But the hangman isn't hangin' and they put you on the street* . . . The coroner estimates the time of death to be between 4:00 p.m. and 8:00 p.m. Friday November thirt . . . *Wheel turning' round and round you go back Jack and do it again . . .*"

I grabbed the radio and turned it in the air, attempting to lock in the elusive signal from Woodville. All I got was static and a verse about a two-timer. No matter, I had heard enough. Time of death between four and eight? Exactly the time Darnell and I were sitting in the Pontiac with Vernon listening to war stories.

I was stunned by the news. Vernon had insisted to anyone who would listen that Gina was dead when he got home. He was telling the truth. It was only then that I realized I had assumed he had done it.

I jumped up. The tree house shook, and the camera tumbled to the floor. The flash attachment slipped over the edge to the pine straw twenty feet below. I put everything back in the case and tossed it in my room on the way to the Spyder bike.

Twenty minutes later I found Darnell up to his elbows in the engine of a vehicle past its prime. He looked surprised to see me. I didn't even give him time to say "Hey, doll." I slid to a stop next to the car in a spray of sand and began talking with the little breath I had left.

"We have to go testify." Huff-puff. "He didn't do it." Huff-puff. "She was dead before he got there." Huff-puff. Huff-puff.

"Hold on there a sec, Toddy Raymer." He extricated himself from the bowels of the engine and wiped his hands on a rag. "Try that a little slower and with more meat." He pushed his glasses up his greasy nose with a greasy finger. "Who didn't do what?" He tossed the rag on the air filter, then looked at me suddenly. "Dead? Did you say dead?"

"Yes, dead. While we were in the car talking to Vernon."

Darnell's eyes narrowed. "You didn't tell anyone we was with him, did ya?"

"That's what I'm trying to tell you. We have to tell them we were with him. He didn't do it."

He stepped closer to me and looked over his shoulder at the house. "We don't have ta tell nobody nothin'," he said with quiet force. "Remember our deal. Just between me and you."

"Darnell, listen to me. Vernon didn't do it. He was with us when Gina was killed."

"How do you know that?"

"I just heard it on the news."

"They said our names on the news?"

"No, no. Will you just shut up and listen? They said the time of death was between 4:00 and 8:00 p.m." Darnell stared at me blankly. "We were with Vernon between four and eight. The whole time." The blank began to fade. "Yes, that's right. While you were sitting in the car all googley-eyed over the war hero, somebody else was at Vernon's trailer killing Gina. Somebody who was not Vernon."

Darnell leaned toward me and whispered, "Then who killed her?"

"I don't know," I yelled.

"You don't have ta holler; I'm right here in the same county, fer cryin' out loud."

"OK, OK, I'm sorry. Look, Vernon is innocent, and you and I are the only ones who know it."

Darnell looked around restlessly. "If he's innocent, he's got nothin' ta worry about."

"Nothing to worry about? Are you crazy? They're going to fry him. They got around the Supreme Court decision last year. They're warming up Old Sparky right now."

"The Supreme Court? They took him ta the Supreme Court?"

"Darnell," I shouted. "Are you even listening to me?"

He looked back at the house and waved his hands, trying to quiet me down. I dropped my voice a few decibels.

"I'm going to talk slowly in words of one syllable. Listen closely because I'm only going to say this once, and then if you continue to talk nonsense, I'm going to bean you with that tire iron."

I pointed at a tire tool on the ground next to the car. Darnell grabbed it at once and held it fiercely.

"The case against Vernon is practically open-and-shut. They have his fingerprints on the murder weapon. They think they have him there at the time of the crime. He has opportunity, he has means—they'll come up with a motive. Heck, all they have to say is he's from Fred and nobody will even ask for a motive. If we don't say something, Vernon will either get fried or spend the rest of his life in Huntsville with a roommate named Ben Dover."

"How do ya know who they will put him with?"

I lunged toward the tire tool. "Give me that!"

Darnell stumbled back. "Hey!"

I threw down the bike I had been straddling the whole time and tackled Darnell, wrestling for the tire tool. With little success. The match ended with me pinned down, the tire tool across my neck.

"I hear Huntsville's not that bad," Darnell said. I thrashed around, pushing back on the tire tool. "Hey, I was just kiddin'." He rolled off me and helped me to my feet. "How about this? What if you go and be the Boy Scout and leave me out of it?"

"I'd beat your brain out with that tire tool if you had one," I said, ignoring the fact that he was the one holding it.

"You and whose army?"

"Think about it, Darnell. If I go to the cops, they're going to ask me if anybody else was there but me."

"So lie."

"Assuming I would lie to the cops, which I wouldn't, then I would be asked under oath if anyone else was there. I'm not going to jail for perjury just because you're as yellow as a buttercup."

"Who you callin' yeller?"

After that it was pretty easy. I told Dad, Darnell told G. B., and the next day we were at the courthouse. If I had started off by telling Darnell I had a plan to cut a day of school, he would have volunteered to testify without an argument.

We had a conference with the defense attorney. He played it cool, but I knew on the inside he was kneeling before us and kissing our hands. After waiting in a back room for the wheels of justice to make a few revolutions, I was on the stand with my hand on a Bible and swearing to tell the truth. Which is why I had come in the first place.

When I sat down, I looked at Vernon. He looked a little thinner. He had a neat haircut and was wearing a black suit. I almost didn't recognize him. He didn't look at me.

The defense attorney walked up to me. "Mark, could you tell us who is your daddy?"

"Matthew Cloud."

His irritation was so miniscule, I was probably the only one who saw it. "And what does he do for a living?"

"He's a pastor." I suppose he was trying to establish credibility. Fat chance. Anybody can tell you that a PK cuts both ways.

"Where were you on Friday, November 30, 1973?"

"I was on my paper route."

"Who is the last delivery on your paper route?"

"Vernon Crowley."

"Could you point him out for us?"

"He's right over there." I pointed to Vernon on the right side of the courtroom. He looked at me without expression, then looked back down to the table in front of him like before.

"Let the record show that he pointed to the defendant. Did you deliver the paper to Vernon at his house?"

"No, I never deliver his paper to his house. I always meet him on a hill a mile away."

"Why?"

"He parks there every afternoon, to watch the sunset."

"Did you meet him at sunset?"

"No, I got there before sunset because I got a ride that day."

"How long before sunset did you deliver the paper to Vernon Crowley?"

"About two hours."

"Let the record show that the sun set at 5:16 on November 30, 1973. And what did you do after you delivered the paper to Mr. Crowley?"

"I sat in his car and drank a Coke and talked about World War II."

"How long did you talk to him?"

"Until after ten o'clock." There was a slight murmur in the courtroom.

"Were you and Mr. Crowley alone during this time?"

"No, there was another guy with me."

"Who was that other person?"

"Darnell Ray. He gave me a ride."

"Thank you. I have no further questions."

I stood up to leave, but the judge asked me to sit back down. The D.A. got up and walked toward me.

"Mark, do you carry a watch with you?"

"No, sir."

"Then how do you know how long it was before sunset when you met the defendant at his car?"

"I time my route to get there just before sunset since I know Vernon will be there then. Halfway through my route Darnell came along and gave me a ride, so I got through the route way early. So we got to Vernon a long time before sunset."

"But it might have been less than an hour and a half?"

I considered it. "It might have been."

"Might have been a half an hour?"

"Oh, no. It was at least an hour."

"And how do you know that since you didn't have a watch?"

"I'd rather not say."

"Be that as it may, you have to say."

"Well, it was still light when I had to pee."

"What?"

"I had to pee because I had two Cokes. And it takes me at least a half hour to drink a Coke. I drink them real slow." There were some chuckles in the courtroom, even in the jury.

"You had to pee?"

"Yessir."

"Do you think you could have drunk those Cokes faster than two an hour?"

"Nosir. I can't drink a Coke very fast. Anybody will tell you that. If I get one at lunch, sometimes I have to throw some of it away when the hour is up. Plus, the sun was still above the house with the girl on the porch swing. I remember seeing it touch the top of the chimney like it was a golf ball on a tee. That would make it a good hour before sunset."

The D.A. gave up and tried for the other end of the window.

"Mark, how do you know what time it was when you left?"

"Because I caught it when I got home for being out so late. I looked at the clock when I got home. It was almost eleven."

He gave up. "No more questions, Your Honor."

The judge looked at the defense attorney. He stood up at his desk but didn't walk up. "So you're sure it was more than an hour before sunset that you met Vernon?"

"Yessir."

"How long of a drive is it from the hill to your house?"

"Ten minutes for most people. About five for Darnell." More chuckles.

"And you got home around eleven?"

"Yessir."

"No more questions, Your Honor."

Then they let me go. I looked at Vernon before I stepped down from the stand. He was looking at me with an expression that was hard to read. But he wasn't happy, I could see that. I walked out of the courtroom confused. I had just given the testimony that would keep him out of prison. I expected him to be smiling.

I waited around while Darnell gave his testimony. Then we went home.

CHAPTER TWENTY-TWO

Vernon was acquitted and back home a week later. On Saturday I did my *Grit* route and thought twice before I took the river road. Ultimately I couldn't keep myself away. I had to know.

The girl was back on the porch swing wearing Daisy Mae shorts that made my pulse jump like a seismograph. The Pontiac was across the road. I faltered, then I pulled up to the driver's side and held out a paper. "Want to buy a *Grit*? It's a newspaper."

His left hand rested on the side mirror, cigarette held between the middle and ring half fingers. He slowly raised his hand to his face, clamped it over his mouth, took a long drag on the Lucky Strike, and blew a stream of smoke against the windshield. "How much?"

"Two bits."

"No news of the war?"

"It's not that kind of paper."

"Get in."

I ditched the bike and slid into the passenger's seat. Vernon handed me a Coke. I checked the clock on the dash. Five forty-seven. I looked at the sun. It was about level with the chimney. Good hour until sunset.

We sat in silence for a long time. Vernon smoked his Lucky Strike. I sipped my Coke. There was a bottle on the seat between us. A frosted bottle with grappa on the label.

He broke the silence first. "I didn't do it, ya know."

"I know."

We had spent most of our time looking straight ahead at the sunset and the girl, not at each other. The look was spontaneous, but once it happened it showed too much all at once. We both looked away. My eyes watered. I blinked rapidly and took another sip.

I spoke first this time. "I just wanted to help."

"I know."

We sat in silence for another while. I considered the girl on the swing. I wondered why she was still there. Since the trial, I had given the situation a lot of thought. When Vernon got home at eleven, Gina was dead from a shotgun wound. Vernon was holding the shotgun, but it only had his prints on it. So either the killer had used gloves or Vernon had wiped the prints off. Why would he do that? I wondered if the girl on the swing would just sit on that porch growing old or if she would finally leave one day. I watched the sun sink. I sipped my Coke.

"I come back ta Texas in '46." The suddenness startled me, but I gave no sign.

"The Krauts give in a year before, but it took us awhile ta clean up the mess." He took a drink from a glass, not a Coke can.

"I couldn't come back here. It weren't the same. I weren't the same. Couldn't face my folks after what I done in the war. Even if I never told 'em. I found a outfit lookin' fer oil in the Hill Country. They had a big truck that would thump the ground with a big pile driver, and they would study the graphs a mile away and figure out what was in the ground. I signed up ta drive the truck and disappeared. We went all over, never too long in one place. That suited me down ta the ground.

"One Saturday I was in Fredericksburg havin' a beer when I was almost run over by a woman draggin' a kid behind her. We was nose ta nose, and when I looked in her eyes, I saw Sarah."

He took another drink and lit another cigarette. It took me a few seconds to dredge Sarah up from my memory. Sarah was the girl he had decided to settle down with in Italy. On D-Day.

"She was the spittin' image of Sarah. As like as two peas in a pod." He clamped his left hand over his mouth and took a long draw. When he talked again, he chewed out smoke with his words.

"She must a thought I was a idiot. She apologized about five times and was leavin' when I come to and offered to buy the kid a soda. He was a little feller, about three or four and sharp as a tack. Her pa was a professer up ta the university in Austin. She give me her address, and a few months later I looked her up. She was surprised ta see me, but she went ta dinner with me all the same. A nice dinner. I had plenty of cash 'cause I worked fer months in the field and didn't have nothin' ta spend it on.

"We had a bottle of wine with dinner, and it seemed ta loosen her up. Afore long I had the whole story. They got out a Paris on one side when the Krauts come in the other and come ta America. How they ended up in Texas it's hard ta figure, but her pa was a wheel in the university in France, and maybe he knew somebody at the university in Austin.

"She come with a husband. He went back ta Paris when the war ended ta find his family, and nobody heard of him since. He didn't even know he had a kid."

Vernon refilled his glass and tilted the bottle toward the girl on the swing with a sad chuckle. "Gina was a piece a work, just like that'n over there. Cute as a kitten and knew it. She was abandoned in a strange country and found a man makin' a good livin' ready ta pick up where the other feller left off with no questions asked. Played me like a fiddle. Didn't mind none. Always did like fiddle music.

"I quit the oil crew and found work in Austin. We went through the paperwork ta cut her loose and got married. We was doin' fine 'til I got word Ma was doin' poorly. We come back here and tended her fer a couple a years 'til she passed on. By then I was hooked up in my business, makin' better money 'n Austin and ownin' the place free and clear. But pretty soon I figured out why the other feller took a powder on her, especially since he didn't know about the kid."

He took a slow sip of grappa. "She was a lot like a cat. Sometimes they'll rub up against ya all affectionate and climb up in yer lap, and other times if ya reach fer 'em, ya get the business end of a claw. She was the same way. Sometimes she would be as lovin' as any man could want, not waitin' around fer me ta start up the romance. But she could turn ornery, get upset fer no reason, and then I couldn't talk sense into her.

"There was no tellin' what she would do when she got like that. She pointed a gun at me more'n once. After the first time I made sure they was unloaded, and I hid the ammunition, but she didn't know that. She would still point 'em at me. Sometimes she'd hurt herself. She wore long sleeves ta hide the scars.

"I took her ta doctors, and they give her medicine, but most the time she wouldn't take it. When I was gone she would flush it all down the toilet. It didn't take long fer me ta have my fill of that, but I couldn't leave her like the first feller. Ever' time I looked at her, no matter what she done, no matter how mean she got, I seen Sarah lookin' back at me, sayin', 'If only you hadn't left that day.'"

His voice broke a little at the end of that sentence, but he covered it with a cough and busied himself, refilling the glass and lighting another Lucky Strike. There was enough light for me to see the moisture in his eyes. He didn't look at me, just stared at the sunset.

"So, whatever happened to the kid?" I asked as if I had no idea who the kid was.

Vernon made a noise somewhere between a grunt and a laugh. "Cut from the same cloth as his ma. Neither one mixed much with the local folk. He got in trouble at school. Always fightin' and smartin' off ta the teachers. But he was as smart as a whip. Got ta studyin' up on the war, askin' a lot a questions 'bout his pa. Gina must a made up somethin' about him bein' a big war hero instead a tellin' him the truth that he run out when the Germans showed up. Not that I blame him none. They was plenty times I was ready ta run out myself."

He took a drag from the cigarette. "But she must a made him sound pretty good. Jake thought he hung the moon."

An electric tingle ran down my back. It was the first time he had said the name. Our suspicions were confirmed.

"When he got old enough, I tried ta tell 'im what war was really like, not some high and mighty glory trail but wallerin' in the mud tryin' ta kill some poor luckless feller afore he killed you. Spendin' days and nights on end pinned down in a ditch with no sleep and bullets and shells flyin' all around ya 'til yer not even human anymore, just a zombie like in them scary movies, so numb ya can't feel nothin' but fear 'til even that goes away and ya can't feel nothin', can't see nothin'.'"

He shook his head. "It ain't nothin' ta wish fer. It's somethin' ta run away from, as far as you can run. But he wasn't havin' any. Nothin' would do but he had ta join up, and the next thing we knowed he was in Vietnam. Didn't hear a word from him fer over five years."

He took a sip of grappa.

"Then one day he showed up at the house. Said the gov'ment thought he was dead, and he was happy ta leave it that way. He was about the same age as I was when I met his ma. But he was hard as a anvil. You could see it in his eyes, a hard look that broke down ever'thing into how he could play the angles. You could almost hear the gears whizzin' in his head.

"He had a idea fer the business, ta branch out. He had it all figured, the connections, ever'thing. All I had ta do was be the broker, just like always. It worked out pretty good. We never seen him after that. He told us he would be gone most a the time, and all he wanted from me was ta keep him supplied. Some days we would get up and find a note on the kitchen table with a list—dried beef, coffee, stuff like that. Never seen him though; never heard him. I would get the stuff and put it in the old family house behind the trailer, and one day it would be gone.

"Sometimes he would leave a note askin' fer cash, several grand. Mine is a cash business, and I don't exactly put it all in the bank. I kept his cut separate and pulled from that. He never got close ta usin' it all. When he asked fer the cash, we wouldn't hear from him for months, sometimes over a year. Then one mornin' we would get up and there would be another note. Last year there was a note on Thanksgivin' mornin'. The next day, the night you and that other feller seen me last . . ."

Vernon stopped. It was pretty dark. A quarter moon was halfway across the sky. In the pale silver glow I saw him staring into the night. He closed his eyes for a few seconds and then refilled his glass, empty- ing the bottle.

"When I come up ta the trailer, the lights was off and the door was open. I didn't like the looks a that. I got away from the car fast and come in from the back and got a flashlight from a closet. I cleared ever' room as I come forward, keepin' the light hid except when I needed it. When I got ta the front, there was a little moonlight comin' in through the door, and I seen something against the opposite wall. I hit it with my light."

He took another drink. "It was Sarah, layin' there with a arrow through her neck. She'd been dead for some time. Her neck was cut up considerable, and there was blood all over. I checked the rest a the house, but I knew I wouldn't find anything. I knew he was gone. Even if he was still there, I wouldn't see him unless he wanted me to.

"I had sipped a few drinks, but I always been able ta hold my liquor. I seen right away if the cops showed up and seen that arrow, they would start lookin' fer the crossbow and that would start a lot of questions and a manhunt, and they would kill 'im 'cause he would never let hisself be taken alive. I couldn't let that happen. There was enough killin' already.

"I took the arrow into the woods and doused it with gas and burnt it up and threw the ashes in the river. Then I went back and loaded the shotgun and used it ta cover up the arrow wound. Then I called the sheriff."

"Jake killed Gina?"

"I reckon he did."

"You knew that the whole time?"

"Yep."

"Then why didn't you tell them? You would be on death row right now if I hadn't testified."

Vernon turned his broad face toward me. "I told ya. They would a killed him."

"But he killed Gina! You're going to cover for him and let him get off scot-free?"

Vernon looked at me steadily. "You think he's free?"

"What?"

"He's paid. He's still payin'. Killin' him won't solve nothin'."

"But what if he kills somebody else?"

"That ain't likely ta happen. He's been back fer six years, and nobody has even knowed he's here. He ain't hurt nobody. I don't claim ta know the why. Probably won't ever know. But I know I'm gonna stop any killin' I can, no matter who does it, the gov'ment or the people."

"You weren't stopping them from killing. They were going to kill you instead of him."

"I cheated death so many times, I figure I owe him one." He drained his glass. "It was the right thing ta do. Yer own pa said so the Sunday before Thanksgivin'."

"Dad?"

"He said there ain't no greater love than ta give yer life fer someone else. I looked it up. Jesus said it."

I started to answer, but he held up his hand and shook his head. "Mark boy, there ain't no percentage in arguin' when yer out of hooch." He held up the empty bottle. "Why don't ya drive me back ta the house?"

He stumbled several times going around the car. I had to help him up the cinder-block steps to the trailer. He collapsed on the couch and told me where to find more grappa, but before I had the bottle open, he had passed out.

I looked around the room. The carpet had been ripped out, the floor and wall scrubbed clean, but the scars from the shotgun blast were visible on the paneling. On the table next to the grappa was a shoebox full of pictures. I looked at Vernon. He was feeling no pain.

There were the usual—baby pictures, birthday parties, pictures of Jake in various stages of maturity, and other stuff, taken mostly in a town I assumed to be Austin. There were pictures of landscapes, a river with cypress and Spanish moss, bluffs overlooking a lake, a railroad trestle over a rocky stream. Under the loose photos I found a few small photo albums, the kind with clear plastic pouches where you put two pictures, one for each side. From the hairstyles and clothes and the buildings, I could see these were taken a long time ago somewhere else, probably France. I found a picture of a teenage girl. In the border at the top "Gianna, 1940" was neatly lettered. I could see why Vernon had been ready to desert the U.S. Army for Sarah. If she looked anything like this picture, she could make a whole platoon go AWOL.

On the other side of the page was a picture of Gina with a dark-looking guy in a uniform. In the border at the top "Gianna e Jacob, 1943" was neatly lettered. I was sure he was the deserter; he looked like an older version of Jake. I had been practicing a little creative dissembling when I told Darnell I had seen Jake's picture in an old annual. The next week I had turned the lie into truth like a predated check by going to the library and digging in the back stacks. I worked backward from

1970 and found him in the 1964 annual in the junior class photos under the name Jacob Crowley. Short, thick dark hair, narrow face, prominent nose, an expression far too serious for a high school junior. Just like the picture I was looking at now.

This page felt thicker than the others. There was a third photograph between the other two, a little smaller and pushed down so you wouldn't notice it. I pulled it out. It was taken at a fair or amusement park. Looked like the '50s. Gina stood in front of a shooting gallery holding a Kewpie doll. A man stood with his arm around her, pointing to the doll. It wasn't the deserter, and it wasn't Vernon. He looked vaguely familiar. A thought nagged the fringes of my mind, like almost but not quite remembering the name of an actor. It was driving me crazy. I squinted my eyes.

It jumped out at me so suddenly I dropped the picture and stumbled backward. It was Deacon Fry. More hair, fewer wrinkles, but Deacon Fry all the same. I realized why it had been so hard to recognize him. He was smiling.

I turned off the lights and left Vernon asleep on the couch. I took the picture.

CHAPTER TWENTY-THREE For the next few weeks things settled down long enough for me to realize I was about to graduate. Throughout the year I had mindlessly filled out college applications and financial assistance forms. Now I realized with a shock that one month remained until graduation. How had my senior year passed by without me noticing? For Heidi and Hannah it was just another summer vacation approaching. For me it was the end of an era. That took my thoughts from Vernon and Jake and Deacon Fry for awhile.

Then a hot Sunday afternoon in the middle of May burned away all thoughts but one: swimming. There was a big pool in Honey Island out toward Saratoga that had been there for decades, but that was a good thirty miles. We only went there on official outings, such as class parties or youth-group events.

Instead, I set my sights on the premier swimming hole in the area—Toodlum Creek. You won't find it on the county map. That's because its real name is Theuvenins Creek, but I never heard anyone call it that. Maybe because nobody could figure out how to say it.

The swimming hole was five miles back from the highway on a dirt road. It was thirty feet across and had a three-foot bank on one side and a ten-foot bank on the other. A giant old oak tree hung out over the water with a rope tied twenty feet up on the first available limb. A rope of that length hanging a third of the way across the creek made for a great arc, particularly because the launching point was four feet above the water. You could do flips off the rope if you had a mind to.

The water was typical muddy creek water and was home to its share of fish, turtles, and snakes, but the critters usually left you alone, especially if you made lots of noise. It was a popular spot. Sometimes even girls would come down and swim. The other big swimming hole was off the railroad trestle on Village Creek. The problem there was that it wasn't as deep, so when you dove from the railroad bridge, you had to pull up pretty quick to keep from plowing sand. After they came along and changed the rails on the bridge, you also had to watch for the old rails, which had been shoved off into the creek. Diving fifteen feet onto a steel rail could ruin your whole day.

Everyone was either busy or gone, so I set out for Toodlum alone. I wasn't worried because there wasn't much chance I would find the creek deserted.

In fact I had a hard time finding a place to park the old '64 Falcon. I recognized the Hound of Hell and yelled a greeting to Darnell as I rounded the corner. I joined a party in progress and spent a few pleasant hours refrigerating my bones in the creek.

Besides Darnell, there was Bubba Culpepper, Turner McCullough and his cousin, and the Beau sisters—Raine, Ella, and Flo—with their little brother, Bo. The girls all had pretty faces but bodies like Twiggy. They made a rather interesting spectacle standing in line for the rope, identically clad in floral-print bikinis, like anorexic Russian nesting dolls.

When I finally tore my eyes away from the scenery long enough to look at my watch, I realized I was going to be late for the Sunday night service. I bid hasty farewells and, still dripping, jumped into the car, pausing long enough to toss the towel across the seat.

The Falcon vibrated down the dirt road at excessive speeds. I utilized the techniques I had seen Darnell demonstrate so many times, including accelerating on curves and sliding around corners.

I approached a blind ninety-degree left curve and pulled a maneuver that would have made Darnell burst with pride. Just as I hit the curve, I turned the wheel hard and floored it. The curve was a sandpit, and as I expected, I rounded the corner sideways. I knew I would be able to pull it back straight as I came through the curve. I might fishtail some, maybe even overhang a ditch for a second, but it was a fairly simple trick.

Then I looked out the passenger window at the road. My heart stopped and my foot jerked off the gas. Fifty feet or so straight ahead was a wooden bridge. A solid bridge that would doubtlessly last for decades, but it lacked what most bridges on these back roads lacked— guardrails. What happened next only lasted a few seconds, but it seemed like hours.

I was plowing through a quagmire of sand, which, like ice, offers little traction, especially when your car is sliding. I could tell that if I were to slam on the brakes, I would just slide onto the bridge sideways, probably with the wheels hanging off either side. I immediately rejected that option as a less than optimum outcome.

Somehow in the midst of my panic I remembered that the only way to gain control of a skidding car is to accelerate. Something about how if you slam on the brakes the car becomes a giant sled because the front wheels aren't turning, so you can't steer it. The rationale was that if you accelerate, the front wheels turn and you regain the ability to steer. It was probably a bit of wisdom gleaned from Vernon while watching the sunset.

It was my only chance. Instead of slamming on the brakes to avoid sliding onto the bridge, I shoved the car into second gear, turned the wheel all the way to the right, and stomped on the gas. To my immense satisfaction, as the bridge rushed toward me with increasing speed, the car started to straighten out.

"Yes! Yes!" I cheered.

It looked as if I was going to make it. "Yes!" I yelled again. The car was only a few degrees off straight. Then, in the final moment, when I felt the thump of the tires hitting the first board, I realized that those few degrees were enough to cause disaster. "No! No!" I screamed. I watched in horror as the front left tire dropped off the edge of the bridge.

The most horrible sound I had heard in my short life followed as the bottom of the car scraped along the edges of the boards with a sickening rasp, and the car rolled off the side of the bridge. At this moment my mind slipped into a parallel universe, and I experienced the sensation of everything happening in slow motion. My mind observed the frantic antics of my body like a coach in off-season listlessly watching the team run bleachers.

To compensate for being abandoned by the brain, my body kicked into autopilot. I watched with detached interest as my hands instinctively reached up and braced against the ceiling, hearing over the grinding noise the sound of a voice much like mine screeching, "Noooooo!" As the car rolled over to the left, my hands walked across the ceiling like a pair of albino tarantulas playing leapfrog. I observed but didn't actually feel the bone-jangling crunch of impact.

At first I just laid there, unable to believe that I had actually driven the family car off a bridge in the middle of nowhere. I was lying on my stomach on the ceiling of the car staring out the passenger window at the rotting branches and brown needles of a felled pine tree, but even this evidence failed to convince me. It seemed impossible that I could do something of this magnitude.

I had done many things in my life that were startling. I had driven a bicycle into a moving mail truck. I had inadvertently loosed a fishbowl full of freshly hatched mosquitoes in the house. I had jumped off a moving car and broken my arm. I had buried the car in a ditch up to the axle. I had broken the tie-rod on the tractor. I had even accidentally set fire to a five-gallon can of gasoline in my best friend's garage.

But I had never done anything on this scale. This was a disaster of such monstrous proportions it couldn't have possibly happened. I was certain of it. Yet here my body was in an upside-down car in a creek.

Meanwhile, my feet were attempting to interrupt the regularly scheduled program for a flash bulletin. With a touch of irritation, my mind tabled the analysis and took a message from the feet. "Water is rushing in this window down here," they exclaimed. As you know, feet are sensitive and easily excited.

That's all they said. Only being feet, they didn't draw any conclusions; they simply reported the facts, knowing that someone higher up would take appropriate measures. And they were right. This bit of information shocked the mind out of its abstract speculation and into positive action. "Water?" it demanded and then instantaneously concluded, "The car is sinking. We're going to drown."

Before the water reached my knees, my mind abandoned its attempt at objectivity and I thought, *I'm going to drown!* I crawled out of the passenger window into a mass of branches and pine needles and scrambled to my feet.

I surveyed the damage. I was standing on a sandbar on the east bank of the creek. The car was lying like a turtle on its back on the sandbar, half in the water. Closer inspection showed that the creek wasn't more than two feet deep anywhere. There had been no danger of drowning.

"Gee whiz!" I hollered, kicking sand at the car. At least I'm pretty sure that's what I said. Perhaps not my exact words but pretty close.

I yelled a few more times and slammed the bottom of the car with my fist. A little too hard. Now I really had something to yell about as I hopped around on the sandbar with my fist between my knees. I tripped over a cypress root and sprawled face first in the sand.

This had a calming effect, and I paused with my face buried in the sandbar to reflect on the situation. In the silence that followed I heard the strains of "Don't Get Around Much Anymore" fading sporadically into "Okie from Muskogee" and back again. In my confused state it took me a few seconds to realize that it was coming from the car radio. The motor had died when the car hit the ground, but the key was still on.

"Oh, no," my jumbled brain exclaimed, "that's bad for the points, and the battery's going to run down!" Spitting sand, I struggled to my feet without the aid of my injured hand and staggered through the pine branches back to the car. I reached up around the steering column, which looked strange projecting down from the dash, and turned off the ignition. However, when I pulled at the keys, they fell out and dropped into the water.

"Golly bum," I muttered and groped around in the water with my good hand. That was when I discovered that the windshield was shattered. I did get the keys, but I also got a gash in my index finger that the murky creek water didn't improve.

Somehow I got out of the car without further casualties. Sitting on the trunk of the felled pine, I took a moment to calm down and assess the damage. The car was lying on its back, half in a creek. The roof was compressed to about a foot from the dash, the windshield shattered. But on a more positive note, the bottom of the car looked fine.

I realized I hadn't checked to see if I had been injured. I'd heard that people hurt in wrecks might not know it due to shock. A quick inventory revealed that all my injuries happened after the wreck, my slashed left hand and what felt like my broken right hand. I used my thumb to keep pressure on the gash in my finger and cradled my right hand in my lap.

CHAPTER TWENTY-FOUR

After a few minutes of sitting on the log, I decided there might be more constructive ways of dealing with the situation. Find a phone, perhaps. I scanned the area and realized the best way to the road was via the car to the bridge. With my handicap, it was with some difficulty that I climbed up onto the car.

Standing on the bottom of the car, staring at the drive shaft and the muffler, the enormity of the trouble in store overwhelmed me and I grabbed my cap, a faded denim railroad cap, and threw it down with renewed imprecations. Not content with the usual options, I branched into new territory, invoking the entire pantheon of Greek and Roman gods and as many of the Norse gods as I could remember.

I was pausing for breath when I felt something cold and slimy stroke my ear. I spun around and came face to face with a lanky mutt, which took the opportunity of my momentary paralysis to lick me in the face. This second outrage spurred me to action. I charged after the dog, which was a hideous orange color, exhausting the remaining pagan deities in my arsenal. The dog flinched back across the road, and I climbed the bridge a lot faster than I had climbed the car.

I took a few swings in the dog's direction, but it remained out of range, its tongue hanging out, lips stretched back in that mocking smile mutts seem to have—an ambiguous mixture of friendliness and caution.

"What are you grinning at, you ambulatory pumpkin?" I snarled, jerking in its general direction. It remained unperturbed. A dog of that color was no doubt used to abuse. Probably immune to sarcasm.

I started walking down the road away from the swimming hole. I had no idea where the nearest house was, but at least I was getting closer to my house, which was a mere twelve miles away.

The dog trotted a few yards behind me. "Shouldn't you be haunting a graveyard or something?" I demanded over my shoulder. It didn't answer.

The road that stretched before me between two fenced pastures was uncharacteristically straight for an East Texas road. It seemed endless, disappearing into the heat shimmers before I could detect a turn or shade. The sun was more than halfway to the horizon, but the sand on the road was still hot. I tried moving to the side, but there were briars and weeds in the ditches. Instead I tracked a zigzag course from one clump of grass to another, hopping like an inexperienced firewalker in between.

As I progressed, I alternated between murmuring at the wreck, cursing vaguely at the dog, and trying to remember where the next house was. After a few months, I detected a curve in the road a quarter of a mile ahead.

Then I heard a sound as familiar as thunder to a nervous child. The rattle of the Hound of Hell.

It was the only time I was glad to hear that sound. I stepped to the right and waved my good hand. Meaning the one that was only cut, not broken. I closed my eyes and felt the sand spray against my legs as the truck skidded to a stop. If tires could screech on a dirt road, Darnell's would have.

When I felt the cloud settling, I opened my eyes. I was almost sandblind, and the relative darkness of the cab looked cool and inviting. His greasy glasses glinted from the shadows.

"Say, doll. Whatcha doin'?"

"Oh, just out for my afternoon constitutional. Want to join me?"

"Ya need a ride?"

I paused as if considering the option. Even in the direst emergency a Fredonian didn't show concern. Detached reflection was the proper attitude. I glanced down at the dog. It was marking its domain on Darnell's tire.

"I guess so." I reached up to open the door, but my right hand hurt too much to push the button and my left thumb was busy keeping the blood in my finger from spurting out. "Hey, could you get the door for me?" I asked as if my hands were full of groceries.

Darnell shoved open the door. He eyed me curiously as I climbed in and shut the door by crooking my right forearm through the window instead of grabbing the handle.

"What's with the hand, doll?" He ground the truck into gear and lunged forward in a spray of sand. I glanced in the side mirror with satisfaction as the mutt disappeared in a cloud of dust.

"Huh? Oh, it's nothing. I think I sprained it or something."

"What about the other hand?"

"I cut it on some glass I didn't see under the water."

We rode listening to the death-rattle of the Hound of Hell in motion.

After a few minutes of skidding around curves and fishtailing down straightaways, he broke the silence again. "Say, doll. Did ya see that car upside down in the creek?"

"Yeah. I saw it."

"I wonder if anybody was in it."

"Nope."

"How do ya know?" He glanced at me as we sailed over a slight hill.

"I looked inside."

Our dialogue was interrupted by the wail of a train whistle. I peered out my window through the trees that lined the road. A train track followed this road for several miles. I could just make out the red of a caboose about fifty yards ahead.

Darnell gunned the motor as if the whistle had been the starting gun for a race. Our speed stepped up from the typical hysteria-inducing pace to the permanent-psychosis-inducing pace. I grabbed the window in spite of the pain in my hand and counted my blessings. At least it was still daylight.

Seeing a moving train acted on Darnell like seeing a running animal acts on a dog. Fortunately the stretch of road that paralleled the tracks was fairly straight. Most of the curves were gentle curves that a train could match.

We inched toward the front of the train. Eventually we sighted the smoke and then the actual engine. Darnell leered at it with a feral intensity.

We pulled up alongside. I could see the engineer leaning on the window. He waved. Reluctant to pry my fingers from the grip on the window, I just nodded back.

"I think we can make it," Darnell whispered hoarsely.

"Make what?" He didn't answer, so I followed his gaze. When I realized what he was doing, my grip faltered. Up ahead, a cutoff formed a Y. The main road followed the tracks, but the cutoff crossed them.

I looked back at Darnell in horror. "No!" I breathed. "You're not taking the cutoff?"

It was as if I weren't even in the car. Darnell kept his eyes on the cutoff as we inched ahead of the engine. The train was blowing the whistle in anticipation of crossing a road. From the nonchalant wave the engineer had given me, I was sure he had no clue as to Darnell's intentions.

The time for Fredonian detachment had passed. "Darnell, don't do this! You'll get us both killed!"

He made no sign that he had heard me.

"Please," I whined. "My dad will kill me!"

This bit of illogic was equally ineffective. The cutoff was rushing toward us. I was certain we were going too fast to turn and would bisect the Y, plunge through the ditch, and soar off the embankment, only to dive under the wheels of the train. My system dumped all available adrenaline into my bloodstream. I turned to Darnell and screamed.

"I can't take this! I've already driven one car off a bridge today, and another wreck is going to freak me out! Stop the dang truck!"

We were already at the cutoff, but I saw Darnell flinch for a second, whether at the confession or the screaming I didn't know. But only for a second. Then he calmly turned on his right blinker, jerked the wheel to the right, and pushed the accelerator to the floor. I was thrown back against the seat. I looked at the train. The horn was blaring and hands were frantically waving out the windows.

Once again my mind detached itself. It began considering the situation as a physics problem of vectors and forces. It calculated the angle and velocity of the train and the truck, factoring in their relative masses, and the resulting angle and velocity of the masses after collision.

The train faded from my view, and I saw it all diagrammed on a blackboard. A very old man wearing a white robe and sporting a knee-length beard stepped up to the blackboard with a pointer and demonstrated the principles involved with a few scribbled calculations. Seemingly dissatisfied with the results, he erased a few numbers and redid the calculations. He was still displeased. In a fit of irritation, he threw the chalk to the floor and slammed the pointer across the blackboard. It shattered.

The chalkboard vanished. I looked out the window and saw the front plate of the locomotive bearing down like a juggernaut. With a sudden surge of speed, we cleared the tracks and the locomotive disappeared from view.

Darnell loosed a maniacal laugh of glee, slammed on the brakes, and turned the wheel. We skidded around in a rainbow of dirt and came to rest facing the departing train. He gazed on the caboose with a look of triumph. It was like seeing Alexander survey the provinces he had captured. No, it was more like watching Satan gloat over the sight of Adam and Eve leaving the Garden for eternity. A look tinged with a trace of primeval scorn.

I quietly opened the door, retreated to the woods, and hid until I heard him tear off in a riot of rattles.

Not far from the tracks I saw a house. I cautiously emerged from the brush and knocked on the front door. Once inside, I called Dad and asked him to come pick me up, saving the worst of the news until I could tell him face to face. I thanked the lady for the use of the phone. She gave me a Band-Aid for my cut, and I went outside to await my fate.

I no longer dreaded the scene with Dad at the bridge. In anticipation it had seemed like the worst possible moment I could ever experience. But now, having challenged a train with Darnell Ray, I knew the depths of despair, and telling Dad about a car upside-down in a creek would be a step up.

I found a stump on the side of the road and dropped in exhaustion, my head buried in my hands. Something cold and slimy stroked my leg. I looked up. It was the orange mutt. I kicked at it and it moved back, hovering just out of reach and panting. Saliva dripped from its tongue into the sand. I picked up a stick to keep it at bay. It took a few steps back, cautious and tired.

I had time for reflection. It would take Dad twenty minutes if he left immediately. Not for the first time I wondered about the photograph of Gina Crowley and Deacon Fry that I had hidden in the hollow book in the Fortress. It looked like it had been taken twenty years ago. Gina appeared to be in her late twenties; Deacon Fry looked like he was in his forties. His hair was full but beginning to recede. He had a good paunch going and a hint of the jowls to come.

His smile didn't look forced, the arm around Gina's shoulder seemed very comfortable and relaxed, and she leaned into him, also smiling. It looked like the union of a cradle-robber and a gold digger, both satisfied with the arrangement, him with his trophy bride and her with her sugar daddy.

Then I thought of the car lying on its back with its feet in the air like something out of a cartoon. What would I tell Dad? What would be a reasonable explanation for driving a car off a bridge? I was trying to avoid a skunk? That sounded pretty good, except the bridge was only thirty yards or so from a ninety-degree curve. Even if I hadn't seen the skunk until I turned the corner, I would have been able to stop if I had been going a normal speed. Plus, the ruts I dug in the road and the feathered spray of sand on their leading edge would tell the story plainly enough.

It was an unpleasant thought, and I pushed it from my mind. Vernon and Jake. It had been more than a month since our talk, and I still didn't like it. OK, so Vernon wasn't going to pay with his life for something Jake had done. Still, he would have if I hadn't stepped in. And Jake hadn't even acknowledged it. Nothing. I knew because every week when I delivered a paper and drank a Coke, I asked him if he had heard from Jake. Nothing.

The longer I thought about it the more it bugged me. Somebody ought to tell Jake what his dad had done for him. Or his step-dad. A wet tongue on my elbow startled me from my reflections, and I whipped the stick around behind me. I heard an orange yelp. The mutt scurried back through the weeds. The price of freedom from orange mutts is eternal vigilance. I swiveled around on the stump and resumed my thinking with my eyes open.

Nobody seemed to know Jake was out there. Ralph had told the story to keep me away from the beer, but he had told it the same way Darnell had told about the ghost trucker. I don't think any of them believed it was really true. And when Deputy Hurst said something about Vernon running moonshine and dope, he hadn't said a word about Jake. If what Vernon said was true, I was the only person in Fred besides him and Gina who had seen Jake since the war.

I saw a bit of orange from the corner of my eye. I turned and waved the mutt away with the stick and also tried to wave away the thought that was trying to sneak up on me. A most unwelcome thought. An ugly orange thought. But it was bigger than my stick. It wouldn't go away.

No way was I going on a search-and-confront mission in the river bottom. Not in search of a crossbow-wielding wacko who had killed his own mother.

But, the orange thought whispered, *he didn't kill you. He had the chance and he didn't. He knew you saw him and he didn't.*

True, but that was more than a year ago. He might have snapped or something. Why else would he kill Gina?

He left the deer for you. Even field dressed it. He likes you. He wouldn't shoot you.

When I hunt him down and tell him I know he killed his mother, he's going to say, "Thanks for coming by. Here, have another Coke." I don't think so.

You know you're going to do it, so why argue?

I jumped off the stump and threw the stick at the mutt. "Go away," I screamed. "I'm not going to do it. You can't make me." The dog dodged the stick and then went over and sniffed it. Then he peed on it for good measure.

Dad pulled up in the Galaxy. It gave me something else to think about.

CHAPTER TWENTY-FIVE

The following Saturday I was sweating in the sauna of the river bottom, slapping mosquitoes and pushing through underbrush that I hoped wasn't poison ivy. And I was telling myself I was a fool.

After a week of wrestling with the unwelcome orange thought, I surrendered resentfully. The decision only replaced one brand of anxiety for another. Early Saturday I pedaled ten miles past Parker's house while it was still cool. I would have used the Falcon, but it was on blocks in the backyard awaiting a new windshield, motor mount, and rear end.

When Dad had picked me up, I had opted for the truth. I was running late and driving way too fast and forgot the bridge around this corner. He didn't speak until he stopped the Galaxy twenty yards from the bridge.

"Where is the car?" He scanned the ditches.

"See the bridge up there?" He nodded. "See those little black things sticking up over the weeds?" He nodded. "Those are the tires."

He walked on the bridge and viewed the underbelly of the Falcon. He looked to the corner at the sand splayed across the road, followed the tracks with his eyes to the bridge and into the creek. He looked at the Falcon some more. Then he looked at me.

"What do you think we ought to do with her?"

I didn't look back at him. I just looked at the car. The roof was almost touching the dash. I could only imagine what had happened to the engine. The crankshaft was probably snapped; the transmission, shattered. All kinds of lines and linkages and whatnot were likely twisted and broken. Fluid was running from the hood down the sandbar to the creek. No telling what shape the frame was in. The thing was more than ten years old and had been overhauled twice. I knew because I had held the work light both times. If I had a tattoo for every maintenance job we had done on the thing, I would have looked like the Illustrated Man. Only thinner.

"I say we strip off the tires and battery and anything else worth taking and leave it there."

He nodded and returned to the Galaxy. The only thing he said was, "I'm glad you weren't hurt."

That was it. It was like watching a grenade fall into your foxhole and waiting for the blast that would obliterate you. But it never came. I waited the entire drive home. I waited through the sermon. I waited after church. Nothing. When I got home, the car was in the backyard on a trailer. It had been winched out and towed while we were at church. Dad had decided to fix it up himself.

The Falcon was the car the kids were allowed to use. Hannah had just turned sixteen, and a car was crucial to her social agenda. Heidi had just returned from her second year of college and had planned a slate of activities that heavily relied on transportation. Although Dad remained silent, the girls weren't reticent about their views on the topic. Neither was Mom. She said something about Nimrod while she was cooking dinner, but I don't think she was talking about the hunter.

Dad's silence grew unbearable. After the news, I went back to the study. Dad was cutting an illustration into a mimeograph stencil for a flyer to advertise our summer revival. Brother Bates was coming back for another fun-filled week of hellfire and damnation. I couldn't wait.

"This thing was my fault. I've got a job lined up this summer at the lumberyard. I'll give you my check every week until it's paid off."

Dad considered it. "How about if we split it? I'll pay half; you pay half."

It was more than I deserved. I took it. Since I had neutralized the only car I was allowed to drive, it was the bike or nothing. I took the bike and set out on a long trek to the river bottom. The unwelcome thought demanded it.

I verified our former campsite from the pile of rusting beer cans a stone's throw from the fire ring and parked the bike there. After scouting around, I located the sweet gum tree where a crossbow shaft had hit just above my head. I ran my fingers over the scar in the bark. Then I wandered through woods, up and down gullies and hills and washouts, hunting for Jake much like I had hunted deer, by wandering bewildered, wondering where a whacked-out Vietnam vet would hole up. Would he have booby traps set up? A trip wire that would send a frame of bamboo spikes flying down at me? Or up at me?

When the sun was straight up, I pulled a bologna sandwich and canteen of water from my backpack. I sat on a log above the high water mark in a gully. A tree above me overhung the log, roots hanging down like tentacles. I ate the sandwich, drank some water, and leaned against the embankment to rest. It was hot, I was tired, I fell asleep.

I woke up suddenly. The sun had barely moved. I had been asleep only fifteen or twenty minutes. I was slumped down behind the log against the dirt wall. I put my left hand down to push myself up, but the layer of leaves didn't give. I tried to brush them aside, but they didn't move.

Looking closer I saw they were attached to brown-green mesh netting. Plywood under the netting covered a two-by-three-foot area behind the log at the base of the hill. Looking directly at it, even while standing on it, it was impossible to tell it wasn't part of the hill. It opened up like a door to a root cellar, leading to an open space under the hill.

The log blocked the leading edge of the door. It was secured by stakes covered with more leaves and netting. There was a small gap hollowed out under it that would allow someone in the hole to push the door up slightly and peer under the log without being seen. It commanded a view of the gully going downhill.

I peered into the hole. There were timbers supporting the sides and roof. I stepped in and looked further. It wasn't a hole. It was a tunnel about two feet square that disappeared into darkness. That made me nervous. I looped a hanging root around the door to hold it open and crawled down to see how long the tunnel was. It sloped down and made a right turn away from the river about ten feet from the door. I crawled to the turn, pushing my pack in front of me.

As I peered around the corner, the root came loose and the door slammed shut. I was instantly plunged into darkness. I ducked behind the pack as if I were taking incoming rounds. When nothing happened for a few seconds, I peered over the pack. There was a little light coming from further in the tunnel. Around the corner the tunnel continued to slope down, and I could see a left turn ahead.

I waited for whoever had the light to investigate the noise, but nothing happened. After several minutes I inched forward and peeked around the corner. The tunnel opened into a room about eight feet wide, ten feet deep, and tall enough for Jake Crowley to stand up in. Which is what he was doing. Looking right at me.

I jerked back into the tunnel, but his hand snagged my collar and dragged me out. The pack tumbled across the ground. He whipped me around and held me with one arm. A knife appeared and pressed against my throat.

"If you make a noise I will kill you, you hear me? If you lie to me I will kill you. And nobody will ever know. You hear me?"

"Yes," I croaked.

"Did you bring anybody else?"

"No."

"Did you tell anybody you were coming?"

"No."

"How many sisters do you have?"

How did he know I had sisters and not brothers? He shook me.

"None." The knife pressed deeper into the skin on my neck. It felt like it was breaking the skin. "Two."

The pressure let up slightly. "I told you not to lie, didn't I? That was your only chance. Another lie and they'll never find your body. How did you get here?"

"I rode a bike."

"What kind of bike?"

"Brown twenty-inch Spyder bike with chopper handlebars and a tiger skin banana seat."

"What's your name?"

"Mark." The knife pushed into my neck. "Cloud. Mark Cloud."

"Did you tell the old man you were coming here?"

"What old man?"

"Vern."

"No."

He threw me across the room onto a cot. I landed hard and hit my elbow on one of the wooden supports.

He stood in front of the tunnel, twirling the knife through his fingers. A very large knife. The blade glinted in the yellow light of a battery lamp set on a shelf on the opposite wall. He was dressed in camouflage, but not the tattered ones I had seen before. His hair was cut short. He looked like the picture of his dad in the photo album, just dressed for a different war.

"Do you really think you were sneaking up on me? Even if you didn't slam the door, you sounded like a freight train coming through that tunnel. If I was a VC, you would have been dead before you finished your bologna sandwich."

"How did you know I had a bologna sandwich?"

"I could smell it. What are you doing here?"

I retrieved my pack and extracted a crossbow shaft.

"I'm returning this." Jake looked at it without expression. "Do you know who I am?"

"Of course. If I need to know it, I know it."

"You remember me?"

"Remember you? I've studied you."

"What?"

"You're the only person who has seen me out here that's still alive. I wouldn't have let you live, but I knew you helped the old man, so I let you go."

"How did you know I wouldn't tell anyone?"

"I watched the first night, when they told you that fairy tale about me. I watched when you called the other guys back after you found the deer. I watched you walk home the second night. I knew you wouldn't talk."

"You watched me?"

"When I'm here, there's not much happens I don't know about."

"When you're here?"

"The less you know, kid, the better. I'm not always here; that's all you need to know. You'll never see me unless I want to be seen. And when I'm not here, this place is booby-trapped. Nobody finds it and lives unless I want them to. I only let you find it to hear what you think you're doing."

"I came here to tell you what Vernon did for you."

"Is that all?"

"You know what he did?"

"I have eyes. I can read. It was in the papers." He sat in a camp chair.

"You know he hid the evidence that you killed Gina and took the blame himself."

"He wasted his time. If the cops had any sense, they would have seen a lot of stuff they couldn't explain. How did they explain the slash marks on her neck?"

"I don't know."

"They didn't. Where was the weapon that made the marks?"

"I don't know."

"And neither do they." He pulled a Bugler's tobacco bag from a dufflebag.

"Any competent coroner could see the shotgun wounds were post-mortem. They catch a guy with a gun that shot a dead body, and they try to put him in the chair. That's justice." He rolled a cigarette. The tobacco didn't look very brown. In fact, it looked green.

"That's the D.A. paying off the coroner so he can climb another rung on the ladder. The most they could get in a fair trial was corpse abuse. The fact it made it past the indictment shows something is up."

He licked the cigarette, twisted the ends, and lit it. He took a deep drag, held it in, and blew it out all at once. It had a sweet smell, like incense.

"He would have been convicted. None of that information came out in the trial."

"True." He took another drag on the cigarette.

"And you would let him be executed for something he didn't do? Something you did?"

He blew the smoke out. "Hey, it's his nickel, kid. Nobody held a gun to his head. I should put my neck in a noose because he's too stupid or stubborn to keep his out?"

"He decided to give his life for yours! That doesn't mean anything to you?"

Jake looked at me long and hard. "Kid, the best you can get for putting your nose where it don't belong is a flat nose. You don't have any idea what you're talking about, so put a sock in it."

I thought I had a pretty good idea what I was talking about. But I was a little surprised at myself for talking so boldly to a murderer. I had expected to tread softly through the minefield of post-traumatic stress syndrome to get my point across without buying the farm. And for a second I thought I was a goner. But once he threw me across the room and told me why he had let me in, I wasn't really scared. He seemed to be as normal as the next guy who lived in a booby-trapped tunnel by the river. And he seemed to believe I would keep his secrets. Maybe I would and maybe I wouldn't. It's a lot to ask to keep the secrets of a murderer.

CHAPTER TWENTY-SIX

Jake sat smoking his cigarette and staring at the lamp for a long time. When the cigarette got short, he pulled an alligator clip from his sleeve and smoked the rest while holding onto the clip.

"The truth is, the old man did kill her. He just didn't pull the trigger until twenty years later."

I waited for him to explain himself. He looked at me for a second. Then he dropped the butt in a snuff can and snapped the lid shut. He went to a corner of the room, pulled a crate aside, lifted a cover from a hole in the floor, and pulled out a can of Dr Pepper, dripping water. He tossed it at me.

"I believe this is your brand, kid. The old man never bothered to find that out, did he?"

He pulled a small brown bottle out of the hole and replaced the lid and the crate. He popped the top off with an opener on his knife and dropped it in a coffee can next to the duffle. He raised the bottle toward me.

"Salute," he said, sort of like how Vernon said it, only it sounded more foreign and less Texan.

I fumbled with the Dr Pepper and popped the tab, held up my can, and we both drank. He took a long pull from the bottle, then sat in the chair and sighed contentedly.

"Belgian beer. Can't get this down at Fred Grocery."

I nodded at the Bugler pouch. "You get that at Fred Grocery?"

Jake smiled for the first time since I'd been there. "As a matter of fact, I did. On sale."

"Aha." I took another sip of Dr Pepper. "What do you mean he killed her twenty years ago?"

"Kid, let's not bother with it. What's done is done, and I'm enjoying this beer."

"From what I hear, Vernon helped you and your mom out of a funky situation. Seems like you would be grateful for that."

He flared up like lighter fluid thrown on a charcoal grill. "Kid, you remember what I said about the flat nose?"

"If I'm wrong, then tell me. Until then I have no reason to think anything different."

"Truth is, we didn't need any help. We were doing just fine living with Nonno."

"Nonno?"

"My grandfather." He took another deep pull at the beer.

"She just had a way with men, could make them do what she wanted. Any man. She thought she could do the same with the old man, but things didn't work out like they had before. Nonno died, and then he dragged us off to the middle of nowhere to watch his mother die.

"He could have just shot her right then. It would have been kinder."

"What do you mean?"

"You take a woman who grew up in Rome, who lived in Paris, who traveled all over Europe, and stick her in the middle of the woods with a bunch of hicks. She practically chewed her leg off to get out of that trap, but she never made it. Somehow she just couldn't do it."

We were both quiet for awhile. He spoke again. "Maybe she realized he wasn't like the others."

"The others?" I thought of the picture of Deacon Fry and Gina. "I thought you were just a kid when they got married, like five or something. How would you know about others?"

"Oh, there were always others. Even out here. Somehow she

would hook them. She had expensive tastes, so they wouldn't be seen around here. She would disappear to Houston or Dallas or New Orleans for a week or two. But she always came back. I never could figure that out. Maybe she realized there was one man who couldn't live without her, and that made it impossible to leave him. I don't know. She usually couldn't stand weakness and would drop a man who showed sign of it."

"Weakness?"

"Yes, weakness. Anything you can't live without is a weakness. That's how they get to you, how they break you, when they find the thing you can't live without."

"So it's a weakness to love somebody?"

"Love is the biggest weakness of all. It will kill you."

"Or make you willing to give your life for someone else?"

Jake shrugged. "Same thing. Either way, you're dead."

How could he have no feeling for the man who had done so much for him? Had taken him in and raised him when his own father had deserted him. For the innocent man who had taken the blame for his crime?

I asked him. Suddenly the cave was a dangerous place again. He dragged me off the cot by the front of my shirt with his left hand. His right hand still held the beer.

"Don't you insult the name of my father," he breathed in my face in a fierce whisper. "He was ten times the man Vern is." He threw me back across the room. I had Dr Pepper all over me.

"He didn't desert us. He was killed in action before I was born. He saved an entire platoon that was overrun by a battalion of retreating Germans. He didn't go hiding out with some woman in a barn while his men were getting slaughtered."

"Vernon didn't hide out. He was caught behind enemy lines and couldn't get back across."

Jake sneered at me. "Oh, I see he told you that story too. Did he give you one of these?" He dug in the bag and pulled out a key chain with a Luger shell hanging from it.

I pulled mine out and held it up. "Yeah."

"He told me that story when I turned sixteen and was talking about joining the army. War is hell and people get killed and they're just regular guys like you and me and all that tripe. I saw it for what it was—cowardice. I've seen it plenty times since then."

"So was he a coward when he covered up your crime and took the blame?"

"No, he was a sucker." He took a gulp from the bottle and calmed down.

"I signed up when I was seventeen just to spite him. Forged the papers. It was 1963, and there wasn't a war happening yet. Shipped to Vietnam in '64. We would hang out at the base in the day and in the bars at night. Spend weekends on the beach. If we got bored, we would go on a patrol and scare up some action, get shot at, shoot back, but if we minded our business, so did they.

"I was there almost two years when the brass decided to hit Ia Drang. That's when it all started. A lot of guys didn't have a clue what they were getting into. We were hit with a wall of lead, and they were just figuring out that the guys on the other side were trying to kill us. Unbelievable. One platoon rushed out and got isolated from the rest. We spent two days and a lot of men to get them back. Some said that was a mistake. Truth is, it forced our guys to stay and fight, and it took three days, but we finally made them turn and run.

"Then we moved to the pickup zone four miles away. A scout patrol captured a couple of VC. I saw right away something was up and took cover and told the guys around me. Some of them just laughed, sitting there smoking cigarettes. But some of them did like I said. Those were the ones that lived.

"It was a slaughter. We lost over 150 guys. They lost over 400, but that's not how you win a war over there. They don't quit no matter how many you kill. They got billions more, and they'll throw them in front of a moving train if they think it'll slow it down enough for them to get on."

Jake finished off his beer and put the bottle in the coffee can. "I spent a year being a walking target with guys who didn't know a booby trap from a booby prize. We would drop in on search-and-destroy missions. The NVRA would come up and give us a good pasting and disappear when they got tired. We would march from one location to another. The NVRA would pick a good spot, ambush us, give us another good pasting, and disappear again when they got tired. Sure we would call in napalm and toast them, but it was like pouring gasoline on a fire ant bed. There was always more. We went around fighting when they wanted to fight, where they wanted to fight, how they wanted to fight, as long as they wanted to fight.

"Any fool knows it's the hunter that controls the time and place. It's the hunted that is shot. I was tired of being ordered around to do stupid things by guys who would spend the rest of their short lives being the prey and not the predator. I finally chewed my way up the line of command until I got a transfer.

"In a few weeks I was in Cambodia on the Ho Chi Minh Trail on the right side of the equation. We gave those poor suckers fits. But even there I got stuck with idiots. The main challenge in life is to protect yourself from what an idiot might do."

He shook his head. "I'm on an op with five other guys and about thirty locals. I have it planned to the last twig on the trail, but one of the guys goes to take an unauthorized dump and gets captured. In a few hours we have half the population of Hanoi on us. I tell the locals to beat it. I get the other four guys out just before the camp is surrounded by forty or fifty NVRA. Not a problem since they don't know I'm in a bunker.

"I designed the camp. They could send hundreds of NVRA through it and all they would find is a deserted camp. I figure they'll spend maybe half a day clearing out the supplies, lose a few guys now from the booby traps and a few more later from the booby-trapped ammo. Then they leave and so do I.

"That's how it should have worked, but a tough guy from Alabama decides to be a hero and comes back for me. Of course they see him, and he gets cut up pretty good from DP 7.62 fire before he falls into my bunker, looking like the wrong end of target practice. I'm behind the stairs with my knife. The idiot says, 'Don't worry 'bout me, Tex, I'm all done in. Jest get on out and I'll cover ya.' Like I'm going to waltz out through four dozen NVRA who watched him come in.

"I tell Bama to be quiet and hold his fire no matter what happens. But when we hear a noise outside the bunker, Bama fires off a hundred M60 rounds up the stairs. Next thing I see is a guy falling down the steps. He's dead, but a grenade rolls down after him. I decide to take Bama up on his offer. I grab the dead guy, throw him on the grenade, and hit the dirt behind Bama.

"It gets very loud and then it gets very quiet. I don't move or make a sound. They're satisfied. Problem solved. They leave. I am about to do the same when I see a set of legs coming down the stairs. I slip back behind the stairs and let down the tarp I put there for this purpose. I watch him through the steps.

"He sees two dead bodies, just what he expects to see. Like I figure, he puts down his weapon and digs around. I lose sight of him, but I can track him from the noise he's making. Then I see toes and sandals under the edge of the tarp. When he pulls it back, I come out on top of him. Problem solved. I take his weapon and slip out without being seen."

He got up from the camp chair and stretched. "Everybody thought I was dead, from the NVRA to the USA, and I didn't do anything to make them think any different. It was time to work without idiots. I only work with the best, and I check them out first. From the guy who hires me to the guys I work with."

"Doing what?"

His expression told me not to ask anymore questions. "Doing what needs to be done. For the right price.

"When you saw me awhile back, I was between jobs. After Christmas I was gone on business for almost a year. I got back around Thanksgiving and went to the house to get some goods. I knew she had got bad, but I didn't know how bad."

He sat down on the crate with his elbows on his knees and stared at the dirt. "I always get the goods and disappear. I never go to the trailer. Never. But something told me to go to the trailer. I don't ignore that voice. Even if it makes no sense. Most of the time danger doesn't make sense because it's coming from an angle you don't understand until it's over. If you wait to understand it before you respond, you're dead."

His voice lowered. It lost some of the authoritarian tone. "I go at twilight because it's harder to see just before it gets dark, which means it's harder to see me. I came in through the back, my knife out, and secured every room starting at the back. They were all empty. When I got to the front, I saw her. I saw her eyes first, and she saw me. She didn't say anything, couldn't say anything, but she didn't have to. I knew.

"She was on the floor leaning against the wall. She had a paring knife in her hand. Her neck was a mess, there was blood and . . ."

He sat up, looked at the ceiling, ran his hand through his hair, and looked back down. "There was blood. She had tried to hurt herself before, just surface scratches on her arms. You could tell that wasn't for real. But this . . . this was definitely for real. She was pale, almost white, bleeding to death. I've seen enough to know when it's too late."

He looked at me. His eyes were moist. "She's never done anything like this before. She never means it."

He was pleading with me. I didn't know what to say, so I didn't say anything.

"I didn't know how bad she had got. I was gone a long time."

I held his gaze until he looked away.

"I could tell she was in pain; she was asking me to end it. I could see it in her eyes. I always carry my bow on my back when I pick up deliveries. I know how to kill instantly with one shot, and the mark won't make a sound."

"When I sighted down the bow, I looked at her face one last time. She smiled at me." He ran his hand through his hair again. "She smiled at me."

I was sitting on the cot, soaked with Dr Pepper, crying. I didn't say anything. Jake didn't say anything. I pulled two pictures from the pack. The picture of Deacon Fry wasn't the only one I had borrowed. I also had taken the ones on either side. One, a face that could have launched a thousand ships. It was a face that had been the undoing of many men, according to Jake. The other was the war hero and his bride. Or the deserter, two stories molded by the same face for different reasons.

I stood up. Jake looked at me. I handed him the pictures. He looked at them, and the moisture in his eyes overflowed. He didn't look up.

I cleared my throat and wiped my face with my shirtsleeves. "Jake, you're wrong about love. Love isn't the biggest weakness. No, maybe you are right. Love is the greatest weakness. It is the greatest weakness that overcomes all. The greatest of these is love."

"No," he whispered, his voice high. "It doesn't overcome anything. Love is death." He cleared his throat and got control of his voice, but still whispered. "He trapped her because he loved her. She stayed because she loved him. And it killed her."

"Are you weak?"

"No," he whispered fiercely.

"Then tell me why you pulled the trigger."

He was silent.

"You did it because you loved her." My voice broke. I cleared my throat. "And you are not weak. So love must not be a weakness."

I stood there for awhile. Neither of us said anything. I grabbed the pack and stepped to the tunnel.

"If you tell anyone about me or this place, I will kill you."

I turned around and looked at him. He looked at me, eyes filled with moisture and blazing.

"I believe you," I said.

I crawled out into the light and squinted. It took a long time to get home.

CHAPTER TWENTY-SEVEN I didn't tell any-

one about Jake. I didn't see the point.

I knew it was wrong. He had killed her. How did he know it was too late? He had seen a lot of death, had caused a lot of death. But every death is unique, just like every life. The truth that is stranger than fiction is full of stories about people who aren't supposed to make it but do. Even doctors are wrong about stuff like that.

I was abetting a murderer. If it came out, I could go to jail. And I couldn't think of any verses that would help me prove that Jesus would let him go. Let him who is without sin cast the first stone. Jesus said that to a woman caught in the act of adultery. Did that apply to murder? Maybe. They were both capital offenses back then.

But I was hedging and I knew it. I should have gone straight to Deputy Hurst. But I didn't. Perhaps Vernon was right. Maybe Jake had already paid enough. And then there was the part about him killing me if I told anyone. I didn't doubt his sincerity or his ability. So I didn't tell anyone about Jake.

The next morning I went to Sunday school in a daze. I was startled out of my trance when I found Mac in the room instead of Scooter and Brenda. He greeted everyone that came in, waiting until the buzzer to explain.

"Yesterday I talked ta Pastor Matt and Scooter. I asked if I could take the class on a special project. It will last through Sunday school and church." He looked around the room. "Looks like we'll all fit in the van."

"Where we goin'?" Ralph asked.

"You all remember Parker Walker? He used to come ta church here. And he used ta have a gazebo out at his place. Awhile back it burnt down. I figured it would be a nice gesture if we was ta go out and help him rebuild it."

"Shucks," Ralph said, "he burnt it down hisself. What makes ya think he wants it rebuilt?"

"Shut up," Squeaky said. "It gets us out of Sunday school and church, so what are ya askin' questions for?" She stood up. "Let's go."

Mac laughed. "They'll announce it in the service so yer parents will know where ta come get ya. I know some of ya come in yer church clothes. I have some overalls and coveralls in the van. We'll go out the back way so as not ta disturb anyone."

At Parker's place a crew was clearing the charred remains from the foundation of the first gazebo. They were hired hands from Mac's family farm. Fortunately there was a decent carpenter among them. Parker's truck was gone. Probably at Elrick's church in Warren. That gave us plenty of time.

We took fresh lumber off a trailer and loaded the burned wood on. By the time that was done there was plenty of wood measured and cut. We banged nails at the direction of the carpenter while the girls cleared the weeds out of the flowerbed. The frame was up, and we were working on the roof when parents started showing. Hannah and I stayed on. Mac was our ride, and he wasn't leaving until it was finished.

Mrs. Harmon brought us lunch. We took a fried-chicken break in the shade of the new roof, washing it down with sweet tea. I worked on the railings while the carpenter worked on the benches. The sound of a car in the drive made me look around.

Parker almost ran into Mac's van. He turned off the engine and looked out at the gazebo for a long time. Mac spun around and rolled up to the truck.

"Don't just sit there while there's work ta be done. We got a spare hammer," he hollered over the sound of hammers and a skill saw.

Parker opened the door and unfolded out of the truck like a crane moving slowly through a marsh. He looked hard at the gazebo and then at Mac.

"Parker, I got somethin' ta tell ya."

Parker nodded at him.

"Back around Christmas you come and told me ya forgive me. I didn't like that much. Didn't like it at all, as a matter of fact. You probably figured that."

Mac paused. Parker didn't say anything. The hammers rang out.

"I didn't like it, but I couldn't get away from it. I drove home and it follered me. I went ta Beaumont and it follered me. For months it follered me around. Finally I had ta face it down, look it square in the eye. And when I did, I seen you was right."

Parker's expression changed slightly. It was hard to say exactly how. Maybe the lines weren't as hard as they were before. Maybe his eye wasn't squinted as much.

"I did cut you out. I had my reasons. I told 'em to ya at Christmas. They were good reasons. At least, I thought they were good reasons. Anybody would agree with me. It was askin' too much."

Mac rolled forward. His voice got softer.

"But when I faced it, I learned somethin'. God asks too much. He asks us ta do what is too much fer us ta do 'cause He wants us ta know it's too much. We keep thinkin' we can do it. We can do the right thing, act the right way, do what we have ta do. *We* can do it. Not Him. Us.

"But we can't. Sometimes we want ta do right but don't do it. Sometimes we don't even want ta do right. That's when we find out how wretched we really are. It ain't pretty, but it's truth. That's what I found out.

"So I prayed. I told Him I didn't want ta change and I didn't even care. I told Him if He wanted me ta do right, He would have ta change me Himself 'cause I was through tryin' ta change myself. And ya know what happened?"

Parker raised an eyebrow, the one over the good eye, but said nothing.

"He did. Just like that. It was like somebody poured a bucket of spring water on my head. I felt a cool feelin' run through me from my head down to my feet, real slowlike. And the next thing I know, I'm won-derin' why it was that I could be so unkind to my best friend."

"So here we are." He wiped his eyes and waved his arm to the gazebo. "Half a year after you forgive me, I ask yer forgiveness. I guess I got it backward, but I hope it's not too late."

Parker stood silent for a long time. He looked from Mac to the gazebo. He blinked and looked away awkwardly. Then he stepped for-ward and held out his hand. Mac took it.

"Ain't ya gonna say anythin' at all?" Mac asked.

"Thank you," Parker said quietly but forcefully. "Where's that hammer?"

Hannah and I got home midafternoon. Mom, Dad, and Heidi were sitting at the kitchen table. All they needed was a casket to complete the mood.

"Have a seat," Dad said. We did.

"You two missed the service this morning, so you haven't heard the news. I had a meeting with the deacons. Tonight there won't be a service."

I didn't understand the somber mood. That sounded like good news to me.

"Deacon Fry wanted to have a meeting this afternoon, between serv-ices, with the deacons and our family, but you weren't available. So he has asked that we have it tonight instead of the service."

"You're canceling church for a deacon's meeting? Don't those usually happen on a week night?"

"This isn't a regular deacon's meeting. This is a meeting to determine if I will be the pastor of this church next week."

"What?" I looked around. Mom and Heidi had tears in their eyes. Hannah was in shock.

"I explained to Heidi, but you and Hannah may not know what has been happening the past few years."

I figured he glossed over our previous conversations on the subject in the interest of client-attorney privilege.

"Six years ago we came to this church full of excitement at what God could do. After a few years, it became apparent there were basic differences between what we thought the church should be doing here and what the deacons wanted. I have tried to reach out beyond the people who always come to church, to bring in folks who don't. Even folks who you would think wouldn't come at all.

"The deacons or, I should say, Deacon Fry seems to see this church as his personal country club that admits people he approves of and excludes those he deems unworthy. And he has a considerable amount of control over the other deacons. It seems he has finally convinced them that we are a bad thing for this church. That's what the meeting is about tonight."

"With all of us?"

"Yes. However, it seems that they are most interested in the activity of the male members of the household. The female members appear to be exempt from their official censure." He smiled. A small, sad smile, but still a smile.

Heidi could no longer contain herself. "Mark, you see what you did? You are going to get us kicked out of here."

"Me?"

"Heidi," Mom said, but Heidi was not to be squelched.

"Yes, you. You go out drinking and hanging out with bootleggers and killers. What did you expect would happen?"

I spluttered, unable to make the words come out one at a time instead of all at once. Dad intervened.

"Heidi, they're not after Mark. They're after me. Mark didn't cause this. Deacon Fry is using Mark as an excuse."

"But if he hadn't given them the ammunition, they wouldn't be doing this now."

"For the record, Mark has done what he thought was right, however misguided he might be at times. No matter what happens tonight, I'm proud of all of you. We both are." He glanced at Mom. "There are a lot of pastors, some I know personally, who have been through a lot of grief because of the behavior of their kids. You all have not caused us those kinds of problems, and we're very thankful."

Mom said, "Yes, I agree although I wouldn't complain if some people stopped trying to kill Bambi with guns and themselves with cars."

I decided this was not a good time to mention Jake and the grass. Maybe later.

"One more thing. This is not a disaster. It is a sad thing; it is an unfortunate thing. But it is not the end of the world. Jesus said, 'Blessed are you when people insult you, persecute you and falsely say all kinds of evil against you because of me. Rejoice and be glad, because great is your reward in heaven.'"

"Rejoice?" Heidi said. "Rejoice?"

"And be glad," I added. "Don't forget that part." I jostled Hannah with my elbow. She turned and with both hands shoved me out of the chair onto the floor. I landed on my elbow, the one that I had hit the day before at Jake's tunnel. I expressed my displeasure.

Hannah smiled. "Now I'm glad."

In the few remaining hours left to me, I sat in the Fortress of Solitude like a condemned prisoner awaiting sentencing. The radio played a poignant blend of "Will the Circle Be Unbroken" and "Stand by Your Man."

It had been a long run. Six years in one place. It was the longest I had lived in one house my whole life. After four schools in four years in Ohio, having six years in the same place had given me a sense of permanence. I felt like a true Fredonian, although only three generations would really qualify me, and even then I would only be eligible for probation.

It wasn't so bad for me. I was graduating in a week. Heidi was already out. But it would be bad on Hannah. She had two years left to go. Like C. J., she would do her last few years of high school among strangers. I felt bad about that. I hadn't given thought to how my actions would affect her.

But I knew I wouldn't have changed anything. Couldn't change anything. I had done what I thought was right. Most of the time. Did what I had to at any rate.

I thought back two years to a dreary summer afternoon and a dusty book in the church library. It was a dangerous book. I should have burned it. No need though. It was such an old, brittle, boring-looking book, there was little danger that many people would read it.

But the ideas in it seemed to get out regardless, with mixed results. Parker did what he thought he should do, and Sonia left him. Jake did what he thought he should do, and it didn't seem to bring him any peace. Vernon did what he thought he should, and it almost got him executed. I did what I thought I should do; it saved Vernon's life and threatened Dad's job. And as Dad had pointed out, Jesus did what He thought He should do, and it got Him killed. It seemed a risky proposition at best.

CHAPTER TWENTY-EIGHT

Oddly enough, we had the meeting in the fellowship hall. It was strange to see the place where we had enjoyed so many covered-dish suppers and Valentine banquets turned into a stage for an inquisition.

The room had been set up with the tables in a horseshoe for some other function. The deacons didn't change it, so we sat down like diplomats negotiating a treaty. Deacon Fry and Dad sat in the middle. The deacons sat down one side; the Cloud family, in stair-step fashion down the other.

I looked across at the panel of inquisitors. They all looked somewhere else. Anywhere but at us. Elmer was coughing into a hanky that he carefully folded and returned to his back pocket. Weldon was digging something out of his fingernail with a paper clip that had been left on the table. Scooter looked at us briefly and then at nothing in particular.

Deacon Fry appeared immune to the epidemic of nerves. He led off with a ponderous prayer as soon as we sat down. Then he flipped open a big black Bible. He cleared his throat.

"James 3:1," he rumbled in a voice that could clean out rain gutters. "Not many of you should presume to be teachers, my brothers, because you know that we who teach will be judged more strictly."

He paused so long that everyone looked at him. He looked up from the Bible over his reading glasses and raked a piercing gaze across all present, saving his most searching intensity for the deacons. They nodded back solemnly. Message received.

Nice system. Make sure that those passing judgment will not be restrained by the thought that the same standard would be applied to them. You had to admire the man, even if you despised him at the same time.

"Romans 16:17–18. 'Now I beseech you, brethren, mark them which cause divisions and offences contrary to the doctrine which ye have learned; and avoid them. For they that are such serve not our Lord Jesus Christ, but their own belly; and by good words and fair speeches deceive the hearts of the simple.'"

He licked his finger and flipped the pages to a red ribbon marker. "First Timothy 3:1–7."

It was the dreaded passage, the one that haunts every PK. Heidi opened her Bible, perhaps hoping to catch him in an error or find a loophole.

"'Here is a trustworthy saying: If anyone sets his heart on being an overseer, he desires a noble task. Now the overseer must be above reproach, the husband of but one wife, temperate, self-controlled, respectable, hospitable, able to teach, not given to drunkenness, not violent but gentle, not quarrelsome, not a lover of money. He must manage his own family well and see that his children obey him with proper respect. (If anyone does not know how to manage his own family, how can he take care of God's church?) He must not be a recent convert, or he may become conceited and fall under the same judgment as the devil. He must also have a good reputation with outsiders, so that he will not fall into disgrace and into the devil's trap.'"

When Fry read the part about managing the family, Heidi paused from reading long enough to look at me reproachfully. I glared back. So much for the united front, shoulder to shoulder, bolder and bolder.

I wondered if there was any other career where a kid had to live in constant fear of costing his dad his job. How many welders had their boss come up to them and say, "Jim, your kids are a mess. If you can't keep your own kids straight, how do you think you can weld a straight bead? Get your lunch bucket and get out of here."

I knew PKs who were constantly reminded that they could be responsible for destroying their dad's career. It cowed some kids into anxious submission, living their lives over a substratum that varied from nervous timidity to controlled terror. But it gave others a unique weapon with which to punish their parents, taking them along in a downward spiral of self-destruction. Either way, it wasn't a healthy way to grow up. But that's just part of the territory, an occupational hazard of being born into a pastor's family.

Fry didn't lead with the family thing. Perhaps he was saving it for the KO punch.

"Brothers, it says right there in Timothy that a overseer must have a good reputation with outsiders. People who don't go ta this church, some who don't even go ta any church, are askin' what is goin' on in our church.

"It says right there in Romans that we should shun them that cause divisions and pervert sound doctrine. And there is no question we have divisions. There are many unhappy folks in this church. There are good folks ready ta leave 'cause we seem ta become a gatherin' of the heathen instead of the holy."

I looked at Dad, who was listening to Deacon Fry in the same way he might watch a slightly boring sitcom. His silence was unnerving but not unexpected. On the way to the church I had asked him what he was going to say.

"I don't know."

"Haven't you thought about it?"

"Not much."

"Why not?" Such complacency was incomprehensible, if not irresponsible.

"When you are brought before synagogues, rulers and authorities, do not worry about how you will defend yourselves or what you will say, for the Holy Spirit will teach you at that time what you should say."

I looked at him blankly.

"Jesus said that," he said with a smile. "To His disciples."

I knew that. It just seemed like a naive strategy. Something on the order of an organized rebuttal of the charges seemed more sensible to me.

As Fry droned on, I stared at Dad, willing him to speak up and defend himself. He sat impervious to my telepathic demands, now studying the expressions of the other deacons.

Fry's tirade continued unabated. "I have heard reports of him goin' into bars up North. Frequenting dens of iniquity with no care for upholdin' a good reputation for his Yankee church."

The man had no shame. Everyone knew Dad went to bars to hand out tracts and to witness. He had said so from the pulpit.

"As if that wasn't enough, I heard reports of him goin' ta other churches that teach error and even heresy. Many times."

This also was no secret. Dad sometimes went to weekday services at other churches that allowed for more freedom of expression than the conventional services in Fred. The other deacons were now beginning to show signs of boredom and impatience. But Fry was only beginning.

"There are reports of our pastor even speakin' in tongues." This accusation brought a mild show of interest from the deacons. And from me. It was the first I had heard of it. Dad leaned back and looked at the ceiling but said nothing.

Failing to hit home with hearsay evidence, Fry fell back on his first tactic. "If that ain't enough, think of what Timothy says."

Uh-oh.

"Second Timothy 4. 'Preach the Word; be prepared in season and out of season; correct, rebuke and encourage—with great patience and careful instruction. For the time will come when men will not put up with sound doctrine.'"

Whew. Dodged the bullet again. Maybe he wasn't going to drag me into it after all.

Fry skewered the deacons with a bloodless gaze. "When was the last time you heard someone correct and rebuke in our pulpit? Not since Pastor Prichart was here. He"–Fry nodded his head toward Dad–"he has ta bring in Brother Bates ta do his correctin' and rebukin' for him. Why is that? Could it be because he can't abide sound doctrine? Could he be pickin' up doctrine contrary ta what we have learned from all these places he goes and peddlin' it ta his trustin' sheep?"

Dad looked on with more interest.

"I think what we have here is a case of cheap grace–forgiveness with no repentance. A cheap grace that lets folks come into the church without confessin' their sins and turnin' away from 'em."

Dad cleared his throat and raised his hand as if he was asking to go to the bathroom. Deacon Fry glared at him. I leaned back, relieved. At last he was going to do something.

"Do you mind if I ask a question?"

"Go ahead."

"When you say *church*, what exactly do you mean?" Fry frowned. "You said cheap grace lets folks come into the church without confession and repentance. What exactly do you mean by 'coming into the church'?"

"You seen it. You encouraged it. You got that bootlegger comin' in ever' Sunday, sittin' on the back row like he owns it. I ain't heard tell he's busted up his still before or after he killed his wife."

"Ah. If that's what you mean, then I have to agree. Yes, I am guilty of what you said."

I jumped forward in my chair. Whose side was he on?

Deacon Fry was speechless, for a second anyway. "You admit it?"

Dad nodded. Fry looked at the other deacons as if to say, "See? I told you so." They looked back, startled. I looked at Dad as if to say, "Have you lost your mind?" Heidi and Hannah looked at each other in confusion. Mom just sat patiently, waiting for these men to finish their foolishness so we could get on with the evening.

"Yes. I am guilty of allowing people to enter the building without first confessing their sins at the door. But I believe that policy has been in effect for a long time. Probably back when your daddy was here and his daddy before him, I would suspect." Dad smiled slightly. Very slightly.

"However, I feel compelled to point out that I don't let people into the church or out of it. I don't have any authority over that. The church is not a building; it is the bride of Christ, and He's the one who lets people in or doesn't."

The girls and I resumed breathing. The deacons looked thoughtful. All except Fry, who looked angry.

"So, if you are going to bring a recommendation to the church that I be dismissed because I have failed to initiate a policy of mandatory confession before coming into the building, I will gladly testify that I am guilty."

"That's not what I mean and you know it," Fry breathed through the gravel of his voice. He shook his finger in Dad's face and boomed, "You preach a cheap grace, Pastor. You keep talkin' about how God loves ever'body, but we never hear about repentin', about countin' the cost and not turnin' back. I don't hear you denyin' that you ain't never preached a sermon correctin' and rebukin'."

"That may be true. I don't have the topics of six hundred sermons at my immediate recall. I am prepared to plead guilty to not calling out people in the congregation from the pulpit on Sunday mornings and publicly rebuking them although I have been sorely tempted at times. I prefer to do correction and rebuke in private, not in front of the entire congregation. Like the time I rebuked you."

"Me? You never rebuked me." Fry's eyes narrowed. "Or had cause to," he added, looking around at the deacons.

If the deacons had been ambivalent before, they seemed genuinely interested now. The Cloud family leaned forward in one accord.

Dad nodded. "I was afraid of that. I wondered if I had been so gentle and subtle that you didn't realize that I was rebuking you. But the rest of the deacons can verify it. They were all there."

"Where?" Fry demanded. The other deacons looked puzzled.

"That would be six months ago. The Sunday after Thanksgiving in my study at the meeting you called. A meeting similar to this one."

"You didn't rebuke me then."

"Oh, but I did. I warned you against slandering, listening to gossip, spreading discord, and keeping away those whom Jesus has asked to come to Him."

Fry looked hard at Dad. He looked at the deacons. One by one their expressions slowly transformed from puzzled reflection to affirmation. Scooter nodded. Fry jerked his head back around as Dad continued.

"As you pointed out, that's the danger of a gentle rebuke. Sometimes it doesn't sink in, especially for people who aren't open to correction. It goes against my style to rebuke from the pulpit, but if you insist that I rebuke you in front of the congregation next week, I will consider making an exception just for you."

I was unable to suppress the laugh although I immediately repented because it drew fire from Fry. A low profile might have allowed me to escape unscathed. But it was too late for that. I discovered that Solomon knew what he was talking about when he said, "Even in laughter the heart may ache, and joy may end in grief." Grief for Mark was the next item on the agenda.

"Pastor, you shouldn't make a mockery of this meetin'. It reflects poorly on you."

"Deacon Fry, I'm afraid I must be painfully blunt. Your immunity to subtlety forces me to resort to a plainness of speech that must necessarily sound harsh. I apologize for that in advance although I realize that it will do little good. My remarks are intended to point out the absurdity of this meeting and of your comments, not to mock you. It was my hope, a vain hope it seems, that when this became evident, you would realize that your position is not only wildly impractical; it also violates the spirit of the gospel."

"Pastor, you can dance around this all ya like with high soundin' language, but puttin' lipstick on a pig don't take away the stink. Yer peddlin' cheap grace, and we don't have ta look no further than yer own family."

Dad nailed Fry with a look of his own. "Do you really think it advisable to beat this dead horse? Or cosmetically enhanced pig, if you prefer. Surely by now even you must realize there is no basis for your accusations."

"Oh, you don't want ta talk about it? What are ya tryin' ta hide? You don't want the church ta know the preacher's own kid goes ta Nigra churches where they dance right in the church, goes out drinkin' and drives a car off a bridge, makes up stories ta let a bootlegger get away with cold-blooded murder?"

"I'm not trying to hide anything. I'm trying to save you some embarrassment. And to spare my family the ordeal of being dragged into this for no good reason."

"Save me embarrassment? I got nothin' ta hide. But I think it's time the church heard how the pastor can't manage his own family." Fry lowered his voice and leaned toward Dad. "Or perhaps you'd rather just resign now and that won't be necessary."

CHAPTER TWENTY-NINE
Dad's voice didn't get any louder, but it took on an edge that would cut stone. "Fry, you may have lived here with the grave of your daddy and granddaddy and who knows what other graves. You may be able to bully people to get your way. But I will not be blackmailed. Do you understand me?"

Dad stood up suddenly, sending his chair sliding back across the puke-green tile floor. He towered over Fry. Fry stood up and looked down on Dad.

"I have changed my mind," Dad said, looking up, toe to toe with Fry. A patina of sweat glistened on his forehead. "Up to now, I have considered you a thorn in my flesh, a stubborn man who sincerely disagreed with me. But I have recently formed a new opinion. You are not just stubborn and annoying; you are evil. You have the ways of your father—the serpent—sneaking around using gossip and innuendo and intimidation to control this church and infect it with the same poisonous legalism that drove the Pharisees to stalk Jesus and kill Him."

"You dare to—"

"Until now, I have considered it my duty to endure you. But now I see clearly that it is my duty to rescue this church from your influence before you kill it entirely. You are the one who must resign. Failing that, perhaps you are right. Perhaps you should be publicly rebuked from the pulpit."

"I'll see you in hell first."

"I'll defer to you as the expert on that topic."

"If yer cheap-grace preachin' wasn't enough of a disgrace, yer boy is bringin' disgrace on this church. The good people of this church ain't gonna sit around and let it keep goin' on. I ain't gonna let nobody bring disgrace on this church."

Dad and Fry were only inches apart. Everybody was leaning forward in their chairs, focused on the two men in the center of the room. The tension was so thick it would have been a waste of good cutlery to cut it with a knife. So when I jumped to my feet and my legs hit the metal folding chair, which folded up and slammed on the floor like a rifle shot, it had a noticeable effect on those present.

Reactions varied among the deacons, from Scooter jerking around suddenly to Weldon's three-second spastic fit of flailing arms and legs. Heidi screamed and fell off her chair. Mom inhaled sharply and clasped her hand to her throat. Hannah, when she recovered, slugged me in the stomach with a backhanded swipe of her fist. I ignored it and glared at Deacon Fry.

"You ain't gonna let nobody bring disgrace on this church? You?"

Dad couldn't have been more startled if he had seen an Irish setter puppy turn into a snarling Rottweiler. He had the look of a man who has seen the natural order of his universe disrupted. Fry focused on me a look of violence. It wasn't the controlled certainty of violence that I had seen in Jake. It was a chaos of passion held in check by a thin tether of civilization.

Such was my outrage and righteous indignation that this vision of my certain bodily destruction scarcely registered.

"*You* are the disgrace. You strain out the gnat but swallow the camel. You shove the kingdom of heaven in men's faces, but you won't even go in yourself, or let in those who are trying to get in. You recognize that one? Jesus said that, talking about people just like you."

"Mark, sit down and let me deal with this," Dad said.

"See? He can't even control his own family in the Lord's house," Fry growled without taking his eyes from me. "Listen here, young man, yer daddy may not be able ta keep ya on a short leash, but—"

"No, you listen. Who is bringing disgrace on this church? I say it's the one who sneaks around to see a woman when her husband is gone. I say it's the one who is having an affair."

I pulled it out of my shirt pocket—the trump card, the secret weapon, my own private Manhattan Project. Since the beginning of the meeting I had been tormented with the weight of the decision that lay before me. I could use it and likely annihilate the enemy. But I had no idea what form the fallout would take. How far would it reach? Who else would become collateral damage?

I was prepared to use it, had even rehearsed my speech, until I heard Dad's strategy that I interpreted as: the best defense is no defense. Then I wasn't sure. Was that what Jesus would do? I thought it was. He had not even answered His accusers, like a sheep before its shearers is dumb. So I sat through the meeting, waiting to see what the Holy Spirit would teach Dad to say.

And as the struggle escalated before us, the weapon of ultimate destruction grew heavier in my pocket, throwing me off balance. Until Fry let out those words.

I ain't gonna let nobody bring disgrace on this church. They rang in my head and rolled around and got all mixed up. Disgrace on this church. Grace on this church. Let him disgrace this church. Can't let him dis-grace this church. You can't let him steal grace from this church. You can't. You. Me.

So I jumped up and pulled the trigger. After the pandemonium faded, in the sudden silence I could hear my heart pounding and Fry breathing heavily through his teeth. The deed was done. I was committed beyond recall.

All eyes were drawn to the object I held out before me.

It was a small pasteboard rectangle. A black-and-white picture about twenty years old. A picture I had retrieved from the hollow book in the Fortress of Solitude just before we left for the meeting.

"The deacons should see this."

I handed the picture to Heidi, who looked at it and passed it to Mom. She looked at it and handed it to Dad.

Hannah leaned over and whispered, "What is it? You didn't let me see it."

My answer was cut short by Dad's question. "Mark, what is this?"

"A picture of Deacon Fry with the wife of another man."

Fry glared at me, at the picture, and back at me. Dad inspected the picture more closely. He looked at Fry. He looked at me.

"Who is the woman?"

"Gianna Crowley, wife of Vernon Crowley. About twenty years ago, I think. Give or take."

Fry snatched the picture out of Dad's hand. "This has nothing to do with the purpose of this meeting."

Dad's left hand shot out and locked Fry's wrist in a grip that belied his shorter stature. Fry winced as fingertips pressed between the bones on his inner wrist. The picture dropped into Dad's right hand. Fry seemed on the verge of explosion but restrained himself.

Dad spoke without taking his eyes from Fry's face. "I propose we add an item to the agenda. All in favor say 'Aye.'"

Everyone in the room said, "Aye." Except Fry.

"All opposed." Nobody said anything. Not even Fry. Dad clamped his hand on Fry's shoulder.

"I suggest you sit down." Fry looked around for support and finding none, dropped reluctantly into his chair. Dad also sat down. "Since you are in this picture, I expect you can explain it."

"I don't have ta explain it. This meetin' ain't about me."

"Correction. It wasn't about you. But the agenda has changed. You might recall a vote. Robert's Rules, even." Fry snorted. "Refresh my memory, Deacon Fry. Didn't you just celebrate your fortieth anniversary? Got married in your early twenties, did you?"

"I don't have to answer your questions."

"No, you don't. But I expect I can get the answers without your assistance. Elmer?"

Elmer nodded. "As I recollect, young Fry here got married back in '33, or was it '34? It were a tough time ta get married. But he was young and had the world by the tail. We all had high hopes for 'em." He hocked a loogie into his handkerchief. "And he ain't disappointed us." He carefully folded the hanky and returned it to his pocket. "Yet."

Dad regarded the photograph. "This appears to be taken in the '50s. So you would have been married around twenty years."

"You can't railroad this meeting into a fishin' expedition. Yer just lookin' ta weasel out of the spotlight and put somebody else into the hot seat." He looked at the deacons.

"I can understand your reluctance to pursue this issue. However, I believe you were the one who brought the topic up yourself. About someone disgracing the church. If you refuse to provide some context for this photograph, perhaps Mark will oblige us."

I was still standing. "I found this picture in Gina Crowley's photo album."

Scooter coughed loudly and held up a finger. "Could the rest of us see this picture?"

Dad nodded to me. I delivered it to the deacons.

"Deacon Fry," Scooter said, "I think you might want ta explain this. I looked at this picture, and it might be Gina Crowley or it might not. But it sure ain't Mrs. Fry you're huggin'."

"Scooter, yer not gonna be hoodwinked by this two-bit seminary preacher, are ya?"

"Deacon Fry, I plow my own rows. I ain't beholden ta no seminary preacher. Pastor Matt and me has our differences. But I ain't seen no picture of him huggin' another man's wife. And if I did, he'd explain it or I'd know the reason why. If it's good enough fer Pastor Matt, I reckon it's good enough fer the head deacon."

Fry looked to the other two.

Weldon shrugged. Elmer snuffled deeply and said, "Ulysses, young Brown here is as right as rain. Ya owe us some kind a story fer that picture. What ya got agin Pastor Matt here is mainly cotton candy and moonshine. I never seen as how it mattered much, but you was so worked up over it I was willin' ta hear ya out and see if ya could make somethin' of it. But Matt's boy has got ya by the short ones. That girl ain't Eunice. She might be yer niece, and I hope she is, fer yer sake."

Reality overtook Fry. He suddenly deflated and sat back in his chair, looking very tired. He looked at me reproachfully.

"This is a private matter. It has nothing to do with this meeting, or the deacons."

"Quite to the contrary," Dad said. "It has everything to do with this meeting. You have set yourself up as the standard of moral rectitude in this fellowship and on that basis have presumed to dictate what will and will not happen. The same passage in Timothy that you were so eager to quote also delineates the qualifications for a deacon. 'Men worthy of respect, . . . with a clear conscience' if I recall correctly."

Heidi looked down at the passage and nodded. "Yes, that's what it says." She looked up and smiled. Everyone ignored her.

Fry sat wordless for a long time. He appeared to be retreating back into himself, flying back over time. "He never understood her. Couldn't understand her. Not the likes of him. She needed help. She needed someone strong. She should a left him, but she wouldn't."

"She?"

Fry looked up, back in the present and annoyed. "Gina. Like the boy said." He gestured vaguely in my direction and turned on Dad. "Look here, Pastor Matt. This ain't the time nor place for this. This ain't got nothin' ta do with you nor this church. It was over and done with years ago."

Dad looked at the deacons.

Elmer shook his head. "Ulysses, you made your bed, now ya got ta lie in it. You set this meetin' up as the place for hearin' accusations and makin' decisions. Seems we got an accusation, and as the deacons and the pastor of this church, we got ta make a decision. You can speak yer piece or not, as ya see fit. But we have ta make our decision as we see fit."

"I don't see as how it's proper ta do it in front of his whole family." Fry looked at me as he spoke. Not a very friendly look.

"Seein' as how ya thought it were proper ta tar and feather Pastor Matt in front of his kids, I reckon it's proper they be here for the rest of the meetin'."

Fry was trapped. If he refused to explain the picture, the deacons would vote based on their own interpretations of its meaning. If he wanted to mitigate the damage, he would have to tell his story in front of the preacher's kids. He looked like Samson, shorn and blinded, used like a donkey to draw water and taunted by insolent teenage punks. From the look he gave me, I knew he held me personally responsible for his humiliation. He chose to take his medicine as quickly as possible.

"There was a time when Eunice and I had some differences. I got a room in Beaumont fer awhile, not far from my job. I come back on weekends. Most weekends. I run across Gina and her boy in a department store. I learned how that bootlegger kept her cooped up in that old house; wouldn't do nothin' with her nor take her nowhere. She asked me if I wanted ta take in a picture show with her, and I did."

Fry looked around the room. "Look here, there ain't no need ta go into all the details. I had my reasons. I'm not sayin' I was right, 'cause I weren't. I'm just sayin' I had my reasons. But after awhile Eunice and me patched things up, and I put that all behind me. A long time ago."

The room was silent for a long time. Then Dad cleared his throat.

"If this ended a long time ago, why is it that your car was seen near Gina's house as recently as last year? Are you one of Vernon's customers?"

"Alcohol has never touched my lips. There ain't a man on this earth that can say different."

"Then . . ."

"I went by to check on her from time ta time. She wasn't a well woman, and she couldn't depend on him. I knew he parked out on that hill and drank himself into a stupor every sunset."

Dad frowned. "You are saying the affair ended years ago, but you continued to go to her home when you knew her husband would not be there? On a regular basis?"

"Don't you go and try ta twist it up into somethin' it ain't. I was just doin' my Christian duty."

"Your Christian duty? Could you refresh my memory on the verse that says it's your duty to maintain a relationship with a woman you lived in sin with after the affair is supposedly over? Would that be the verse about avoiding every appearance of evil? Or the one about being above reproach? What happened to the concern about reputation you trot out in front of me every time you see Vernon in church?"

"He mistreated her. I seen the marks on her myself. I seen enough ta know he's the one that killed her, no matter what the courts say. I tried ta get her ta leave before it was too late."

Elmer snorted loudly. "Does Eunice know you go to another woman's house while her husband's gone?"

"No."

"Does she know about the affair?"

"No."

"Deacon Fry," Dad said, "I seem to recall you complaining that good decent folks were being forced to sit next to sinners. Do you consider yourself one of the good decent folks or one of the sinners?"

"I ain't never said I was perfect. But I repented of my sin. Yes, it was sin. I admit it. And I turned away from it. That's what Jesus said. Go and sin no more. When I was in sin, I didn't disgrace the church by comin' in and actin' like I was as good as the next feller. I did the proper thing and stayed away. If that bootlegger wants ta repent and turn away from his sin, fine. Until then, he should stay out of the church and let decent folks be."

"Ulysses," Elmer said, "I'm gonna give ya some good advice. You go home tonight and ask Eunice ta forgive ya."

"I don't see no reason ta go courtin' trouble. It's over and done. There ain't no reason ta cause her grief over the long gone past that she don't know nothin' about."

"Don't talk nonsense, Ulysses, like a dang fool teenager. There ain't a woman alive that wouldn't know. She knows you sinned against 'er. She knows you ain't asked forgiveness."

If she doesn't know now, she will soon, I thought. You can't have eight people hear a secret and expect it to stay one for long, even if they are deacons. Or PKs.

CHAPTER THIRTY Five days later I felt like a tamale wrapped in a cornhusk and steaming over a slow fire. A senior tamale in a black cornhusk with a mortarboard and a tassel. Graduation had sneaked up on me. I wasn't ready. Or rather, I was ready enough to get out of school, but I wasn't ready for whatever would follow.

I had churned through the college applications and the financial aid forms and the standardized tests. But I hadn't given any thought to what would happen the day after. My senior year had been overshadowed by other concerns—Gina's death, Vernon's trial, Jake's tunnel, a car in a creek, and the looming showdown with the deacons.

Dad had been right. It wasn't the end of the world although Deacon Fry may have disagreed. The vote that placed Scooter as head deacon was not likely the outcome Fry had anticipated when he called the meeting. But there was little he could do. It took a vote of the congregation to add or remove a deacon, but the position of head deacon was determined by the deacons and the pastor. The silver lining was that there would be no public rebuke of his behavior. His resignation had been announced as the passing of the baton to the younger generation. It was a Pyrrhic victory rendered more hollow by the certainty that everyone in Fred would know the story in less than a week. Even those who didn't go to any church.

The valedictorian completed her speech. The class stood. One by one we filed to the front, shook the principal's hand, received a blank piece of paper rolled up and tied with a ribbon, and moved our tassel from right to left. The poor guy in front of Jolene went up with his gown tucked into the back of his pants, his fate for having a last name that started with C. He walked up on the stage proudly, smiling to the enthusiastic crowd. Cutoffs and cowboy boots with a stretch of pale white legs visible in between. Nice touch. Jolene looked back at me and winked.

At the end we threw our mortarboards into the air and hugged each other and promised to stay in touch and a lot of other things we really really really meant but would never do. Really.

An hour later I was driving the recently restored Falcon, my tassel hanging from the rearview mirror. It was a night for celebration. The gang was meeting at a picnic area in Town Bluff for the festivities.

They were sitting on top of a picnic table under a mercury vapor light; boots propped on the seats, watching the traffic go by. I skidded to a stop in the gravel and switched off the key. The engine did not go gentle into that good night. It sputtered and coughed and shivered before it gave up the ghost. A sprinkling of sand sifted down from the roof into my hair, a gentle reminder of my most recent act of folly.

I was halfway to the table when Jimbo jumped to his feet. "Hey, where's the ice?"

"Ice?"

"You was supposed ta bring two bags of ice."

"Oh, yeah." I shrugged my shoulders. "But I did bring this." I held up a six-pack of Dr Pepper.

Jimbo left in disgust to get some ice. Bubba and I opened Dr Peppers. Ralph decided to wait for the ice.

Darnell pulled out a bottle of grappa. The previous weekend, at Vernon's request, I had talked Darnell into taking me on my rounds. When we arrived at the Pontiac, Vernon had made a laconic presentation of a bottle of grappa for each of us. In light of recent events, I thought it prudent to decline. Darnell had gleefully accepted both bottles.

I held up my can. "A toast."

"Wait," Ralph said. "I don't have anything to toast with."

Darnell handed him one of the Dixie cups I had swiped from the fellowship hall and poured him a generous portion of grappa. Flecks of wax floated on the surface. We all held up our drinks.

"To the Class of '74," Ralph said.

"To the future," Bubba said.

"To Peterbilt," Darnell said.

"Salute," I said.

We all drank. Then Ralph began coughing.

"What is this stuff?" he gasped.

"Grappa."

"What's it for? Cleaning drains?" Ralph asked, his eyes watering.

"Is it that bad? I've never tasted it, but Vernon didn't complain when he drank it. He said this was the good stuff."

Bubba snared the bottle and peered at the label in the thin light. "Can be used on glass, porcelain, Formica, linoleum, and metal. In case of contact with skin, wash immediately in soap and water. If taken internally, call a poison control center. Do not induce vomiting."

Ralph took the bottle from him. "Does it really say that?"

"You gonna finish that?" Darnell asked.

Ralph handed him the cup. We watched him drink it down without a flinch and open a warm beer.

"Give me one of them things," Ralph said. I handed him a Dr Pepper. He swished some around in his mouth and spat it out, then took a gulp. We sat in silence, watching the occasional car pass on the highway.

Ralph spoke up. "Hey, Darnell, remember in sixth grade when you brought your go-cart to school and Jimbo drove it through the halls?" Bubba and I laughed.

Darnell scowled. "Yeah, and I also remember when you took Jolene ta the drive-in and she hid the distributor cap while you was in the bathroom and left ya there." Bubba and I laughed.

Ralph said, "Hey, Bubba, remember when yer house caught fire and you tried ta put it out with a garden hose wearing Jolene's prom dress?" Darnell and I laughed.

"Is there a point to this?" Bubba asked.

I elbowed Bubba. "Don't take it personally. We're just remembering the funny things that happened through the years."

"Oh, you mean like the time you got crowned Li'l Abner in front of the whole school with yer zipper open, and Jolene pulled the chair out from under ya?"

Everybody laughed the loudest at that one. Except me. We eventually ran out of things to remember and drifted back into silence.

Ralph tossed his can at the trash barrel and missed by several feet. "So, you goin' off ta college then?"

I nodded my head.

"Yep," Bubba said.

"What?" Ralph and I said in unison. Darnell choked on his beer.

Bubba smiled. "Yep, Pastor Matt give me a recommendation to a Bible college. They accepted me."

"A Bible college," Ralph said flatly.

"Yep."

"Yer gonna be a preacher?"

"Might be. We'll see."

I looked at him suspiciously. "Which Bible college?"

"East Texas Baptist College."

"That's where I'm going."

Ralph turned to me. "You gonna be a preacher too?"

"Absolutely not."

"Then why you goin' to a Bible college."

"They teach other stuff too. Music, math, science, psychology, the works."

"Which one you gonna study?"

"I haven't decided yet."

"I'm goin' ta school too." Darnell tossed his can into the trash barrel on the first try and freed another from captivity.

"You gonna be a preacher?"

"Nah, truck driver." He popped the top.

I looked at Ralph. "How about you?"

"My dad's gonna see if he can get me on at the refinery."

I nodded. We sat on the picnic table, considering the future and slapping mosquitoes.

Bubba, a preacher. Who'd a thunk it? He might make a good one. Being the brother of Jolene, he knew suffering and so could identify with the suffering of others. But a hick white boy certified as possessing soul who thinks that whatever Jesus would do it would probably upset religious folks. His life wasn't going to be boring.

Everybody seemed to have a handle on the next step. Bubba was going to be a preacher. Darnell was going to become a truck driver. Ralph was going to do what Jesus did: work with his dad.

Is that what I should do? Follow in Dad's footsteps? After all, I knew the real job description. Which was exactly the problem. From what I could see, the only way anybody in his right mind would set out to become a preacher was if he didn't have any idea what it was really like. If God were to show up right then and give me the choice between becoming a preacher or running a mile down the highway naked with a yellow stripe painted down my back, I would have asked, "North or south?" and started unbuttoning my shirt.

Maybe you felt differently if you got the call. If that were the case, I simply wouldn't answer the phone. I would let the answering machine get it. But that didn't seem right. Screening calls from God to avoid answering? That's hardly what Jesus would do. He was more of a "Not my will but Thine" kind of guy.

But there was no way I could do it. I knew it deep within me, where you just know things. Like when you hope you don't throw up, and then, suddenly, you know you're going to. I just knew I could never be a preacher. I had seen what it took.

Listening to people complaining all the time about stupid things like the color of the new carpet or why their daughter wasn't picked to be Mary in the Christmas play. Counseling people through their grief because they got a scratch on their new Cadillac while the lady who just lost her only child waits to talk to you. Pouring your heart out to a room of people in various stages of catatonic stupor. Listening with a straight face as someone promises you something you know they will never do. Calls at all hours of the day and night. And after doing all this for half a living wage, then being the target for every bitter, power-hungry hypocrite who gets joy from making you miserable. I didn't have Dad's talent for silver linings.

I couldn't do it. I wouldn't do it. Absolutely not. It was asking too much.

Then it hit me, what Mac had said to Parker. God asks too much. He asks us to do what is too much for us because He wants us to know it's too much. So we can see Him do it in us. Through us.

Could it be that God expected me to be a preacher because He knew I couldn't do it and therefore would be forced to rely on Him? What a dirty trick.

What was it Mac had said? He had prayed, "God, if You want me to change, You will have to change me." And then he felt cool spring water running down his head and through his body, and he was changed. Just like that.

Was that what I should do? Is that what Jesus would do? Somehow I thought it might be. Did I have the guts to do it? Probably not.

I looked around at the guys. Darnell was opening another beer. Hmm, binge drinker. Not a good sign for a future truck driver. Ralph and Bubba were talking about what kind of girls go to a Bible college.

I got up and nodded toward the bushes like I was going to answer nature's call. Instead, I stepped behind a pine and leaned back against it. I was sweating. I rolled up my sleeves. I undid another button on my shirt.

I looked in desperation for some way out. I did not want to be a preacher. Please, anything but that. I would even consider deacon. Well, that might be taking it a bit far. No sense in going over to the enemy.

I knew if I was going to do it I would have to do it all at once, like going for an ocean swim in California. You just have to commit and dive in; wading in slowly was much worse.

I spun around, braced myself against the pine with both hands, and leaned my head forward, looking down at the pine straw. My fingers dug into the flaky bark, peeling off a few layers. They drifted to the ground like feathers.

I closed my eyes tight and prayed in utter terror. "God, I don't want to be a preacher. I know I'd be a miserable failure. Even with Your help, I'd probably mess it all up. But if for some completely crazy and impossible reason You want me to be a preacher, I'm willing to do it. Back in Barstow I made my choice, and I don't go back on my choices. I am a man of my word. If You give me a sign, I'll do it. Not my will, but Thine. Amen."

I stood motionless, eyes squeezed shut, hoping I would not get a sign. For a minute that seemed like an hour I clutched the bark of that pine and pleaded for the complete absence of all signs. Nothing. Complete and blessed nothing.

Then, just as I relaxed and released the tree to wipe the sweat and tears from my face, I had the sensation of ice-cold water pouring over my head and down my sweat-drenched shirt.

"No," I screamed.

Could this really be the sign? When Mac felt the cool water pouring over him, his mind and heart were changed. But I didn't feel changed; I felt betrayed. How could I get this sign but still feel the same?

Then I heard laughing and opened my eyes. Jimbo was standing next to me, an empty ice chest in his hands. I looked down. My shirt and pants were soaked with water. Ice lay all around my feet.

"I reckon that pays ya fer that time ya clobbered me with that log. Remember that one?" He grinned and tossed the ice chest aside. His grin faded when I lunged at him and hugged him.

I blurted, "Thank you!" as he tried to disentangle himself from my embrace. We danced awkwardly, tripped over a branch, and rolled apart in the grass. Jimbo jumped up and grabbed the lid of the cooler, holding it out like a weapon.

I lay on the grass, laughing. Bubba, Ralph, and Darnell came over. They stood above me in a semicircle.

"Did he have some grappa?" Ralph asked.

"Well, don't give him anymore if he did," Jimbo said.

"I'll drink to that," Darnell said.

"A toast," I exclaimed, struggling to my feet. Jimbo backed up and brandished the cooler lid. I went to the picnic table and grabbed a fresh Dr Pepper. "Pick yer poison, boys," I hollered.

Ralph handed a beer to Bubba. He looked at it and handed it to Jimbo. "I guess, since I'm headed ta Bible college, I'll have ta develop a taste fer Dr Pepper." Ralph opened a beer. Darnell grabbed the grappa.

I leaped to the top of the picnic table and held my can aloft with a dripping hand. Around me, four arms went up. Maybe I wasn't going to be a preacher, but Dad's blood flowed in my veins, and I felt his eloquence stir within me.

"A half score minus four years ago, I came among ye as a stranger in a strange land. And ye received me not." They looked at me strangely. "Yet did I sojourn through many grievous trials, through Roller Coasters and Brakemans' Daughters, through Pastor Bates and hunting trips, and yea, verily even unto the end of the bridge, wherein my Falcon faileth, but was raised again."

I gestured grandly to the car. They looked at it in confusion, then at each other. I could see the time had come to wrap it up.

"To Fred," I shouted.

"To Fred," they echoed back.

I drained the can and smashed it beneath my heel.

ACKNOWLEDGMENTS Winning the 2004 Christy
Award for First Novel for *Welcome to Fred* was an unforgettable moment.
Because only a handful of people were there to hear my thanks, I want
to repeat them here. Thanks to Robin Hardy, who is largely responsible
for me being published, and to Gary Terashita and the other good folks
at Broadman and Holman for believing in my book even more than I
did. And that takes some doing!

After finishing book 1, I was concerned about being able to improve
on my effort for book 2. Winning the Christy increased the pressure. But
after six months of perspiration (literally, my office is not air-conditioned
and it can get pretty warm writing on summer afternoons in Hawaii, or
even on winter afternoons), I think I've done it. However, like any large
effort, I didn't do it alone.

Thanks to the Woman for the excellent input, as always; Mark
Spyrison for supplying some excellent last-minute suggestions; Gordon
Brown for vetting the Vietnam chapters; Charles Rex Jehlen Jr. for the
help on the WWII chapters; Rae Dryzmala for loaning me Band of
Brothers; Sam Lott for help on the cars and villains; Merle Bobzien for
proofreading, grappa research, and the Big Bear final draft weekend;
Don Woodliff for suggesting that Mark might actually hook up with
Jolene; Guy Clark and Lyle Lovett for unknowingly assisting in creat-
ing Vernon Crowley; CRJJR, Clyde and Marcia Combs, Dan and
Linda Barnnett, and Don and Judy Woodliff for housing on the book
tour; Gary Terashita for making sure I don't commit professional sui-
cide, Lisa Parnell for making sure I don't commit grammatical suicide,
Kenneth Stephens and David Shepherd for remembering my name,
FredNotes subscribers for naming Gianna and Jacob; the PK list

(groups.yahoo.com/group/preacherskids) for sharing their stories, none of which appear in the book but all of which amaze and inspire me.

I don't know how anyone ever wrote a book before the Internet was created. Of course I greatly relied on biblegateway.com, allmusic.com, dictionary.com, and google.com. But even more amazing are the obscure sites that will tell you the time of sunrise/sunset and moonrise/moonset on any day in the past, the dates of the phases of the moons, what TV shows played at what times in what years, and the myriad other little details that work together to lend that air of verisimilitude to a good story. So thanks to all you other guys too.

— BRAD WHITTINGTON —
www.fredtexas.com